---

# TEXT ME, CUPID

all four scandalous episodes

---

## M. JANE COLETTE

# TEXT ME, CUPID

Cover Art: Marco Garrincha/iStockPhoto
Cover Design: Sean Lindsay

*First Paperback Edition 1.0, 2018*

*GENRES were made to be BROKEN*
121, 104-1240 Kensington Rd NW
Calgary, Alberta T2N3P7 Canada



ISBN: 978-1-989297-00-1 (paperback)
ISBN: 978-1-989297-01-8 (hardcover)
ISBN: 978-1-989297-02-5 (audio)
ISBN: 978-1-7751809-9-9 (ebook)

**mjanecolette.com**

*For Lolly, in gratitude*

# Contents

Episode III
## BITTERSWEET HALLOWEEN

Episode IV
SAVING CHRISTMAS

---

## Text Me, Cupid

### A (SLIGHTLY DIRTY) LOVE STORY FOR 21ST CENTURY ADULTS

---

Meet Will and Florence. He's freshly divorced and in denial. She's twice-burnt and prickly. They're a terrible idea. They know this. But every time their eyes meet, their clothes come off.

---

This collection includes all four *Text Me, Cupid* episodes, previously released (and still available) as individual e-novellas:

- Episode 1: *Messy Christmas*
- Episode 2: *Delayed Valentine*
- Episode 3: *Bittersweet Halloween*
- Episode 4: *Saving Christmas*

as well as the bonus shorts, "Will and Florence, 25 years later" and "Awkward Cupid," not available in other editions.

If you enjoy the book, please consider leaving a review for it with your favourite bookseller and on GoodReads.

And, of course, tell all your friends about Will and Florence.

Thank you very much for your support!

*mjanecolette*

---

To find out what's coming next from M. Jane Colette and to receive a **FREE** copy of *Taste Me: The Thinking Woman's Erotica*—a gift available exclusively to M. Jane Colette's newsletter subscribers—ask Jane to send you love letters:

## YES! MY LIFE NEEDS MORE LOVE LETTERS!

*mjanecolette.com/loveletters*

---

For audiobook samples, outtakes, and extra peeks into Will and Florence's love story, visit

*mjanecolette.com/TextMeCupid*

# MESSY CHRISTMAS

*For Brandy,*
*who got me to write the first 500 words in 15 minutes*

## PROFILE: notanightingale

*38, Straight, Woman, Single, 173 cm, Fit,
Caucasian, Speaks English and Other,
Attended high school ?,
Religion Other (and laughing about it),
Never smokes, Never drinks, never does drugs, Carnivore,
Has kid(s) and doesn't want more, Sagittarius*

K, I've done this before, looking for a partner or soul mate or someone-to-grow-to-love, and you know what? I'm done with that. Honestly: I'm just looking for some casual sex. Specifically, during December. It's a weird season over-loaded with memories and childhood trauma—and adult trauma for that matter. Which is already more than you need to know. All I'm interested in is a one night stand, or several—not all of them with you, I'm just making it clear that I'm interested in playing with multiple partners. I don't want to get attached and I don't want you to get attached.

And seeing as that's what I'm looking for, you don't

really need to know anything else, right? Look at the pics. If I'm cute enough, message me.

I don't respond to creeps, children, married men, or fat people. Sorry. I am that shallow. I might consider couples, if you're both fit and cute. (Shallow. Really shallow. I'm not kidding about that.)

December sucks. Let's make it more fun for each other for one night.

## The Challenger
### SUNDAY, DECEMBER 3

**iwillornot sent you a message!**

*iwillornot*: Are you for real?

**notanightingale:** Are you?

*iwillornot*: Meet for coffee to find out?

*iwillornot*: I'm Will, by the way.

**notanightingale:** Will, or not? LOL.

**notanightingale:** Do you understand and agree to my terms?

*iwillornot*: I'm reeling from a recent divorce and incapable of having a meaningful relationship, possibly even a meaningful conversation. Or, at the moment, a meaningful life. The only upside to my situation is that after fifteen years of monogamy I get to chase all the strange I want. And

December sucks. And I'm damn fit for a guy a couple of years past forty. Also—bonus—I still have all my hair. So, yeah. Bring it on, Florence.

**notanightingale:** Did you just figure out my real name from my handle? Oh, Will. We will have fun.

*iwillornot:* It was rather obvious. So. Coffee. Saturday morning?

**notanightingale:** One night stands begin in the evening. Wednesday night? Also, you're not teasing about the hair? I can do bald, but only if it comes with killer abs.

*iwillornot:* Fucking full head of hair. Although there's more salt than pepper in it—as you can tell from the pics if you look. Premature greying. It's because I'm so fucking brilliant.

*iwillornot:* Also, I do have killer abs. Thank you for inferring.

**notanightingale:** Also, you like big words. LOL. So— Wednesday night?

*iwillornot:* Wednesday night. Cafe Blanca near Eau Claire convenient for you? My apartment's just upstairs.

**notanightingale:** Perfect.

One Night Stand Gone Wrong
WEDNESDAY, DECEMBER 6

She was gorgeous. Much better looking than her photos, which were typical online tease—half-profile, sunglasses, hat. They had made it clear that she had a lot of a red hair—fuck, *a lot* of red hair—and a very triangular chin. But they didn't make it clear that she was... outrageously, ridiculously hot.

Will tried not to drool. He allowed himself to feel a twinge of regret that she was already in the cafe, sitting down, so that he wouldn't get to see her walk, move towards... flow towards him? Dance? She sat as if she knew how to move. How could a woman convey that much promise in the way she crouched on the edge of a chair?

He smiled again. Tonight was going to be a good night.

"Hi," he said. "Will." He extended a hand and she took it while standing up in a graceful, fluid motion. In his head, she was already naked. Was she going to be covered with freckles? Fuck, yes—freckles everywhere. He would find every single one.

Best thing—she looked nothing like his ex-wife. The first four or five women he went out with—the first women he attempted to date since Amanda asked him to move out —were his ex's clones. The worst thing was, he didn't realize he had dated Clone Number One until he found himself sitting across a coffee shop table from Clone Number Two. They could have been sisters.

And then, he hooked up with Clone Number Three. And Four. And then Five...

"You have a type." Niko, his sponsor, laughed when Will told him. "Nothing wrong with that."

Everything wrong with that when that type's your *ex*-wife, right?

Anyway—Florence. Red-haired. Gorgeous. Not Amanda's clone. Fuck, yes. And she was probably covered with freckles, everywhere. He was going to kiss every single one.

Maybe bite a few too...

She was standing and shaking his hand and he was getting hard.

Fuck.

"Florence," she said, letting go of his hand but not of his eyes. He liked them too, and her gaze. Her eyes were a delicious shade of hazel. She smiled. Her bottom front teeth were a little crooked. He felt his cock twitch again.

Anticipation.

*Thank you, God, for this December present.*

"You're sitting in the guy's spot, you know," he said, sitting opposite her.

She smiled.

It was delicious.

She was delicious.

"It's the spot of control," she said. "Nothing to do with gender. Back to the back to the room, eyes to the front—you see who's coming and going—it's the place of control." She paused, tilted her head a bit.

"And safety," she added, just as Will said, "That's why it should be the guy's spot."

She laughed.

Pink tongue.

Will fought the impulse to put his hand on her hand. Or his cock. He was already putting her tongue places. Imagining his in others...

"Is that where you usually sit?" he said instead.

Florence nodded.

Smiled.

"Are you going to get a drink?" she asked. "This is a very fancy cafe. As I suppose you know if you live upstairs. They serve beer and wine. Ooh-la-la."

Will paused for a split second. He didn't want to think, or talk, about drinks.

He swallowed.

Where were they?

Right. Control.

"See, I've only known you for five minutes, and I already know you like to be in control," he said. "We're going to change that."

She laughed. That fucking tongue. Will leaned forward and saw freckles on her throat.

"You're fun," she said. "But you know what this means? Even though I desperately need to pee, I now cannot go to the washroom, because you're going to take my spot when I'm gone."

"Unfortunately, you're right," he said. "Can you hold it until we get to my place?"

But he wouldn't let her pee right away. He would make her squirm and beg and then maybe explode all over the hallway floor, half a foot away from the bathroom door, because his hand would be...

*Yes.*

His eyes closed and he was suddenly aware of how he wasn't looking towards the cafe's small selection of drinks. He opened his eyes to look at Florence again, and started to smile.

She had been smiling, he was sure, but suddenly, her face looked frozen. As he tried to catch them, her eyes went left. Right. Down to her hands—so pale, fingers so very lightly freckled—and then slowly back up to Will's face.

She shook her head and her entire body changed shape and expression.

"This is not going to work out," she said.

"What?" Will flinched. "What did you say?"

"This is not going to work out," she said. "Don't you think?"

Will stared. What the fuck? Had it even been five minutes? He had just come in—chemistry. Teasing. Banter. That pink tongue and those hands and the hair, and his apartment right upstairs, December sex with no obligations, no need to explain the ex-wife and the kids and why did you get divorced and what are you looking for—and now this? What? How?

"I thought it was going rather well," he said. Felt stupid, awkward. Sitting in the girl's fucking spot, playing her game. She was, after all, just a tease.

Her freckled fingers moved across the table and grasped his hands.

Fucking thunderbolt. What was she doing?

"Oh, you're very sweet," she said. Smiled. Fuck. Beautiful smile—he loved her smile. Those crooked teeth. "And cute," she added. Leaned closer towards him across the wobbly table. Dove into his eyes and he wanted her to stay there. "Totally as advertised. Fit. Hair. Also, as tall as your profile said, which is a bonus. Do you know that almost all men on dating sites lie about their height? They add two inches. And not just to their cocks. Seriously."

She laughed, and he laughed with her.

"To be fair, women lie too. Mostly about their weight, though," she said.

He laughed again. The clones he went out with were both shorter and... curvier, the kind word was *curvier,* than advertised.

Not that he minded curvy. Amanda had not been... well, never mind that. He looked at Florence again. She was wearing a very loose sweater. What she had under there had to be left entirely up to his imagination.

He imagined. His cock approved.

"But it's not going to work out," Florence said. Smiling still, or again. And looking into his eyes.

What the fuck?

"Say it," she invited him.

"What?"

"You just thought something angry. Obscene?" she asked. Eyebrows up. "Did you call me a bitch? Or something worse?"

"I just thought... 'what the fuck,'" Will said. "I thought... I thought it was going quite well. This."

"It is," she smiled. "You're sweet. But it's not going to work out. I already know."

"Why not?" he asked.

"Because," she smiled—fuck, why did she keep on smiling? He needed her to stop smiling so that he could hate her. He would go home alone, and masturbate to the fantasy of hating this teasing redhead and doing nasty things to her, things that she hated, because... "Because," she smiled again, "you're sweet. And I'm not."

"I'm not that sweet," he said.

"Why?" she laughed. The next time she laughed, he

was going to jump across the table and kiss—no, slap her. "Because you're imagining me tied to your kitchen chair with... what? Nipple clamps on, or a mouth bit? While you whip me? Or suspended from a beam in a garage and you're fucking me ruthlessly while I scream and beg you to let me go?"

Will started.

"Handcuffed in the shower," he muttered.

"Nice," she smiled. He half-rose. "Oh, Will. You're a darling. And this is not going to work out, however much I'd enjoy being handcuffed in your shower. If you managed to get handcuffs on me. I like to fight." And she laughed again and his hands fell on hers and clamped around them. Hard. She pulled hers away—he thought about clamping down harder so she couldn't, but what sort of ass would do that?— and put them in her lap.

"You're too freshly divorced," she said.

"What the fuck?" Will said. "I haven't said boo about my wife."

"You don't have to." She shrugged her shoulders. The motion of the bones under the bulky sweater was intoxicating. "I've been around." She tilted her head again. The triangular chin pointed at him. "Tell me. What are we going to do on our second date?"

"I was thinking skating at the Olympic Plaza," he said. Fuck. She laughed.

"See? This is supposed to be a one night stand," she said. "And you're totally falling in love with me. And you know nothing about me, so I don't even take it as a compliment. You're—you're this uber nice guy. And your last relationship... how long were you married for?"

"Fifteen years," Will said mechanically. He brushed a hand against his pant leg and crotch. Invited a thought of Amanda, at the moment she was saying to him, "His name is Ranveer—we didn't plan it, Will, it just happened," into his mind, the ultimate anti-aphrodisiac. His cock obeyed, fell.

"See, you only know how to do one kind of relationship. Long-term, loving, committed," she said. "Which is wonderful. And what most women want."

"And you're not most women," he finished her sentence. She shrugged.

"Sorry," she said. "I am entirely as advertised. And you're a liar, because you said you wanted a casual encounter, but you are so shopping for Mrs. Will Number Two."

And this time he wanted to slap her not out of lust and desire but out of sheer anger. His fingers curled and he took a deep breath.

She looked at her watch.

"I had high hopes too," she said. "I have hours to go on the babysitter."

He nodded woodenly.

"Do you want to go... dancing?" she asked.

"What?"

"Well, we don't have to waste the night," she said. "We agreed it's not going to work out as we had planned. But we could go dancing. I love to dance. Do you?"

He stared at her.

"You're fucking unbelievable," he said. Got up. Turned around. Walked out of the cafe alone.

Had absolutely no idea why or how he was pressing Florence's half-naked body, the sweater shoved up to her shoulders, her tiny breasts cupped in his hands, against the hood of a parked car.

"What the fuck?"

"I'm willing," she gurgled.

"I mean, how the fuck did we end up here?"

He really had no idea.

Witch.

He was leaving. Pissed. And?

"I followed you out of the cafe to apologize. You... well, you kissed me," she whispered. "And... here we are."

She smelled like heaven.

He sunk his teeth into the thin line of flesh between her sweater and her hairline.

She moaned.

"But Will? This is a one night stand."

"Would you, for fuck's sake, stop talking?"

"Are you going to fuck me, *sans* foreplay, on the hood of someone else's car parked in front of the cafe that's apparently on the ground floor of your apartment building?"

He pressed her into the car hood. Stroked her almost bare back. Unsnapped the bra strap.

The light was insufficient to see if she was covered with freckles. A police or fire truck siren mewled in the background.

"No," he said. "Let's go upstairs."

They didn't quite make it. She unbuttoned his shirt in the vestibule, and he tore off her sweater in the elevator, and by the time the elevator door opened, she had soaked the outside of his pants, and he had covered her belly with cum without feeling her hand around his cock, never mind her cunt.

Pussy.

He shouldn't call it a cunt.

He wanted to. Call it, possess it, lick it, inhale it. He fell to his knees as soon as they made it across the threshold of his apartment, but she pushed him away.

"Not that," she said.

"I told you not to talk," he said. But he got up and met her mouth with his. "To the bedroom."

Clone Number One and Clone Number Two both ended up in his bed and bedroom. So did, um, the others. The sex was... well. It was sex so it was good. It was with real women and not his hand, so it was better than good. It was with women who looked and moved and tasted just like Amanda so it was both good and awful.

He and Florence didn't make it to the bed. He fumbled for condoms while they rolled on the floor, managing to reach the nightstand drawer without really looking at it, knocking the pack to the floor. He pushed her face down into the hardwood floor, belly down—fuck, her legs went on forever, freckles on the backs of her thighs, calves, behind her knees—and managed to get the condom on almost as quickly as he wanted to.

And then he paused.

He flicked on the bedside lamp, and its light was suffi-cient. She was covered in freckles everywhere and he needed to kiss every single one. So he did. And she moaned and howled as though every kiss was giving her a mind-blowing orgasm, and this time, when, after rolling her onto her back he moved his head between her legs and disap-peared between them, she did not push him away.

Face soaked, he kissed his way up her torso to her neck. Mouth. Slid his cock in. She wiggled off it and, curling underneath him, rolled onto her belly again.

He rolled her over again.

"I want your eyes and lips too," he said.

"You're too greedy," she said, wiggling.

"You're too contrary," he said.

"I like to fight," she agreed and arched her back hard, and fought, and her strength was quite incredible, but he kept her on her back and his cock inside her and relished every bite and claw mark. When she paused for breath and he felt her body melt, exhausted, he dove into her mouth.

"Fuck."

"We did." She laughed. He let the weight of his body rest on her completely and felt her stillness.

"Will?" Her voice was muffled. "I can't breathe."

He lifted himself slightly onto his elbows.

"Can we move to the bed now?"

He nodded and got up off her. Pulled her to her knees, then onto the bed.

"And look, we kept the sheets clean for your next one night stand," she laughed again.

"Could you fucking stop talking?" he said.

"No," she said. "Because this is important. Will? Come here." She wrapped her arms and legs around him, tight.

"Best sex ever?" she asked.

He didn't, wouldn't answer.

"It sure felt incredible to me," she answered herself. "Fucking amazing. You know what that is, Will? Chemistry, and restlessness. And lust. And desire. And perfect timing, and stressful December. It's not destiny or meant to be. It's just sex. Fucking fabulous sex. But just sex."

Will smiled.

"Me thinketh the lady doth protest too much," he butchered Shakespeare.

"I've been around," she said. Kissed his shoulder. Neck. Ear.

"One night stand," she said, unwrapping herself from around him and moving off the bed in search of her clothes. Will closed his eyes, exhausted. When he opened them, she was dressed and at the bedroom door.

"Florence," he said. Stopped. What was he going to say?

"You should say, 'Thank you for coming,'" she instructed. He laughed and she joined him. "Will? I had a really great time. But if you text me, I won't answer. That's what a one night stand is. Ok?"

His cock seemed to sigh with happiness. So Will nodded.

"I'll let myself out," she said.

Blew him a kiss. Walked out.

Before he fell asleep, Will saw her bra and panties on the floor, beside the nightstand.

Like a teenage boy, he fell asleep with the panties grasped in his hand, the bra under his pillow.

---

## Panties, Penises & Bank Vaults
### THURSDAY, DECEMBER 7

---

Waking up with a woman's lacy panties (black, of course) grasped in your hand is, Will reflected as he brushed his teeth the next morning, both... fucking amazing and, well, pathetic. Fucking amazing because... well, sex. Phenomenal sex. Gorgeous redhead. And she left his house without her panties. Fucking amazing.

Pathetic, because, well... he stopped thinking. That was self-evident. Still. It was really more fucking amazing than pathetic. He smiled.

Waddled from the bathroom to the kitchen naked. There weren't a lot of ups, as he saw it, to living alone after fifteen years of marriage. But wandering around the apartment in the morning—any time, really—without having to put on pants rocked.

Was that pathetic?

Will frowned. Commanded himself to think about something else. Like... freckles. Freckles all over—he was pretty sure he kissed everyone one. Maybe missed two. Three. Next time.

Except there wasn't going to be a next time. She said.

*She might change her mind,* he reasoned as he made himself a protein shake for breakfast. It was, after all, fucking fabulous sex. And everyone always said the first time with a new partner was not the best sex you were going to have, right?

*She will change her mind,* he decided as he downed a cup of coffee before heading out the door. *She'll text. I won't. I told her I wouldn't. But she'll text. She'll say…*

He checked his phone and the OkCupid app. Three new likes. Two new messages.

None from Florence.

*Ping.*

"Good morning, Daddy."

"Good morning, Munchkin. All ready for school?"

"No. I can't find my purple socks. You know, the ones with the elephants?"

He knew. He bought them for her for her seventh birthday.

"Have you asked your Mom?"

"She says she's too busy to look for socks in the morning."

A wave of anger at the fucking… at Amanda. A wave of shame—he'd say the same thing. He said the same thing, how many times? "Polly, just put on the blue socks, ok? Why does it have to be the unicorn socks today? We don't have time to look for them. And none of this would be happening if you just put your laundry away on Sunday the way Mom asked you to."

But now, he wasn't there to be asked about the socks, to not look for the socks, to get frustrated by the socks.

"Look under the bed, Polly," he texted.

*Ping.*

A message from Amanda.

"Will, don't undermine me with Polly, please. Let me deal with the fucking socks. You're not here."

*And whose fault is that,* Will thought, and this time, he finished the thought—*you fucking bitch?*

You should not, Will knew, call the mother of your children, the woman who was the love of your life, the woman whom until six, nine months ago you were certain you were going to love and live with till death do you part, a fucking bitch.

But sometimes, it was hard.

"Whose fault is that?" he typed back without thinking.

"And this is helpful?" she shot back.

*Fucking bitch.*

*Fucking divorce.*

*Think of something else.*

Bra under his pillow. Panties on the sheets.

He left them in the bed. He liked them there.

As he started on the short walk to his office, he forced himself to think neither about Florence nor how much he hated Amanda for... There was a silver lining. *This walk was a silver lining, right?* He no longer commuted, he lived downtown, among the bars, the cafes, the restaurants, he was within walking distance of his work, he was living the life he had dreamed of having when he was twenty-six, twenty-eight and already the owner of a house with a double garage in the suburbs, because Amanda wanted to plan ahead for when they would have a family.

And he missed the house and the... but this was good. This was good. There was a bra under his pillow and... Will smiled, and started to indulge in a fantasy. Florence would... well, Florence wouldn't. Fine. One night stand. But he would... today, tonight, he'd hook up with someone else. Maybe on OkCupid, maybe on Tinder—maybe, it'd be a genuine old school in-person encounter—she'd come to the bank, and he'd solve all her problems, or she'd bump into him on the street, he'd meet her when he was getting his afternoon coffee... ok, move on, Will, it doesn't matter how you meet, you just meet, and she's fucking hot, way hotter than Florence, and you end up at your apartment, and into the bedroom, and she says, "What's that?" and pulls those lacy panties from underneath her naked ass, and you just take those panties out of her hands and toss them on the floor, and say, "Those are from last night, don't worry about them."

Will smiled. His penis agreed, and he was grateful for the bulky and long winter coat.

*Ping.*

Polly again? Amanda? His son?

No. Niko. Of course. Checking in, as he did every Thursday.

"Coming to the meeting tonight?"

"Of course. When was the last time I missed one?"

"Six years ago. And I'm still paranoid."

"I'll see you at 7, dude. And no beer afterward."

"LOL."

Will laughed. There should be nothing funny about a sixty-five-year-old man texting "LOL." But everything about it was funny.

He suddenly wanted to send a poop emoticon to Polly.

A picture of his cock—still twitching—to Florence.

"Still thinking about you," he'd say.

He didn't think, actually, that he'd ever send a picture of his penis to anyone. But apparently that's what not just the kids, but *everyone* did these days. Amanda had pictures of Ranveer's penis in her texts, as he had the misfortune to find out.

And, like cold water. No more erection.

Florence.

And it was back.

Amanda and her new lover's penis.

Gone.

Florence.

Ouch.

"Will? What are you doing?" He was standing in the hallway of the bank, just outside his office. Rosie, the executive assistant he inherited from the bank's previous VP Strategy six years ago, was staring at him. With amusement and affection.

Maybe, with a twinge of lust. The thought gave Will both pleasure and—after a quick image of Rosie naked in the bank's vault (every bank employee's fantasy)—guilt and... he stopped thinking.

He adored her. He was so happy he managed to keep her, after... he flashed her a big smile.

"I'm playing this stupid game," he said. "Never mind."

Rosie frowned.

He was pretty sure she could see his erection. He walked into his office quickly.

Would she text?

She'd text.

Florence.

It was a nice bra.

She'd miss it.

Fuck. Wait—maybe she left it on purpose?

"Can I take your coat?"

Rosie stood in the doorway, looking at him quizzically.

She had totally seen his erection. She was not... taking his coat was not in her job description. And if it had been, that would have been one of the things she'd tell him she didn't do on day one of the job. "My job is to help you do your job more effectively," she had said. "I don't get you coffee, I don't pick up your dry-cleaning, and I don't buy presents for your wife and children."

"Can I get you coffee?" he had asked.

She thought about it, very seriously.

"Yes," she said. "Every morning, and sometimes, when you're acting like an ass, in the afternoon."

"We're going to get along just fine," he told her.

And they did. Always. Even through the...

"Seriously, Will, you ok? Give me your coat." Rosie stepped into the office and put her hands on his arm.

Will pulled back.

"Not just yet, Rosie. I'm..." He paused. His cock ached. "A little chilly."

---

## The Negotiation
### MONDAY, DECEMBER 11

---

**notanightingale:** Did I leave my bra—black lace, *Empreinte* label—at your place?

*iwillornot:* Let me check. The brand's *Empreinte*, did you say?

**notanightingale:** I'm proactively giving it to you in case you have a collection of black lace bras under your bed.

*iwillornot:* Well, what can I do when your sex is so careless with your precious possessions. Yes, it's here. With a matching panty.

**notanightingale:** You can keep the panties, they're cheap. The bra, however, is not and it's my favourite. Can you leave it for me at the cafe where we met?

*iwillornot:* I'm so flattered you wore your favourite bra for our one night stand.

*iwillornot*: Leave it at the cafe? And say what? "My friend left this here—she'll be by to pick it up later?"

**notanightingale:** You'd put it in a bag, idiot. They wouldn't know what was in it.

*iwillornot*: I'd feel awkward. Why don't you just come pick it up here?

**notanightingale:** I don't want to come to your apartment again.

*iwillornot*: Come meet me in the cafe.

**notanightingale:** I don't want to see you again. Remember? One night stand?

*iwillornot*: Cafe, in the middle of the day. I promise we won't have sex.

**notanightingale:** LOL.

*iwillornot*: Besides. You want to see me again. Just a little. Right?

**notanightingale:** I want my bra back.

*iwillornot*: Right.

**notanightingale:** Could you please just leave it at the cafe?

*iwillornot*: No. If you want it back—now, I'm no expert on

women's lingerie, but *Empreinte* sounds French and thus expensive... hold on, I'm going to google it... Holy fuck, who pays this much for a bra?

**notanightingale:** Women who want to be good to their breasts.

*iwillornot:* Jesus Christ, is that underwire made of gold? Or platinum?

**notanightingale:** You pay for the lace. And the fit.

*iwillornot:* Seriously? Anyway. My point is—expensive bra. Favourite bra. Want it back? Meet me for coffee.

**notanightingale:** What do you think is going to happen, Will? I meet you for coffee and I realize that we were meant to be together and we walk out of Cafe Blanca holding hands?

*iwillornot:* We'll have coffee, I'll give you back your bra, and we won't have sex in the cafe washroom, although we'll both think about it. A little.

**notanightingale:** LOL.

*iwillornot:* And I'll make you laugh. A little.

**notanightingale:** Ok. Next Saturday morning?

*iwillornot:* It's my weekend with the kids. Friday or Monday?

**notanightingale:** This Friday, at noon?

*iwillornot:* Friday at noon, Cafe Blanca.

**notanightingale:** Would it be possible to meet across the river? At Weeds Cafe, on 20th Avenue? I'm going to be running between jobs, and Cafe Blanca's a bit out of the way.

*iwillornot:* Sure, I know where that is. See you there, Friday, noon.

**notanightingale:** Don't forget my bra.

*iwillornot:* I won't. I might bring the panties too if I'm feeling generous.

**notanightingale:** LOL. I told you you could keep those.

## Cute, Fab In The Sack, Not
## Interested, Also, Psychic

FRIDAY, DECEMBER 15

Being Senior Vice-President, Strategy at one of Canada's largest banks had several disadvantages. For example, Will couldn't, at a dinner party, answer the question, "And what do you do, Will?" with "I'm Senior Vice-President, Strategy" without sounding like a grade-A self-pretentious prick, and saying "I work in a bank" made the other guests visibly bored. Will usually compromised by saying "I'm a financial planner," although, as he was discovering on the post-divorce dating circuit, that answer made a certain type of woman—a type that he didn't think existed any longer, but, oh, it did, it did—perk up.

Other disadvantages included having to wear a suit and uncomfortable shoes to work. It was expected, and Will never bothered to fight it, not even with flamboyant ties and designer shirts. He shed the corporate suit as soon as he got home, replacing it with jeans and a T-shirt, although now that he was living alone, he usually just stripped down to his boxers and wandered around the apartment like that until it was time to go out again.

The advantages of being Senior Vice-President, Strategy at one of Canada's largest banks meant that he could take two hours for lunch any time he wanted to—unless of course there was a client meeting scheduled at noon—and so he got to Weeds Cafe at 11:30. In plenty of time to assess the space, choose a table, and take the seat of power. Back to wall, eyes to the front of the room... when they weren't pretending to be looking at his phone.

His heart was beating just a little faster than usual.

The bra, in the little gift bag he had bought that morning—he had slipped a thank you card into it and scribbled his phone number on it—was on the floor beside his chair.

She wasn't going to show.

She was going to be late.

No, she wasn't going to show at all.

He checked his phone. No messages on his app. He checked her profile. No activity on her profile since their last conversation.

A text from Amanda.

"You've hired my cleaning lady to do your apartment? Are you out of your mind, Will?"

What the fuck?

Whatever. Let it go, don't think about Amanda.

Think about Florence.

Who was late.

Who wasn't going to show.

Who... came through the door at 12:11, breathless.

"I'm so sorry," she said, striding across the cafe towards him, breathing hard.

"Were you running?" he asked. His heart pounded.

"Walking very fast," she said. Blushed over her freckles.

She was wearing a paint-splattered T-shirt over yoga pants and her hair was tied back into a messy pony tail.

There was a smudge of something, paint or dust, under her left eye.

She looked... fucking hot.

"Nice suit," she said.

"Do you mean it or are you being sarcastic?" he asked.

She laughed.

"Does it matter?" she asked. "My bra?"

"Coffee?" he asked, nodding his head towards the coffee bar.

"Coffee," she agreed.

She didn't sit down when she returned with a cup of steaming hot something—coffee or chocolate, he couldn't tell—slathered in whipped cream. Instead, she stopped and stared.

"You're in my seat," she said.

"Place of control," he agreed.

"Because you have my bra?" She laughed. Slid into the chair opposite him. "I don't think so."

"I feel sanguine," Will said.

"Big word," she mocked.

"I didn't text *you*," he said. "You messaged *me*."

"I wanted my bra back."

"Maybe you left it behind on purpose."

She laughed. He reached for a hand—she withdrew it. Shook her head.

"Oh, Will," she said. "I adore you. Really. You are so nice. And so cute. And so fucking *phenomenal* in bed—I won't pretend otherwise. It was a fabulous night. I am still tingling. But I am so not for you, and you are so not for me. And also, I come here all the time, and the washroom is awful—it is the last place I ever want to have sex."

"Florence," he said. "I like you."

"I know," she said. "I'm cute. I'm hot. I'm fab in the sack. It doesn't change anything."

"You're annoying. Obnoxious, actually. Everything you say makes me want to strangle you. But I like you. And..."

She put her hands on his in an abrupt gesture. "Will. Stop."

He froze.

He didn't have a script, or a plan. She texted. He seized the opportunity... and again... fuck. Freckles. Tongue. A pink tongue that poked out of her little mouth over those crooked teeth and seemed to be the same colour as her lips and nipples. He wanted that tongue... in all sorts of ways, and places.

"I came at least in part, because... Will, you're... I like you too," she said. "And I'm really happy to see you again, actually. With clothes on." She laughed. Was she nervous? She was. She was totally nervous. Will perked up. "But this will never work. You're nice. I'm not. And... other things."

"Tell me," he said. "Tell me the other things."

She stared at him and her face was beautiful and gentle and loving and he wanted to devour it.

She looked into his eyes so intently he felt... fuck. He was going to drag her into that washroom anyway...

Except why did she look so sad?

"Say it," he said.

She shook her head.

"You don't get to just drop me," he said. "I feel—sitting here, looking at you—I feel all the reasons why we're here, again. And why there should be a third meeting. So tell me. Tell me why there shouldn't be one."

She looked down at the table. Then the floor.

Raised her eyes up to his face.

When she spoke, the words were an assault.

"You're an alcoholic."

Coffee came spewing out his mouth and nose.

"Oh, Jesus, I'm sorry." She grabbed napkins. Patted his tie and shirt with them. He pushed her away.

"I am not an alcoholic," he said. So fucking angry. "I haven't had a drink in six years. And before that..."

"Stuck on step one, are you?" she said. It wasn't unkind, exactly.

"That's not how it..." he started to say. Stopped. Felt his rage rise. Stared at her with something akin to hate. "And you know, how? Takes one to know one?" he demanded.

She flushed and looked away.

"You can think that if it makes you feel better," she said. He looked at her. She was looking away and she looked tired and sad and broken.

"You were married to one," he said finally. He recognized the look. He saw it in Amanda's eyes one night—on their first wedding anniversary, after he... Well, he saw it. It sent him to AA. She didn't have to say a word. He saw it all —in her eyes.

He didn't see it again, not until six years ago.

Fuck.

Florence.

"You were married to one," he repeated.

"Two," she said. Brought her eyes to his. "There won't be a third. You understand?"

This, actually, he understood. He wanted to say things in his defence. Six years dry. Before that, more than that. Almost a decade. Well, nine, almost nine years. Fuck, he was dry... He realized... he *realized*. He had to see that look on Amanda's face once, only once—the fear, the despair, the hopelessness. Bucket of cold water, and he knew what he had to do. And six years ago... One night. Only one night. Massive major fuck up, but...

"Is that why your wife left you?" Florence asked.

"What?"

"Is that why your wife left you?" she repeated.

*Fucking. Bitch.*

He reached below his chair and grabbed her bra out of the pretty gift bag that she was not going to get. Threw it at her. It narrowly missed her face, bumped off her shoulder and rolled onto the table.

"Here you go," he said.

"Thanks," she said. Then looked at him and in one smooth motion pulled her T-shirt off, unsnapped the front clasp on the pink bra her striptease revealed, shrugged it off and replaced it with the black lace one he threw at her. Pulled the T-shirt back on.

"I've missed it," she said. The pink bra lay on the table between them.

"Good bye, Florence," he said. Got up. Left the cafe.

She didn't follow.

He didn't hope that she would.

Yes, he did.

But she didn't.

## Routine To The Rescue, Sort Of
### MONDAY, DECEMBER 18

Will never minded routine. Well, not quite true. Most of his life, he didn't know what routine was, exactly—his early childhood was... disorganized. Yes. That was the gentlest euphemism. But when Niko introduced it to him—and boxing—when they met at AA, Will recognized routine for what it was immediately. A way to organize life. A way to anchor himself to sanity.

A way to keep himself from thinking about, and taking, that first drink. Thursday meetings. Boxing on Tuesdays and Sundays. Gym on Mondays, Wednesdays, and Fridays. Running Club on Saturdays...

Routine kept him sane, routine kept him sober, routine kept him grateful, routine kept him alive. Routine kept him from strangling Amanda. Or fucking Rosie in the bank vault (although, fuck, that was a good fantasy).

*Don't think about fucking Rosie in the bank vault. Or her apartment.*

Too late.

*Florence.*

Fuck. No. Don't think about Florence.

*Oh-my-fucking-god, penis, STAND. DOWN!*

Routine kept him from thinking about Florence and her freckles 24/7.

He allowed himself to think about her in the morning, while he brushed his teeth. He made himself stop thinking about her while the blender whirred his breakfast protein shake. He did not think about her as he texted with his kids in the morning.

Fuck, he missed them.

He hated being a weekend dad.

Although—he looked down at his naked body—he did like being naked in the kitchen. Who knew? It turned out he was a closet nudist.

That made him laugh, and that made him think of Florence's laugh, and that made him stop laughing.

Witch. Witch, witch, witch.

How did she know?

He ran over every detail of their first meeting in Cafe Blanca in painful detail. What did he say? How did he betray himself?

*"Are you going to get a drink?"*

He wasn't. He didn't. Didn't. Even. Look. Was that... was that it? Was that enough?

*Stop it. Don't think about it, don't think about Florence.*

*Think about the kids.*

The kids missed him, too, but they liked the Daddy weekends, he could tell. He had never given them that kind of focused attention on weekends. There was always some-thing—he tried not to bring work home too much on the weekend, but it happened. And if not work, then the boxing club, gym, or a marathon—or training for a marathon—or work dinner parties, or dinners or brunches arranged by Amanda. Yard work or family shopping for a new couch— Amanda liked shopping and redecorating, and she also liked it when they all four did things together, even if it was boring-ass shit like couch shopping.

And even when there weren't other things, there was just the sheer exhaustion from the week's work. "Daddy doesn't want to play," he'd say. Fuck, how many times did he say that, and how often now did he wish those words unsaid?

These days, from the minute he picked them up after school on Friday, he was theirs completely. Possibly excessively—Niko shook his head and disapproved the last time Will described to him his full-on weekend with the kids, which included a day trip to West Edmonton Mall's Waterpark, a sushi dinner, an afternoon at the pool, a movie, and a trip to the Lego store.

"Kids don't want a Disneyland dad, Will," he said. "They just want a dad."

"I get them for 48 hours out of every two weeks now," Will said. "The occasional mid-week afternoon, at Amanda's goodwill. I need to make the most of it."

"There are other ways of making the most of it," Niko said. He had two children himself, all grown up now, and six grandchildren. There was a picture on his phone screen of all six of them crawling over the mountain of a man that Niko was. Niko looked in heaven. And Will knew—Will knew what purpose that picture served, and why Niko pulled out his phone while they were eating wings and not drinking beer.

He never looked at his phone to check for texts. Only to look at that picture.

"There are other ways of making the most of it," Niko said, pulling out his phone and looking at his screensaver. "But I won't lecture you, man."

That was what Will liked most about Niko, actually. He'd make his point. Always. But he'd never belabour it.

Like that night, six years ago.

Will shuddered.

Thought of Florence.

Smiled.

Then got angry.

Then saw—the paint-splattered T-shirt over her head. The quick unclasping of the pink bra. Those tiny delicious breasts, nipples as pink as her lips and her tongue.

Fuck.

The pink bra, laying on the table where she dropped it when he left.

Did she take it?

Routine kept Will from thinking about the bra—and Florence's breasts—and her freckles—fuck, what was wrong with his head—24/7. It kept him from messaging her. It actually kept him from going on OKC to message someone else or to window shop for potential lovers, because he knew that was all a slippery slope to creeping her profile again, filling out the elusive dating site photographs with the details he now knew.

Like the freckles that did splatter her skin *everywhere*.

*Freckles. Everywhere.*

But he still thought about her a lot.

Too much.

Which was how he ended up at Weeds Cafe at the end of the day.

What the fuck was he going to say?

"Hi," he said to the barista behind the counter. The barista was bearded, pierced, and tattooed. Will pondered briefly what he'd look like in a beard. Did Florence like beards? Probably not, he decided. She didn't look like she'd go for... he looked at the barista critically and realized he was examining him as Florence's potential lover. Oh-my-god. What was wrong with him?

She was right.

He was obsessed and planning their wedding. Or at least... well, fantasizing about meeting three. Four.

For their one month anniversary, he'd take her to Cafe Blanca again and fuck her on a parked car. This time thoroughly. So thoroughly the police would come, and it would be embarrassing, but also hot.

*Shut. Up. Brain.*

His penis twitched to suggest that perhaps it was not the brain that was in control.

"Can I help you?" the bearded-pierced-tattooed barista said, and Will realized he was repeating himself.

"Sorry." He shook himself. "Um. I was here last week. With a friend. She... we... this is a little embarrassing. We left a pink bra on the table..."

The barista laughed.

"Yeah, I got it," he said. "She said you'd come back for it."

"What?"

"She left it here for you. She said you'd come back for it. I'll go get it."

Witch.

Fucking witch.

Also, other things.

No, there was no other word for it. If she was here... Will closed his eyes.

"Here you go." The barista handed him a ziplock bag. Pink bra.

"Do you have a pair of scissors I could borrow?" Will asked.

The barista shook his head.

"I mean, I do," he said. "But she said you'd ask for a pair, and that I wasn't to give them to you."

"What?"

"She said…"

"I heard you." Will held the baggie. There was a piece of paper tucked into one of the cups.

Her phone number?

His heart made a loud, ridiculous thud, and his throat felt dry.

He reached in.

"Will, I'm sorry. I'm right. But I'm sorry."

And that was all.

He dropped the note on the floor and left the cafe.

"Are you going to take the bra?" the barista yelled after him.

"You can keep it," he snapped over his shoulder.

But when he made it to his car, he turned around and went back.

"You can keep the bra or toss it," he said. "But… I do want the note."

He fiddled with the note all day. Even as he logged onto OkCupid and made a last minute "Let's meet for coffee after work, and see if we're up for more" date with a gorgeous black-eyed, non-red-haired, non-freckled nurse whose real passion was her cello.

*Fuck. You. Florence.*

He tore up the note.

Taped it back up.

Tore it up again.

*Get a grip, Will.*

Routine.

Date.

*Red-haired witch.*

## Methadone Fail
### MONDAY, DECEMBER 18, CONTINUED

"I'm sorry," Will said. He felt like a jerk. "This just isn't going to work out."

"What?" The woman sitting opposite him looked nothing like Amanda. Nor Florence. She was cute and sweet and perfectly nice. Also, fucking cello player. Was there a sexier instrument?

*Fucking work it, Will. Cello. Between those thighs. Come on. Penis. Twitch!*

"I'm so sorry. This just isn't going to work out."

He was a jerk.

Also, fucking *déjà vu.*

Was she going to say, "I thought this was going quite well?"

"I thought this was going quite well," she said. "I thought..."

"You're lovely," he said. "I'm just..."

Thinking about another woman's freckles and nipples.

*Don't fucking say that. Say something else.*

"I'm so sorry," he said.

*Fucking lie, Will. She's about to cry.*

"I'm just realizing... and I'm so sorry, I'm realizing it right now, sitting across the table from you—but I'm just realizing I'm too freshly divorced. You know? I'm not ready for this."

She reached for his hands.

"It's all right," she said. "I'm not looking for anything serious."

Except she was. He saw the lie and longing in her face —is that what Florence had seen in his?

Fuck.

"I'm so sorry," he said. And he took her hands to his lips. Kissed the knuckles of each of her ten fingers. Rested his forehead on her wrist.

Went home alone.

Thought about Florence.

---



---

He couldn't believe it.

He fucking couldn't believe it!

And by text, too!

He closed his office door. Picked up his landline. Dialled.

"Look, Will, I know this is hard," Amanda said as soon as she answered.

"It isn't hard, it's fucking unfair," he said.

"Don't swear at me," she snapped.

"I'm not swearing at you. I'm expressing my anger at the situation." He paused, because he also really wanted to swear at her. And just generally scream, "Fuck, fuck, fuck, fuck!" at the entire world. "You don't unilaterally decide I don't get to spend Christmas with my children."

"It doesn't fall on your weekend," she said, and they both knew it sounded lame. "Look, Will, I know it's hard, but it would be so..."

"How difficult would it be for you to... we're doing well, right? I mean, compared to most people I've seen go through divorces. I'm not happy. You know I'm not happy. But I am not being a dick. We are generally being civil. I've given you pretty much everything you wanted, including a custody arrangement that's killing me because it's suppose to be better for the kids. Fine. You don't get to just decide I don't get to spend Christmas with them. How hard would it be, Amanda, for you to endure two hours of me in your house— our fucking house!—on Christmas Day, so that I can spend Christmas Day with my children?"

"Will..."

"And how do you think they will feel? This Christmas is going to be hard on them too!"

"Will, I wish I could. But Ranveer will be here, and..."

"Oh-my-fucking-god, your fucking new lover gets to spend Christmas with my children and I don't?"

He didn't know what she said next, because he ripped the headset off the phone, then slammed it down so hard on his desk, it bounced... and then yanked the cord out of its socket and threw the entire thing to the ground.

Kicked it.

"Fuck!"

Rosie knocked on the door.

"Will?"

He stared at her, furious.

"You need to go run on the treadmill," she said.

"My ex-wife is a fucking bitch," he said.

"Run on the treadmill, and then box, and then run some more," Rosie said. "No. I don't care what she did. I don't care if she flipped out because you hired your old cleaning lady, I don't care if she's sending you pictures of Ranveer's dick, I don't care if she's demanding that you donate a pint of blood a week for some warped science experiment and if you don't you lose custody of your kids. Go run on the fucking treadmill, and we can talk after."

He hugged her and then kissed her on both cheeks as he went out the door.

"What would I do without you?" he called over his shoulder.

"Get fired or go to hell in a hand basket," she yelled after him.

Fuck. Rosie.

He adored her.

He had kept the break-up of his marriage a secret from her for the first three weeks. Because... well, he just did. During which time he apparently metamorphosed from the best boss in the world (Rosie had bought him a mug that said so, on their three-year anniversary) to a Grade-A asshole.

He didn't remember what he did, exactly. But it was after three weeks of sleeping on Niko's couch, three weeks of daily texts and phone fights with Amanda, and he was going out of his mind.

So. He snapped. Barked.

Rosie first snapped back, and then sat him down and said, "What's going on?"

"My life is over and I'm going insane," he told her. And then he told her everything. Well, almost everything. He didn't tell her about how that night six years ago... No. He couldn't. But he told her about Niko and AA, and patterns.

And his greatest fear.

"What helps?" she asked.

"What?" He didn't understand.

"When I fall apart, I dance. Or do yoga," Rosie said. "That's what helps me. What helps you?"

He thought about it a little.

"Running, punching people, and lifting heavy shit," he said.

She blinked.

"I mean, boxing," he corrected. "Not punching random people. Although I do think slugging fucking Ranveer would make me feel better," he added. Wistfully.

Rosie laughed, and he tried to smile.

"When was the last time you went to the gym?" she asked.

"Three weeks ago."

"Ok. Go now. Run half-a-marathon, and then come apologize to me."

"Rosie?" he said when he came back from the gym, limping, exhausted but in slightly less pain, that time. "I don't deserve you."

"I know," she said. Patted him on the head as if he were a little boy.

He was really, really grateful he didn't fuck it all up by sleeping with her... again.

It would have been so easy. It would have felt so good. In that moment... so good. And she wouldn't mind... she would actually like... he felt the thought coming, and backed away from it.

He ran on the treadmill, not thinking about Amanda. Nor Florence. Nor Rosie. Nor drinking.

Not thinking, not thinking.

When he came back from the gym, Rosie had hooked the landline back up.

"It still works," she told him. "Your wife... your ex... er, Amanda called on it."

"It's probably not such a good idea that I talk to her right now."

"As you wish." Rosie shrugged. Put the pink slip in-between his fingers. Punched his shoulder and walked out.

"Call Amanda." Underlined.

He texted instead.

"I don't want to yell at you again. I'm still pissed."

"I'm sorry, Will," she wrote back immediately. "I was, like you said, unilateral."

They were so fucking civilized.

They decided he would take the kids on Christmas Eve-eve, and have them that night, and have all of Christmas Eve day with them. Deliver them to Amanda's house—their former house—apparently, now, Amanda and Ranveer's house ("Is he living there?" he asked Amanda, and she didn't answer, which probably meant yes)—at 8 p.m.

Amanda graciously forgave him for stealing her cleaning lady. Will did not mention that she had been *their* cleaning lady for five years. And it wasn't stealing. It was asking—it was saying, "Hey, Karla, do you have time in your schedule to clean my condo once a week?" Although apparently, it was unthinkable that, post-divorce, the same woman vacuum and scrub their *separate* households.

"I'll get another," Amanda said.

"I don't ask her a fucking thing about you, you know," Will said. "I don't even ever see her."

Amanda conceded that perhaps it didn't make sense, but she just didn't want... she just didn't. "Ok, Will?"

Will didn't press the point, but he did mention that it was perhaps unfair to fire a loyal employee just before Christmas. Amanda, after a pause, agreed, and decided to give the cleaner her notice after New Year's.

So fucking civilized.

Rosie gave him a much-too-sympathetic hug when he told her about the "compromise."

"I can't offer to spend Christmas Eve being depressed with you because I have a crazy party planned," she said. "To which you can't come, because you have a penis."

"Sexist bitch," he muttered.

"I love knowing that if I had to, I could get your ass fired six dozen times for workplace inappropriate behaviour,"

Rosie said. Then they both blushed. "Anyway, trust me, you wouldn't enjoy it. But if you're desperate on Christmas Day, text me, ok? You can have dinner with me and all my hungover friends."

"Are they as cute as you?" he volleyed half-heartedly.

"Cuter," she said. "And even gayer."

They laughed.

Will felt better.

Not good. But... better...

---

## Lies, Groceries & Plans
### THURSDAY, DECEMBER 21

---

At the Thursday meeting, Will lied to Niko and told him he was feeling fine about the Christmas arrangement. He wasn't. But it was as good as he was going to get. And what did Christmas Day matter, anyway, if you were a *de facto* atheist? He and the kids could have Christmas Day morning just as well at his place on Christmas Eve.

"Did you go overboard with the presents?" Niko asked.

"Totally," Will confessed. They laughed. Wished each other merry Christmas, and Niko went off to the airport for his annual Christmas golf vacation in Maui—after he retired from the ring, Niko became an avid golfer, although Will never did manage to picture the former boxer with a golf club in his hand... what would that look like?—and Will went to buy his children more presents.

And, to get a tree for his apartment. A wreath for the door. A kitschy red tablecloth covered with white reindeer for the dining room table.

He did not buy Christmas-themed dishes, but he thought about it. He wasn't sure about groceries—should they go out for dinner? Maybe. But then, breakfast?

He went to Sunterra and bought everything, including an outrageously priced organic turkey.

"Holy fuck," he said when the cashier rang it through.

"I know, outrageous, isn't it? But you're lucky we had any left," she said. Smiled. Was she flirting with him? He paused and looked at her. She was adorable. Looked nothing like Amanda. Or Florence. Or Rosie. Jesus. What was wrong with him?

She smiled at him more fully. "Plans tonight?"

He could take her home. She'd show him how to make the fucking turkey.

"Yes," he said. "Have a good night."

------

## Fake Christmas Eve Fails & Victories



------

Will ended up taking Polly and Matthew out for steaks on Christmas Eve-eve, because, first, the turkey wouldn't fit in his apartment-sized oven, and, second, googling revealed that even if it had fit, it would take almost five hours to cook, and not the 45 or so minutes he had allotted to dinner preparation.

The failure to provide a proper Christmas dinner for his children made him feel like shit. And angry. He should have planned ahead, he should have bought a smaller turkey —he should have just bought a chicken and slathered it in cranberries.

The dinner out was a disaster. Polly was whiny and Matthew was sullen. Will's steak was overdone and Polly's was too raw, and it didn't occur to them to just switch them, because they were both too busy being miserable.

So it was shaping up to be a horrible Christmas Eve-eve... until they came back to the apartment, and the kids saw the tree, and Matthew found the turkey in the bath-tub, and they all tried to cram the bird into the oven to prove him wrong—and failed—and they laughed, and he gave each of them a can of cranberries to eat as a bedtime snack.

They watched *How The Grinch Stole Christmas* in his bed, and when Polly fell asleep, he decided to just leave her there. And then Matthew didn't want to leave the bed either, and instead of arguing, Will let him stay too.

He woke up on Christmas morning with a crick in his neck, but Polly in one armpit and Matthew in the other, and so he was very very happy.

They ate cranberries and pumpkin pie and Black Forest cake with real whipped cream and cherries for breakfast. Then Will made them fruit smoothies liberally laced with protein powder, which Polly left untouched and Matthew poured into the sink. Then they went skating at Olympic Plaza, and had hot chocolate and greasy hamburgers for lunch, and then they went sledding, and then chilled in the hot tub at his condo.

And it was a wonderful, amazing day and Will didn't even hate Amanda that much when he dropped them off and chose to stay in the car, just in case Ranveer was already in *his* former house.

"Merry Christmas, Dadda!" Polly said, using the diminutive that she now thought, at seven, she was too old for.

"Merry Christmas, Dad," Matthew said very seriously, nine and already practicing being a teen. But he let himself be kissed like a little boy.

"Merry Christmas, you boogers," he said. And they went home, and he drove back to his apartment, where he would be spending Christmas Eve proper, and Christmas Day, alone.

He was aware of every bar he passed en route. He took certain turns just to avoid passing *that* particular bar, *that* old haunt. He didn't stop at a single one. He made it to the underground parking garage of his building safe.

*Safe.*

There was a liquor store on the ground floor of his building.

He knew this, of course. Thought it ironic.

He had never been inside, not even to get sparkling water.

It was really nice.

Fuck, it was beautiful.

He walked up and down the aisles, just enjoying the...

...he was just here to enjoy the aesthetic arrangement of the bottles and the...

...oh-my-fucking-god what was he doing?

He would just buy a small...

One drink. Not even one night. Just one drink.

And if it was one night—if he had a binge night one night every six years, what difference would it make?

Rosie, that morning, when he came to, started to explain: "Shit, Will, you fucked up."

One night, Rosie! One fucking night!

Amanda, five years later: "I never got over it, Will. Do you understand? I never got over it!"

One night. One drink.

The best of reasons, right? His first Christmas without his kids.

He'd just get...

"Looking for anything in particular?" the clerk asked him.

*Tell him.*

"Just trying to decide," he choked out.

*Help me.*

Jesus. What was he?

*Don't do this, Will.*

He went into the corner with the beer coolers and put his head against the glass. Cold.

Ok. He knew the drill. He had this. Never again.

*Help.*

Get help.

Phone.

Amanda.

No.

Never, never, never.

Niko. That's why... that's the whole reason...

"Call me. Anytime."

Lifeline. Yes.

Will dialled.

Voicemail.

Fuck. Of course. Niko was on his way to Maui. On a plane. Or at the airport.

Rosie.

No.

Will not ruin her Christmas Eve. And will not ruin... will not.

Will. Not.

Have to.

"Sir? Are you okay?"

*Break a pane of glass and they will call the police and you will be safe.*

"Just very undecided," Will said. He was surprised how... sane his voice sounded.

"Ok, just let me know if you need anything."

Phone.

What the fuck was he supposed to say?

Fuck.

He stared at the shelves and bottles around him. Snapped a photograph. Hit send.

Rosie: "LOL."

And a picture. Her face, smiling, grinning. Wearing a hot pink dress.

Plunging cleavage.

Think about cleavage.

*Come on, Will.*

She didn't understand.

Call her.

Don't.

Don't ruin her night.

Her life.

*Your life.*

"Sir? Are you sure you're all right?"

*No! Help me!*

Help.

*Someone. Please. Help.*

Florence's voice: "You're an alcoholic."

Fuck.

Florence. She knew. And. She was lost to him anyway.

Florence.

She never gave him her phone number. And who would be checking OkCupid messages on Christmas Eve?

He tapped the app.

Typed.

"I'm in a liquor store. Help me."

Send.

Jesus.

Run.

She responded immediately.

"Address?"

He was sitting on the floor, in the corner beside the beer coolers, his head between his hands when she found him. Slid down onto the floor beside him. Said nothing for a long time.

Then, suddenly, kissed his cheek.

"You did good," she said. He shook his head. She shook hers and then, put both her hands around his head and shook it. He swatted at her. "You did good," she said. Looked around. "Nice place," she commented. Frowned. "Isn't your apartment just upstairs? Oh-my-fucking-god, Will, do you live on top of a liquor store?"

"I thought it would be... you know, ironic. Like a private joke? Between me and my... demon?" His voice was... very normal. A little distant. Tired.

"Or, stupid," she said. "Well. Come on, let's get out of here."

"Where are we going?"

"To your apartment," she said. "My babysitter is charging me an extortionate three-hour minimum, last-minute, holiday rate. I'm getting some mind-blowing orgasms out of this rescue trip."

"So... you're paying someone to have sex with me? I'm flattered," he attempted a joke. It was a terrible joke. She laughed anyway.

"You can think that if you like," she said. Pulled him to his feet. "Let's go."

## Sex, Stick & Carrot



He didn't bend her over a parked car this time. Nor kiss her in the vestibule. And she didn't touch him either, not until he pushed the elevator button, and that's when she leaned into his shoulder—just a lean, her forehead brushing the bottom of his jaw.

And he lost his mind, again, and by the time the elevator doors opened, she was half-naked and he was all hard, and Mrs. Ziernicka, the chair of the condo board, almost swallowed her dentures.

"Mr. Ornot!" she shouted stepping out of the elevator. "Are you drunk?"

"So fucking sober, Mrs. Z," he moaned through a mouthful of Florence's hair. "Merry Christmas."

She unbuttoned his coat and shirt in the elevator, but he didn't let her do much else—he was too... he couldn't stop to let her touch him, he needed his hands, his mouth, his nose, everything—touching her, squeezing, pulling. He pulled her out of the elevator by her breasts and she moaned with such pleasure and pain that he dropped them and fumbled with his belt and zipper because the pressure of his clothes on his cock was unbearable.

"Keys, keys, keys, apartment, apartment," she whispered, then dropped to her knees and lunged for his cock, and he grabbed her breasts again and pulled, then lifted his hands to her hair and dragged her, on her knees, his cock in her mouth, towards his apartment door. He mouth-fucked her, holding her head with one hand while fumbling for his keys with the other.

"Fuck, god, Florence." He made inarticulate sounds, and thought *If she laughs, I will slap her*, and hoped she would laugh, but she didn't—just eased off his cock for a second.

"Keys?" she said.

"Keys," he groaned. Let go of her head with his other hand. Keys. Pockets. Cock. Mouth. Tongue. Teeth. Thrust. Thrust—and hold still. Gag. Withdraw. Oh-fuck.

He felt her hands on his legs, under his coat.

"Keys." She fished them out of his pocket, placed them in his hands, then returned her mouth and attention to his cock.

He had no idea how he managed to open the door, but he did, and he dragged her across its threshold, still on her knees, her mouth still on his cock, and then pulled out of her and crashed on top of her. Eyes. Nose. Cheeks. Chin. Lips. Mouth full of hair.

Clothes, too many clothes.

They went flying, coats, scarves. His shirt, her bra. His pants. Her leggings.

"Fuck, I love this dress," he said. It was soft and pink and velvety, trimmed with soft fur. Outrageously kitschy. Outrageously gorgeous.

"Did you change into this just for me?" he said, pulling

it down over her chest and belly, and then yanking her breasts out of the V-neckline.

"Lesbian engagement party," she murmured into his neck. "We all had to wear pink and fur." She laughed, and he... he didn't dare slap her, he was too keyed up to control that, but he covered her mouth with his hand. Did not pull off the dress, just shoved it up higher, and pulled the panties down between her knees. Kept them there too.

"They will tear," she whispered, trying to wiggle out of them.

"Leave them." He stopped her. Kisses. Freckles. Neck. He pressed her face against his chest, just to feel... just to feel.

*Fuck. God. Florence.*

Her hands on his cock.

Her voice in his ear. "We need condoms."

Fucking condoms.

His hand between her legs. So slick, so soft. Heaven.

"Florence?" he said her name, and its syllables were a nightingale's song in his ears, head, heart. "We need to make it to the bedroom. That's where the condoms are." He spoke very slowly as if drunk, but he was so sober and he was so happy. "We can do it. But don't you fucking dare stop kissing me as we go," he said, and he kissed her, and wrapped his arms and legs around her. "And we can't get up."

"We can't get up?" she said, tangling her limbs with his.

"We can't," he said. "The world will end. Can we do it?"

"Or die trying." She chewed on his neck. Clavicle.

He slid his hands under her body and heaved her forward. "Don't stop the kissing," he reminded her.

She didn't. Fuck, she didn't, and by the time they made it to the bedroom and he was sliding the condom on, he was also thinking—or not thinking so much as feeling—that there was no need for the condom, for penetration, for orgasm—this was utter bliss and heaven and fulfillment, but then, cock covered, he slid into her, and oh-my-fucking-god, there was more bliss.

"What did you say?" she asked after he came. They were still laying on the floor, although he rolled off her and brought her up on top of him—more than that he couldn't do. They were both wet, slick with sweat, and Will was getting cold...

"Are you cold?" he asked her.

Florence shook her head.

"What did you say?" she repeated.

"I thought the word bliss, repeatedly, for perhaps the first time in my life," he said into the hair just above her ear. "Before coming, no less. Very unmanly."

Florence laughed.

Kissed the tip of his nose.

"Come to the bed," she said, pulling him up.

They slid under the covers, and she climbed on top of him, resting her pussy just above his spent cock, and then sliding it onto his left hip bone.

"Will? This is no way a reflection on your performance, which was fabulous," she said, moving her hips up and down and then grinding herself against his hip. "So fabulous, in fact, that I desperately need another orgasm just because I'm laying here beside you."

He kissed her and reached for her ass.

"No." She breathed into his chest. "You don't need to do... anything."

He lay still, one hand on her ass cheek, one hand in her hair, and felt her moving and felt her breathing and felt her explode on his hip, and then he held her close so he could feel every single vibration.

"Fuck," she said.

*Bliss,* he thought.

*Sleep,* he thought, and tightened his arms around her. But she was wiggling out.

"Babysitter," she said. Kissed his nose.

"You did good, Will," she said, as she had in the liquor store earlier. "I'm proud of you."

It didn't sound patronizing.

He watched her move through the bedroom, into the hallway, hunting for clothes.

He was going to see her again. Did she know that?

"Florence?" he called.

She came back into the bedroom, her fur-trimmed pink dress pulled down over her ass and pussy, her leggings in one hand, her bra in the other.

"I'm not leaving you my bra this time," she said. "Although I can't find my panties."

"Ok," he said. "But, Florence."

"And I'm glad you texted me, but this is still a one night stand," she said. "December-sucks-Christmas-is-hard-let's-have-animal-sex. You know?"

"Florence..."

"Will." She was stern.

It didn't matter. He was going to see her again. It was only a matter of time. He didn't have to fight her right now.

"Ok," he said and smiled. "Thank you—thank you very much for coming."

"You're welcome," she said and smiled her beautiful smile, and turned around. Looking at her back, Will suddenly saw himself waking up tomorrow, Christmas Day, alone, and texting his kids and knowing that they were in his house—former house—spending Christmas without him, and...

She turned around.

He was standing, shaking. A little.

"Will. Talk to me," she demanded.

"Tomorrow is going to be a hard day," he said. "I'm afraid... I know you can't come. Won't come. I know... but can... can I just text you? And say... it's hard? And you can... I don't know, kick my ass, so I don't..." He stopped. "I'm afraid," he said.

Sexy. Fucking cowardly loser. Well-played, Will.

He was never going to see her again.

"Get on the bed and lean back against the pillows," she said. "No, not under the covers. On top. Yes, like that." He followed instructions, confused.

Saw the phone in her hand too late.

Snap.

She laughed.

"Look." She showed him the photograph. "Post-coital shrinkage is such a cruel thing, isn't it? So this is what you're going to do, Will. Tomorrow, every hour on the hour from when you wake up until midnight, you're going to send me a message on OKC, you're going to say... do you prefer dry or clean?"

"Dry," Will said.

"You're going to say, 'Dry.' And I'll send you a thumbs up. I know you won't lie. But if you miss an hour—this photo goes up on my Facebook and Twitter and Instagram, and my kids' SnapChat, for good measure, and I'm going to ask all my friends to share it, and we're going to call it Will's Eenie Weenie Penis."

"Jesus Christ, Florence, what's wrong with you?"

She laughed.

"I'm making sure you don't get tempted into half a drink tomorrow," she said. "Don't you think it will be effective?"

He fucking hated her and loved her at the same time and his penis twitched and grew.

"Could you take a picture of this instead?" he asked. And they both laughed.

"Deal?" she asked, leaning in for a kiss.

"Deal," he agreed. "But... give me an incentive too."

"What?"

"Well, the photo is the... stick. Give me a carrot. If I make it... when I make it... what do I get?" He slid his hands under her dress and rested them on the softness of her belly. His fingertips started seeing her freckles, and then his eyes wanted to see them too. He started to lift the dress up. She pulled it down.

"What do you want?" she asked, moving away.

*To see you again, you infuriating creature.*

"A date on Valentine's Day," he said.

She was in the bedroom doorway again and half-turned. "What?"

"A date on Valentine's Day," he said. "Pro-actively. I definitely don't want to be alone and moping and feeling sorry for myself on Valentine's Day."

"That's... six, seven weeks away. You'll find a date by then."

"I'm booking a date now. With you. As... my carrot, Carrots. Incentive."

She laughed and twirled her crazy red hair.

He loved the way she laughed, and he also wanted to shove his cock into her mouth every time she laughed.

"Ok," she said. "You can cancel if you find Mrs. Right by then."

"Ok," he said.

"This is still a one night stand," she said. "Because of... extenuating circumstances."

"Right," he nodded.

"Merry Christmas, Will," she said. "You don't have to see me out."

"Merry Christmas, Florence," he said. Stayed sitting on the bed. "I'll see you on Valentine's Day."

He couldn't see her anymore, because she was in the hallway. He heard her open the door.

He heard her say, very quietly, "You will."

He was asleep in minutes, and he dreamt of nothing but freckles. Woke up happy.

# Dry



*iwillornot*: Dry.

**notanightingale:** You made it. Congratulations.

*iwillornot*: Thank you.

**notanightingale:** Don't mention it. Seriously. Don't mention it again.

*iwillornot*: I won't. I'll see you on Valentine's Day. And I promise not to message you once before then.

**notanightingale:** You'd better not.

*iwillornot*: Won't you miss me?

# DELAYED VALENTINE

*For my Nicole,*
*who taught me how to dance with a mop*

---

## Bringing In The New Year


---

Florence did not think about Will on Boxing Day, when she took ten-year-old Isaac sledding while Ethan and Sammy, her two elder boys, insisted on going to Marlborough Mall to check out the post-Christmas sales. She did not think about him—very much—as the week between Christmas and New Year's unfolded, deliciously and slowly. Seven days off in a row, no work, no toilets to scrub or floors to mop except for her own. And she wasn't going to do them, not now. She was just going to let the house crumble around her for a week and do a big clean on New Year's Eve. She was going to sleep in and hang with the boys and cook—and let the dishes pile up until she argued Sammy into emptying the dishwasher and Ethan into filling it back up, and she was going to read trashy romances and watch Netflix and solo-chill and not think about Will at all.

She thought about him, a little, each time OkCupid told her she had a new message. But it was never from him. And she was pleased—*not* disappointed—that he wasn't messaging her. He promised he wouldn't and he wasn't.

She was pleased.

Not disappointed.

She was not disappointed. Why would she be disappointed? She wasn't.

She was not thinking about him. At all.

She expected to hear from him on New Year's Eve, she admitted that to herself when she noticed she was compulsively checking to see if there were new messages. Not a... well, it was another holiday, right? But not a family holiday. He'd be ok. He wouldn't need her.

She didn't want him to need her!

"Fuck, Florence, shake it," she told herself sternly. And did not think about him at all for the rest of the night. She and the boys bundled into snowsuits—well, except for Ethan, who just put on his leather jacket although she did manage to nag him into stuffing a beanie and gloves into his pockets—and piled into the rickety Civic—"Please, God," Florence murmured as she turned the key in the ignition, "let it start," and it started, Hallelujah!—and went to Olympic Plaza for First Night. They met Santokh and Michelle, who were wearing matching Canada Goose parkas, Santokh's white turban poking out from the hood, Michelle's hood tossed back to reveal her cloud of black hair.

"Is it too cute? Too ridiculous?" Santokh whispered into Florence's ear.

"Your turban is always ridiculous," Florence said and ducked as Santokh swatted at her. "What? A white woman in a turban? I don't get to make fun of that? Come on!"

"I'm talking about the parkas!" Santokh wailed. "It was Michelle's idea. She said Korean couples wear matching outfits on their honeymoons. And that we should get matching something. And we needed new coats. So we bought these matching parkas. Do we look like dorks?"

"You look like total dorks," Florence said. "Isn't

Michelle Indian? Sort of? I mean, Canadian, but aren't her parents from New Delhi?" She was quite proud of herself that she remembered this, because she tended to stop listening when Santokh talked about Michelle, which was often.

"She taught English in Korea for a few years before grad school, remember?" Santokh said. Florence didn't remember that, but she nodded as if she did, and she smiled at Michelle and said something nice about the parkas and enjoyed watching Michelle's glower—Michelle glowered often, and more often still when looking at Florence—turn into a glow and a responsive smile.

And it was a great night as they sang along to the bands on stage and goofed around, and the boys Jedi-fought with glow sticks—even the all-grown up, seventeen-year-old Ethan—and they called in the New Year in style, and Florence was happy. Nothing bothered her: not Michelle's random bouts of jealousy, sometimes directed at her, sometimes at some random stranger who happened to look at Santokh and smiled, not Santokh's goofy white turban, which really was a silly thing for a white woman to sport *ever*, much less under a parka, not Sammy's intermittent "Can we go home now? I want to game more!" She was happy, happy, happy, and she did not think about Will or OKC or messages or anything at all.

And she was pleased—not disappointed—that there was no Happy New Year message from him in the morning.

No, she wasn't.

She was disappointed.

So. Fucking. Disappointed.

"Fuck, Florence, shake it," she told herself again. "Shake it. Don't think about it, don't think about him. You don't want this. Shall we make a list of all the reasons why you don't want this?"

His hands on her breasts, dragging her out of that elevator on her knees, oh-my-fucking-god-yes, that was so...

*Stop!*

"All the reasons you don't want this!" she told herself again.

"Why are you talking to yourself, Mom?" Isaac asked her, popping up beside her elbow. "Want to play Battleship with me?" She didn't. But he was her littlest baby, and she was too conscious of how Ethan never wanted to hang with her anymore, not for years, and Sammy, only two years older than the ten-year-old Isaac, was less and less interested in spending time with her too, so she played, and when Sammy brought out Settlers of Catan, she played that with them both, and then happily settled into an *Iron Man* marathon with all three of them for the rest of the night, until Ethan popped out to hang with his friends—"Are you sure it's not too late to be going out?" she asked him and he rolled his eyes—and Sammy wanted to get back to his gaming and Isaac started yawing and she convinced him to go to bed at a reasonable time.

She checked OKC.

No messages.

She did not click on Will's profile. It took effort.

She did not—fuck, yes, she did—jump when she got a message.

*"Hi, gorgeous."*

Not Will.

She logged out. Went to bed... and did not think about Will's fingers or tongue or hands—Jesus, the things that man could do with his hands—and she did not think about laying on top of his torso and rubbing herself against his sharp hip bones, and then she did and she dropped her hands to her clit and slit and...

Oh. Fuck, yes.

Well, maybe she'd think about him, a little. As a masturbatory aid. That was ok.

He'd probably text her next week.

# Disappointment
### MONDAY, JANUARY 8

He didn't.

## Not Thinking

### SUNDAY, JANUARY 28

"I'm very proud of him," she told Santokh. They were doing their usual Sunday deep-clean of the reproductive health clinic. It was their most lucrative contract, and in many ways their easiest one, although to get through it quickly, they worked at a sprinter's pace, and rarely in the same room.

Unless one of them—usually Santokh—needed to talk. In which case, they slowed down a little and worked side-by-side, and Santokh talked about her newfound domestic bliss with Michelle, and how she couldn't wait for the wedding, and would Florence's boys really dress up in bridesmaids' dresses for it? Michelle really wanted it. And the cake—were plastic figures on a cake really kitschy? Because she wanted two bride figures on it so much.

And would Michelle get less jealous after the wedding? "I love her, I love her so much, I never look at anyone else—but she's jealous of everything! Everyone! Even you, Florence, even my students—I think the only reason she takes yoga with me is so that she can keep an eye on me, and it boggles my mind, and I just don't understand these fits at all!"

Florence listened patiently and tried not to roll her eyes.

Now that Florence was talking, Santokh was clearly trying to do the same.

"Uhm," Santokh said.

"I was sure he'd find some reason to text me before Valentine's Day," Florence said. "I was so sure. And he didn't. I'm really impressed."

"You're so full of shit," Santokh said, and Florence blushed—caught sight of her face suffused with red and that made her blush even more. The curse of redheads, she thought. When Santokh blushed, she looked beautiful—alluring, excited, sexy. When Florence blushed... ugh.

At least Will wasn't here to see it.

What the fuck? How, why was she having thoughts like that?

"I'm really impressed," she said again. Santokh shrugged. Florence took a deep breath, and dared her friend to roll her eyes by rolling hers. Santokh responded and they both exploded in laughter and Santokh returned to the vacuum cleaner and Florence to the mop.

She mopped and Santokh vacuumed, and Florence focused on rejoicing that she had found Santokh—how many years ago now? It must be almost ten, maybe more. Ten years ago, she looked at the awkward and shy yoga teacher at the Y with a smile, and that awkward and shy yoga teacher smiled back. She still went by Emily then—it was before she joined her cult full on and received her spiritual name and insisted everyone, including Florence and Michelle, use it *all the time*. It was only a few months later that they were working together as Karma Klean.

The Karma was Santokh's idea. Of course.

For Santokh, the cleaning business was a way to fund

her yoga practice and then yoga studio (cult, as Florence always called it, half-teasing, half-serious—after Santokh went into the practice full on and started wearing white all the time, and then a turban). For Florence, it was part career, part inherited family business—all salvation. It was the safety net that saved her when she walked out of the house she had bought with her second husband and showed up on her mother's door step, with three children and two suitcases. No money. No skills.

She remembered the phone call that made her return possible, suddenly, sharply. "You can come home now." Martha's voice. Sad. Tired. Exhausted. Coming when she was at her wit's end of what to do, where to go. She had jumped from the frying pan into the fire—fuck, she hated clichés, but that one just kept on defining those stages of her life—once already. But she wouldn't go back into the frying pan...

*Oh-my-fucking-god, I am incoherent and I am thinking ridiculous thoughts. Stop it, stop it, stop it, think about something else.*

Will.

*No, not him.*

Fuck, he was sexy.

*Think not sexy thoughts!*

Mom. Martha. Cleaning. Martha worked as a house-cleaner most of Florence's life. Her clients adored her. At the point that Florence moved back in with her, most of her clients planned their lives around Martha's schedule. Martha got Florence her first house to clean. Then another. Florence got the next few contracts herself. And the bank. Enough money, so very quickly, to get a place for herself and the boys.

She remembered Martha's disapproval.

"Florence, it's a trailer park!"

"Mom, it's a really nice mobile home. And it's a really nice trailer park. And it's my own!"

"But Florence—it's a trailer park!"

"But Mom—I love you, but I swear to God, if we keep on living together, I will kill you!"

They were, then, working together still, although Florence was doing more and more jobs on her own. And Martha started to say, more and more often, that she needed to slow down, and could Florence take over another commitment? And perhaps this one?

And Florence could, but suddenly there was too much work, and she decided to take on a partner.

Santokh.

Impulse decision, spontaneous decision, best decision.

She smiled at the back of Santokh's turban.

"I love you, you cultist!" she yelled over the vacuum cleaner. Santokh turned around and gave her the finger.

"Worst guru ever!" Florence sang at the top of her lungs as she danced with the mop. And did not think about Will. Look at her not thinking about Will.

Wait.

Was thinking about not thinking about Will thinking about Will?

Fuck.

She was insane.

Stupid.

A twelve-year-old girl with a crush.

*Stop. It.*

She let herself think about Will briefly as she cleaned the mop and emptied the bucket. Fine. Think about him. She was thinking about him. But she would not mention him to Santokh again—that was foolish, it made her look... foolish.

She would not mention him to Santokh at all.

"Thinking about your boy again?" Santokh murmured into her ear from behind.

"No!"

"You looked all dreamy!" her friend teased.

"I was wondering…" Florence struggled for a thought… "I was wondering how the hell I was going to cope. During your honeymoon. Selfish bitch."

"I was wondering that too," Santokh said very quickly and very seriously. "I have an idea, actually." And she started talking about the concept of service and *seva*, and how her students…

"Wait, wait, wait, are you suggesting that your students would work for us for free because they'd be fulfilling some sort of karmic cult duty?" Florence exclaimed. "Oh-my-god, we're going to be rich! We're going to have an army of them, cleaning every house and bank in Calgary, and…"

"I'm saying my students would be happy to help out," Santokh said. "One of them, Uttamroop, already offered. And we will pay them." She paused. "A little less than we make."

Florence punched her lightly. "Such a bad, bad guru you are," she said. "If they're going to help, they've got to come on a couple of jobs with us before you're gone, ok? So I can train them up a little."

"You know Uttamroop—she was at the engagement party," Santokh said. "You liked her."

"Which one was she?" Florence sang. "One of the ones in the kitschy pink dress, like me? Or one of the weirdoes in a turban?"

She danced away from Santokh, singing, "I'm going to have an army of yogic cultists cleaning for me and life will be so great, la-di-dah."

She didn't think about Will.

Yes she did.

She couldn't stop thinking about him.

Fuck.

But she'd stop. She wouldn't think about it him at all. And maybe they'd go out on Valentine's Day or they wouldn't. She wouldn't get her hopes up, she wouldn't have expectations.

Did she have expectations?

Fuck. She had expectations.

She had to kill them. If she had expectations, she couldn't... she wouldn't...

She would not think of him at all. Not until Valentine's Day.

Unless he messaged her before that. Surely, he would.

---



# Disappointment, 2
### MONDAY, FEBRUARY 12

He didn't.

---

Anticipation


---

"Tomorrow?" Santokh asked. Slyly.

Florence flicked her turban.

Santokh accepted the taunt, and Florence thought about how the white clothes and the turban were just part of her now. She just was... Santokh. As she used to be Emily. And that belonging to her weird yogic cult didn't change the essence of who she was at all.

"Tomorrow," she said. "Maybe? I still haven't heard from him. But you're working tomorrow, and I'm not, no matter what."

"Of course," Santokh said. "I've negotiated it with Michelle and everything."

Florence flushed, suddenly embarrassed. She forgot that the price of her having a Valentine's Day date meant that Michelle and Santokh wouldn't have theirs. She started to say something, but Santokh put a finger to her lips, so she stopped.

Thought about Will.

Jesus.

Will. Will. Will.

"Still impressed?" Santokh asked. They pulled up in front of their new Tuesday job, a new contract midwifed by Martha—"Florence, please? It's an old client of Karla's, and you know how much I owe Karla. She's difficult, but Karla's sure you can handle her. Please, Florence?" It would usually be Florence's job alone, but the client was new and, as Martha had forewarned them, demanding, and they were still breaking her in and getting to know the house and its inhabitants' idiosyncrasies, so they were doing it together.

After two cleans, the client was already in the doghouse, and Florence was pondering for how many more weeks they would be able to endure her bullshit, Martha's attempts at soothing and facilitation notwithstanding.

"There's a note again." Santokh giggled as they walked through the door. Florence rolled her eyes.

"Here we go," she sighed. "'Dear Florence. Thank you for the WONDERFUL job you are doing on my precious house.' Oh-my-fucking-god, this woman makes me want to puke. 'I noticed that neither last week nor the week before did you clean under the children's beds.' Oh-my-fucking-god, is that even a sentence? 'Could you please do so this week? Thank you in advance.'"

"Are we cleaning under the brats' beds?" Santokh stared at Florence in mock shock.

"God, no. We are writing the lady of the house a note." Florence scrounged around for a pencil. "Ok. Here we go... 'Dear Mrs. Park. I regret to inform you that the contract does not include cleaning under children's beds, and the time allotted'—'allotted' sounds like the type of word she'd like, doesn't it?—'for cleaning this house does not allow me to add this task to the list regularly. I would be very happy to arrange for an additional day to come in and do a deep clean under your children's beds, at my usual rates.' Mmmm. Let me think. 'However, I should like to point out that given the ages of your children, which I'm inferring from the toys and books in their rooms'—what do you think about the word 'inferring'? She'll like that word too —'they're old enough to start cleaning under their own beds and keeping their rooms in a state a few degrees above filthy pig sty.'"

"We're going to get fired." Santokh sighed.

"I kind of hope so," Florence said. She remembered Will's use of the word 'inferred.' For some reason... flushed. "I don't really like this house. It's beautiful." She looked around. "It's beautiful," she repeated. "But man, the children are slobs. And so are the parents. Slobs, and also, probably werewolves. I fucking feel like I pull out an entire dead cat out of the shower drains every week."

Santokh laughed. Went to the vacuum cleaner.

Florence smiled. Returned to the note and added, "'Thank you in advance for respecting my time and work. Respectfully'—although she wasn't feeling particularly respectful—'Florence.'"

Then she turned her attention to the muddy floors. Seriously. Did they just not take their shoes off in the house? What the fuck?

Did not think about Will.

Totally thought about Will.

Did not mention him to Santokh, though.

Except when they met at the landing, and Santokh gave her a silent, sly look, and Florence pirouetted and gave Santokh a hug.

"Yes, yes, yes, tomorrow!" she yelled. "If he messages me. And he's going to. Right?"

Santokh just smiled an infuriating cultist smile.

---

## In A Mood
### WEDNESDAY, FEBRUARY 14

*iwillornot*: Happy Valentine's Day.

...

**notanightingale:** Happy Valentine's Day. Are we still on?

*iwillornot*: No, I met my soulmate last night. I'm going out with her. Sorry.

**notanightingale:** Oh. Ok. Well, have a nice VD. Don't get an STD.

*iwillornot*: I'm joking, Florence, Jesus. Of course we're still on.

**notanightingale:** Not a good joke.

*iwillornot*: No?

**notanightingale:** No.

*iwillornot:* Mad?

**notanightingale:** No.

*iwillornot:* So what's up?

**notanightingale:** Nothing. Just not a good joke.

*iwillornot:* I apologize. Forgive me?

**notanightingale:** Eventually. So we're on?

*iwillornot:* Of course. I've been looking forward to this day for six weeks. Haven't you?

**notanightingale:** Maybe. What time should I come over?

*iwillornot:* Where?

**notanightingale:** To. Your. Apartment. Are you extra annoying today, or did I just forget about this part of you?

*iwillornot:* Are you extra touchy today, or did I just never see this part of you?

**notanightingale:** You ARE extra annoying. What time should I come over?

*iwillornot:* No, no, no. This is a Valentine's Day date. A

proper date. A reward, in fact, remember? I want romance and seduction and dinner. And flowers.

**notanightingale:** You want me to buy you flowers?

*iwillornot*: Definitely. Not roses—too cliché, don't you think? I like tulips, actually, a lot. But it's probably too early for tulips. Gerbera daisies. Or freesias. You pick the colour.

**notanightingale:** You seriously want me to buy you flowers?

*iwillornot*: What I want, really, is to bring you flowers. But I think you'd make this face, and feel all uncomfortable, and possibly go stuff them down the restaurant toilet. So instead I'm asking you to buy me flowers, yes.

...

*iwillornot*: Florence? Are you going to?

**notanightingale:** I'm thinking about it.

*iwillornot*: Are you mad?

**notanightingale:** I'm something. So where are we having this romantic dinner? Or am I supposed to plan that too?

*iwillornot*: How about I come pick you up at 7, and you'll find out the rest as the night unfolds?

**notanightingale:** No, I'd rather meet there. I need my own wheels anyway. For getting back home.

*iwillornot*: I'll drive you home.

**notanightingale:** Will? Where the fuck are we having dinner?

*iwillornot*: Notables, in Bowness. Do you know it?

**notanightingale:** I'll google it. At 7?

*iwillornot*: The reservation is for 7:30.

**notanightingale:** Ok. And you want freesias.

*iwillornot*: Florence? Would you rather I brought you flowers?

**notanightingale:** No. Notables. 7:30 p.m. And Will? Please try to switch moods before you get there? You're being obnoxious and I don't like it.

*iwillornot*: I'm making you uncomfortable and you don't like it. Different. No? Anyway. I'll see you at 7:30. Dress up for me. And maybe skip the panties.

**notanightingale:** Granny panties it is. See you at 7:30. xo

*iwillornot*: LOL.

## Someone Special?
### WEDNESDAY, FEBRUARY 14

As always these days, Ethan rolled his eyes when Florence reminded him that Martha was coming to stay the night with them. "Why?" he asked. "Seriously, Mom, why? We're gonna game—well past when you'd chase us into bed, and we're gonna love it, by the way, we love it when you go out for the night and we wish you'd do it more often—and we'll still be asleep when you come home."

"Because I am a responsible adult and I will not leave you alone overnight. Ever," she said. And she tried not to make too big a deal out of it, but her voice trembled and Ethan remembered, she thought, what happened the one and only time she did leave them alone in the house overnight two years ago, when he had insisted he was old enough to take care of his brothers and they didn't need a babysitter. His face and body went rigid.

Florence hugged him. He tried to shake her off.

"Hug your mother," she commanded. He relaxed into her a little.

"Can I ask you a weird question?" she asked him after he wiggled out of her hug.

He shrugged.

"Mebbe?"

"Is it weird... I mean, how do you feel... how do you feel when I go out? On a date?" she asked.

He made a face and then shrugged.

"I dunno," he said. "How do you feel when I go out on a date?"

"Terrified," Florence said frankly.

He laughed.

"I don't really care that much," he said. Paused. "You never... I mean, you never bring anyone home. Or introduce anyone to us. So, it's like..." he paused. "I dunno. It's not that big a deal. Why are we talking about this? I don't want to talk about this."

Florence laughed. Loved him.

When Martha arrived, the boys were fed and Sammy was loading the dishwasher while screaming at Isaac to not touch his computer. Ethan, who had the night off chores, was already sequestered in his room.

"You look nice," her mother said. Florence kissed her cheek. She always said this.

"Someone special?" Martha asked. She always said this too. Florence was careful not to... she usually didn't plan overnight dates. A few hours and home by midnight. A self-inflicted curfew reminiscent of her adolescence. She remembered joking with an old boyfriend—"I need to get home by midnight. Because, you know, you can only get in trouble on a date after midnight."

Ironically—she didn't like this memory, but it was a true one—she was pretty sure she got pregnant with Ethan during an "afternoon delight" session with Jo... but don't think about that, don't go there, don't think about that.

Thinking.

She always hated the phrase "afternoon delight" since.

Will.

"Just a date," Florence said, as she always said. Martha nodded and didn't press. She was, Florence suspected, relieved. She didn't want a thrice-divorced daughter anymore than Florence wanted to be a thrice-divorced wife.

Martha greeted her grandsons and started scrubbing the kitchen table.

Florence laughed.

"Seriously, Mom?"

"I just don't understand how someone who cleans for a living can tolerate such a messy kitchen!" she said. "Really, Florence, if it wasn't for me, this table would be a breeding ground for bacteria. It probably is anyway. Have you cleaned it properly since the last time I was over?"

"Probably not," Florence said. "I haven't scrubbed the tub in two or three weeks either, and your grandsons are filthy, filthy beasts."

She kissed her mother on the cheek, and skipped out to the car.

Will. Valentine's Day. Date.

Flowers.

Did he really want flowers?

Did she have time to?

Should she?

She wouldn't.

# But Not Freesias
WEDNESDAY, FEBRUARY 14

She did.

# Saying Hello, Properly
## WEDNESDAY, FEBRUARY 14

Florence arrived at the restaurant at 7:05 p.m. She was not jittery. Yes, she was. She did not like their morning text exchange—it left her off-balance. She didn't know why.

She held a tiny pot of tulips in a bag and felt stupid. She should have bought the freesias. She shouldn't have bought anything. Why dinner? They should just go to the apartment and fuck. That's what they both wanted to do, right? Another night of mind-blowing sex? Why pretend and dress things up with dinner and flowers, and...

"The rest of your party isn't here yet, and your table isn't ready," the hostess said. Apologized. Offered her a drink and a seat at the bar. Florence refused. She'd just sit and wait at the front... no, you know what? She'd go for a walk. She'd go for a walk around the block, and...

But she didn't want him to be sitting at the table waiting for her.

She didn't want to be waiting for him here either. She just wanted to be at the table.

*Fuck. Florence. Get a grip.*

"A drink and a seat at the bar would be lovely," she told the hostess.

She was sitting at the bar sipping her club soda, not thinking about the tulips at her feet or the underwire of her bra—too tight, new, but a bad call, she didn't like it—digging into her rib cage, when she felt a hand on her hip and breath on her ear.

"Hello," Will said, standing behind her.

But he didn't kiss her.

"Hello," Florence said, turning to face him.

Fuck, he looked good.

She leaned forward, just a little... He smiled and leaned in too. Took her hands. Did not kiss her.

"Come on, our table is ready," he said.

She decided to leave the tulips under the bar stool. It would be better that way.

But the hostess, damn her, brought them to the table with the menus.

Will grinned.

"Thank you," he said. "I was hoping, at the most, for a single freesia. Thrown, ungraciously, at my face at some point during the night."

"Disappointed?" Florence asked. "I could throw the pot at you. It might hurt."

"No. Too precious. I told you, tulips are my favourite flower," Will said. Moved the pot closer to him. Touched a petal with a long finger. "It's too bad they have virtually no... scent. But one can't have everything, in a flower."

Florence disappeared behind the menu.

Unsettled.

*Get a grip, Florence.*

He looked so very good. And she was pretty sure she could smell him. And she wanted him already and it was possible the entire restaurant could smell her.

"How was your day?" she asked, still behind the menu.

"Kind of shitty, actually," Will said. She raised her eyes over the menu—he was now hidden behind his.

"Want to talk about it?" she asked.

"Not even a little bit," he laughed. "How was your day?"

"Perfectly ordinary," she said.

"Want to talk about it?"

"Not even a little bit," she echoed him. He laughed again. She felt...

Disappointed.

They ordered appetizers and salads. Florence demurred on the main. The prices were outrageous.

"I don't think I want—I don't think I need more food," she said. "I'm just not that hungry."

"Do you want to split... oh, I don't know, the lamb, maybe?" he suggested.

She shook her head. Did some mental math; half this meal would cost her a night's work, and if he expected her to pay for the whole thing...

"Florence?" A long-fingered hand on hers. "It's a fact universally established that the person who picks the restaurant pays. That's me."

She pulled her hand away.

Tears threatened to swim in her eyes, and she felt exposed and shamed. And angry. And—oh...

She disappeared behind the menu.

"I'm just not that hungry," she said.

Also, she had thought... she expected that he would bring her flowers. Fuck, she did. Why?

Stupid expectations.

Stupid Valentine's Day.

Oh-my-fucking-god, she was going to cry. Why?

"Excuse me." She got up too quickly. "I have to..." and

she went in the wrong direction, as it turned out, and through bleary, tear-filled eyes, had to be redirected to the washrooms, which had her passing Will at the table again—she turned her head away carefully so he wouldn't see her face, and she walked as fast as she could without running—washroom, sanctuary, where?

Door. Hand on handle, push, and...

Arms around her from behind.

"Ssshhh." Hot breath in her hair.

The restaurant's washrooms were unisex, each room a single-occupant style stall with toilet and sink. And Will was pushing her into one.

"I need some privacy," she hissed.

She heard him latch the door with one hand, still holding her with the other. She could pull away.

She didn't.

"Florence."

She loved the way he said her name.

"I figured out what was wrong," he said. His face was still hidden in her hair. She couldn't see him. He couldn't see her. She closed her eyes and felt the tears come.

He kissed her neck.

"We didn't," he said, and lifted her hair up a little, kissed a lower part of her neck, "really say," he yanked at her dress's neckline and kissed her shoulder, then her back, "say hello properly."

She swivelled around to face him, to find his lips, then remembered her tears and tried to turn back around.

He swivelled her back. Kissed a cheek, then the other, then her nose.

"I wish you hadn't put on make-up," he said. "I want to devour your eyes."

"I can wash my face," she said.

"Do it," he said.

She leaned over the sink and splashed cold water on her face, then warm. Scrubbed her cheeks. Each eye.

He was behind her, his hands on her hips, then on her thighs. Under her dress.

"Where are those granny panties you promised me?" he asked. She felt him kneel down. Hands on her bare ass. Between her thighs. Kisses on her thighs and ass cheeks.

She moaned.

"Keep on washing your face," he said. "I don't want you to stop..." he stopped talking and busied his mouth... "washing your face."

The bite was sudden and hard but she didn't cry out.

"And yes, don't make a sound," he said.

She had no idea how she managed that. She had no idea what it was that he did. There was touching, biting, kissing —tongue and fingers—in each hole and everywhere in-between—and he found a spot on her thigh, first with his fingers then with his teeth, that was connected directly to her g-spot, apparently, because when he finally released it, and pulled her down onto his lap, he was kneeling in a puddle, and there were rivulets of water still pouring down her legs.

"Hello, Florence," he said, putting one hand under her chin and kissing her lips. Then each eye. "Nice to see you again."

"Hello, Will," she said, putting both hands around his neck and kissing the line of his jaw that she had not been thinking about for the past six weeks. "How've you been?"

"Thinking about all the places I would stick my tongue into you when I saw you next took up a lot of my time," he said, a hand between her legs now. "Should we eat?"

"I'm not really that hungry..." Florence said... "for food." She ran her fingers down his chest, then belly to the bulge made by his cock.

He laughed.

"I, on the other hand, am starving," he said. "Let's clean up a little... and let's eat."

The knees and shins of his pants were wet, and after she had sat on his lap, so was his front. But his pants were black, so he looked mostly fine as they walked back to their table. Her dress—red—was splattered with her cum. Her face, washed with cold water and harsh restaurant soap, was stripped of tears and make-up, but she was pretty sure the mascara removal left her with racoon eyes.

Their appetizers and salads were on the table. The waiter gave them a look.

Florence laughed.

Will shrugged.

They ate in silence. Every once in a while, Florence would feel Will's leg against hers. Shin to shin. She'd catch his eyes, he'd catch hers, and they'd smile.

She was soaked. She was getting wetter. She wasn't thinking—she was happy.

When the waiter took their salad plates away, Will called him back.

"We've had a change of plans," he said. "Can you just bring the lamb to go?"

She was very happy. But looked away, feeling awkward, when he paid the bill.

"I took a cab," he said when they went outside and she asked him where he parked. "You have to give me a ride home. It's all part of my plan to get you into my bed."

And she was happy again, and then self-conscious about the ancient Civic, but it was dark, and it started easily, and she was happy again, and then happier as, while she drove, he pushed her dress up above her waist and traced shapes and figures on her thighs and mound and belly... and occasionally flicked a finger at her clit.

When they parked—on the street, right in front of his building—he lowered his face to her pussy and gave her a few slow, lazy licks, then kissed her.

And she was even happier.

"Come on," he said.

This time, the ride up the elevator was uneventful. He had an arm around her—the packed-up lamb dangling from the other hand. She was... calm.

"Tulips!" he said suddenly.

"What?"

"I forgot the tulips. We have to go back!"

She laughed.

She wanted him.

But not with a frenzy. She was... partially sated.

She wondered if they would finally fuck in his bed.

And laughed at the thought.

"Will you forgive me if we don't go back?" he whispered.

She nodded and he leaned in and kissed her.

"It's been so very boring opening this door without you in my arms," he said at his front door. She was kissing him by then, still not in a frenzy... but almost.

The lamb entree leaked and stained her dress, his clothes.

"We are going to need a shower," he said. "Would you like that?"

She nodded.

# The Word Is Ostentatious
## WEDNESDAY, FEBRUARY 14

The bathroom was outrageous. He was kissing her and covering her with suds and soap, and she couldn't stop fixating on the fixtures. The size of the shower and the adjacent jacuzzi. The shower head looked like a chandelier, and could be repositioned at will. The jacuzzi looked like a swimming pool.

"Do you want to have a bath?" he asked her, kneeling down now to soap her legs. He inhaled. "You still smell like lamb," he said. Laughed.

Lamb. Jacuzzi.

She touched the tile backsplash of the shower.

She didn't know very much about these things, but it was probably imported from Spain. Or Italy. Where it was lovingly hand-painted by celibate monks in...

"Are you ok?" Will asked her, standing up.

"Yes," Florence said. Made herself kiss his nose. It didn't matter, none of it matter. Think of the fabulous sex, Florence, she told herself sternly and leaned into his mouth. Biting.

"More gently," he commanded, and then pushed her

against the shower and was not so gentle himself and when they left the shower, she was very sated.

He sat her down on the couch, wrapped in a towel. Brought her a blanket.

Turned on the fireplace.

"The switch is convenient," he said, walking away from it. "But I miss the real thing."

She knew, without him needing to elaborate, that he had a real fireplace at his old house. His ex's house. His kids' house.

"This apartment is nice," she said. Because she felt she had to say something. And then she looked around. Fuck. Yes. It was nice. More than. Vaulted ceilings. Huge windows. The building hadn't really looked that fancy. Nice. But not... what floor were they on? She never noticed. Was this a penthouse?

He shrugged.

"It's just a place where I sleep, really," he said.

Sat down on the couch beside her. Looked around. Shrugged again.

"Although I really like this couch," he said. "Oh. And let me show you the dining room table."

He grabbed her hand and pulled her up off the couch. She followed fluidly.

"This, I love," he said, drawing his hand against the smooth wood. Florence looked on, amused. She listened as Will talked about the craftsman who made it, how long it took him to track the "piece" down. How old the wood was, and the forest it probably came from.

She tried not to roll her eyes. It was cute. A boy with his toy. A new speaker system, a new car, a new phone... a new kitchen table. She understood nesting. She should not be judgmental. She could appreciate his joy in...

"How much did it cost?" she asked suddenly. Wished

she hadn't, because she knew, immediately, why she had asked.

Will looked at her.

"It wasn't cheap," he said. Named a sum that made her gasp. He didn't notice. "But beautiful, unique things are worth... you get what you pay for, you know? A mass-produced table from Sears or IKEA—it's just a table. This... this is a work of art."

Florence thought about her kitchen table. Which looked dirty, no matter how hard her mother scrubbed it. Which was third-hand to her. Originally, perhaps, from IKEA. Maybe even the United Furniture Discount Warehouse.

Will looked at her expectantly.

"What?" she said.

He laughed.

"Do you not see them?" he asked.

She stared at him.

Then realized, in the middle of the table, which Will had been caressing and she had been standing next to, stood a vase. Filled with a dozen—no more, two at least, maybe three—dozen roses.

She didn't even think—romantic.

All she could think was... expensive.

He looked at her expectantly. Then, with a frown creasing his forehead.

"Too much?" he asked.

Florence remembered the pang of disappointment in the restaurant when... when she wished he had brought her flowers. What had she wished for? What would have made her happy?

A single rose.

A small gesture.

Maybe not even that.

She was...

Fuck. She shouldn't be here.

Wrapped in the towel, she walked out of the dining room back into the living room. Sat down on the couch.

Leather.

She touched it.

Soft like a baby's bottom, she thought irreverently and irrelevantly. Stroked it. Expensive. Like the table. Like the dinner.

Like Will.

"Ok." Will came back and sat down beside her. "I fucked up. I don't know how, but I'm not quite as dense as the average guy, Florence. I get I fucked up. Wanna tell me how?"

She looked at him.

He was adorable.

An adorable, expensive... out of her league but it didn't matter because she didn't want to go there anyway... alcoholic.

She shook her head and forced a smile.

He leaned in and kissed the corner of her mouth.

Sat beside her.

"Let's talk," he said.

It was an invitation to... what? Explain her mood? She swayed back and forth a little and tried to make a catalogue of where, in the apartment, her clothes were.

Mostly, she thought, in the hallway. The bra with the uncomfortable wire was in the bathroom.

It could stay there. She wouldn't want it back.

"I'd start," Will said. "But I don't want to fuck up again. So, how about you start. Say something. Ask something."

Ask something.

Sure.

She looked at him—he was looking at her, eyes full on, forehead still creased, the lines around his eyes so fucking gorgeous she suddenly wanted to leap into his lap and kiss them—choked down that impulse—reached out, though, and touched his cheek gently.

"What do you do for a living, Will?" she asked.

"Work?" Will raised his eyebrows. "Um, sure, we can talk about that. I guess you don't really know anything about me... Well, I work in a bank. One of the Big Five. I'm a... well, I have a stupid and complicated title. I'm really a financial planner on a macro-scale. I help people and companies..." he paused... "Nominally, I help people save money," he laughed. "But I develop products, programs that probably just help them spend money. Less foolishly than they'd do it without me, maybe?"

He stopped talking and looked at her. Waiting for what?

Conversation, Florence thought. This is a conversation.

"Do you like it?" she asked.

"Does it sound boring?" he asked in turn, taking her hands into his. He rubbed his thumb into the space between her thumb and index finger and then flipped her hand over and started drawing lines—hearts? fuck, was he drawing hearts?—on her palm. "I don't mind it. I'm good at it." He paused. "Do I leap out of bed every morning with excitement and think, 'Woo-hoo, I get to go do some financial planning today! Derivatives! Yes!' Not so much. But I don't mind it. I work with good people. My assistant—she's been with me for years, you'd love her. She's amazing. Reminds me of you, a little. And... you know, it's a stable job as things in this economy go."

"Stable," Florence echoed. Looked around the apartment again—its sparseness now harsh and luxurious. Everything looked... not tasteful but ostentatious. Expensive. She was conscious of the dining room table that she couldn't see that cost as much as a year's worth of payments on her... trailer park house.

The softness of the couch under her suddenly chafed.

"Are you condemning me as a boring wage slave?" he asked, voice teasing, kissing the palm of her hand. The inside of her elbow. "A sell-out?"

She shook her head and wanted to pull back her hand. Desperately. And she didn't want him to let go. And she didn't want to hurt him.

And she had to leave.

"What do you do, Florence?" he murmured, lips again on the inside of her elbow. Crawling up her arm.

Fuck. She closed her eyes. She loved this... too much.

She pulled back.

"What do you think I do?" she asked.

He took her hands again in his. Moved his fingers over them. It felt like he was counting her freckles, trying to touch every single one.

She fucking loved it.

She had to leave.

"I think..." he said... "Well, I imagine... No, I almost know. I didn't, the first day. But when we met in Weeds Cafe, you know, when I so ungraciously gave you back your bra, fuck, Florence, that memory—look at my cock, it loves it... Anyway, and you ran in, breathless, in those old yoga pants and that old T-shirt... your hair pulled back... a smudge of something under your right eye, did you know you had a smudge there? I saw it." His voice was dreamy. "I knew then."

She waited.

"You're an artist," he said. "I'm pretty sure—a painter. Not a sculptor. You don't smell like clay or wood or... But I can see you... your hands... a paintbrush... maybe charcoal sticks? Making beautiful things."

Florence laughed and her laughter was an unpleasant, unhappy sound. She took her hands back and he released them.

"I'm a janitor," she said, getting up. "Evenings and weekends. In the mornings, while my kids are at school— I'm a cleaning lady. I clean..." She looked around. "...places like this."

She walked into the hallway quickly, gathering up her clothes and pulling them on.

There were things she wanted to say, but they all sounded mean and defensive and stupid. Fully dressed, she turned away from the door, half-expecting to see Will there, behind here.

He wasn't. She couldn't see him, but she knew he was in the living room, still sitting on the soft-as-a-baby's-butt couch.

Well. That made things easier.

She wrapped her coat around her and went out through the door.

Panic, In Texts
WEDNESDAY, FEBRUARY 14

*iwillornot*: Florence? What the fuck happened?

*iwillornot*: Florence, I ran out after you when I realized you left. You were gone. I couldn't find you in the building, in the lobby. By the time I made it outside—wearing pants and nothing else, by the way, and barefoot to boot, your car was gone.

*iwillornot*: Florence, message me and tell me what happened. Or come back. What did I say?

*iwillornot*: Is this some sort of stupid 'I make more money than you do' thing? Or you think I'm judging you, or am no longer interested in you, because you're a janitor? Because that's bullshit, Florence, and you know it.

*iwillornot*: Florence, you're a beautiful, sexy, fascinating, INFURIATING woman and all I can think about is how much I want you naked in my arms. Tonight. Another time, sometime in the vaguely undefined future. I don't care what you do for a living.

*iwillornot*: Is it because of the roses? Was that it?

*iwillornot*: Fuck, did you suddenly think, OMG, he has such a small penis, I can't endure it? Because, remember, post-sex, cold-room shrinkage.

*iwillornot*: Ok, bad joke. I shouldn't be joking. Florence, you're upset, and I want to know why.

*iwillornot*: Florence, this can't possibly be about the janitor/banker thing. Can it? Is that it? Because that's fucking stupid, Florence. It doesn't matter.

*iwillornot*: Fuck, Florence, fucking message me. This is fucking unfair. You don't just storm out on someone like that—ok, you didn't storm, you more sneaked out, I didn't even hear the fucking door close. But you don't do that. Not after—I mean, Florence, you were there, right? In the shower? In the restaurant washroom?

*iwillornot*: Please say something. Message me.

---

*iwillornot*: Florence? Whenever you're ready to talk. Message me. I'll be here, and I'm going to listen, and I'm not going to be an obnoxious ass. Ok? Whatever it is that happened, whatever it is that I said, or did, that upset you—I will listen. I don't know if I can fix it. But I will listen.

Tears

THURSDAY, FEBRUARY 15

Florence didn't stop driving until she was clear of the down-town core. Then pulled into one of the residential streets of Sunnyside, bent over the steering wheel, and burst into tears.

Why? Why the fuck? It didn't matter. Why didn't she just stay and have a good, fun night—have one more round of raucous, mind-blowing sex, taste God again, disappear in the folds of Will's arms and then surface afterwards, exhausted but so-sated... why didn't she just?

She pulled out her phone.

"Sorry to interrupt Valentine's Day wedding planning bliss. Can I come sleep at your house tonight?"

Santokh's response was immediate.

"For sure."

No questions, not even a curious look when she arrived —Santokh let her in and gave her a hug. The couch was made up for her. Michelle was sitting in the arm chair with a book, and she got up, and gave Florence a hug too, and while it wasn't a warm one, it didn't feel particularly resentful.

"I don't want to explain things to my mom," Florence said through a volley of tears. "You know?" They both nodded, said nothing. Tucked her into the blankets on the couch as if she was a child. Santokh kissed her on the forehead and Michelle on the cheek, and then pulled Santokh away and into their bedroom.

And Florence thought she would cry again and hate herself again, but she didn't. She closed her eyes and disappeared.

And dreamt about roses and showers and public restroom sex.

It would be fine, she thought when she woke up in the morning. It would all become an easy memory. A fun, pleasant—fuck, the sex was so good—kind of memory. She wouldn't dwell on, she wouldn't pay attention to those last minutes. She wouldn't examine her motivation.

Her insecurity.

"Do you think I'm insecure?" she asked Santokh, without any context, as they drank their morning coffee. Michelle, who was teaching an 8 a.m. class every day that semester, had already left for the university.

"Not insecure," Santokh said after a few minutes' reflection. Florence loved this about Santokh—the silences that punctuated their conversations. Santokh never said anything too quickly, too rashly. She'd fall silent... and think. "No, not insecure. But you are... prickly."

"Prickly?" Florence laughed. And hugged Santokh. Who also laughed.

"Prickly is the word," she said. "Defensive. Not insecure. But... you won't let anyone... you won't risk being attacked. Breached. Harmed."

"Those are not bad things," Florence said. Defensively.

"I didn't say they were," Santokh laughed. "Shall we?"

Florence nodded. They drove to their Wednesday

morning house and cleaned like the wind. As always on Wednesdays—and Mondays and Fridays—Florence dropped Santokh off at the yoga studio at 11:45. Then checked her phone.

"Kids all had a good night. I made lunches. Even for Ethan. Drove Isaac to school. Ethan and Sammy took the bus. Hope you had a good night, honey."

Fifteen messages on OKC. Were all of them from him?

She wouldn't even log in.

She wouldn't think about it. Him. Anyone.

# Here



*iwillornot:* Florence? I'm still here. Anytime you want to message. You don't even have to explain, ok? Just—fuck, I don't know. Send me a happy face or something.

# Wedding Dresses & Turbans
## TUESDAY, FEBRUARY 20

It was the longest, most horrible week of Florence's life.

No.

Reality check.

The week after she left Ethan's father... the week, the month, the year! after she left Sammy and Isaac's father—fuck, David, why, why, why did you make it so difficult and so inevitable and so right but so fucking hard?—those were way harder. Ok. Perspective.

Yes. Perspective.

Much worse.

There were many longer, more horrible weeks.

Definitely.

Except right now, this one felt the worst.

Florence felt... stupid. And ashamed. And lonely.

And, horny.

So horny.

And masturbation didn't help. At all.

And she was afraid to log on to OKC or restart her Tinder account, because... well. She didn't want to. That was all.

She didn't want to.

She wanted... she just didn't want to think about him.

The effort required not to think about someone who you couldn't stop thinking about was...

"Fuck!"

"Did you just swear, Guru?" Florence teased.

"You almost killed us!" Santokh was pale, and holding onto the dash in front of the passenger seat of the Civic, the knuckles of her hands white.

"I did not. I came to a very rapid but controlled stop." Florence took the last turn into the residential neighbourhood. "You're overreacting. And failing to take advantage of the opportunity with which I've just provided you to... you know. Practice your mantras or breathing or shit."

"You really are the world's most unsupportive friend," Santokh muttered as she got out of the car. "Do I mock you?"

"I haven't joined a cult," Florence said. Then ran around to the curb and hugged Santokh abruptly. Santokh accepted the embrace. Returned it. Florence wished, desperately, that she could say... ask... but she didn't.

They walked into the house arm-in-arm.

"Fuck," Santokh said again.

"Seriously, worst guru ever," Florence said. "I'm writing a note to your cult leader. Don't swat at me. And do your breathing exercises to calm down. You know we're not fired: if we were, she'd text us. And take away our keys."

"Maybe she wants to fire us with a note," Santokh said. "Well. Read it."

Florence picked up the note, propped up against a vase on the hallway table. The flowers in the vase were dead. Irreverently, Florence wondered if they were a Valentine's Day bouquet that Mr. Park bought for Mrs. Park... and that neither remembered to refresh the water for?

She read the note quickly. And snorted.

"Fucking. Bitch." She tossed it at Santokh.

"'Dear Florence,'" Santokh read. "'It is not your job to give me advice on how to raise my children. Please keep in mind that you are very, very replaceable. And it's Dr., not Mrs. Dr. Park.'"

"Fucking bitch," Florence said. With, she realized, immense pleasure. "Santokh, put your coat back on."

"What are you doing?" Santokh said.

"Firing her uptight ass."

"Why? Seriously, Florence, your note was a little..." Santokh stopped, because Florence wasn't listening. She scribbled, enthusiastically, on the other side of the paper.

"'Dear Mrs. Dr.,'" she read to Santokh with satisfaction. "So are you.' Should I add, 'Enjoy cleaning up after your slobby children?' No. Overkill."

Santokh smiled.

"It is nice... to have options," she said. "Do you think we'd be this sanguine about firing her when we were starting out?"

Florence shrugged. "There are always other toilets to scrub," she said. "Sadly. Oh, the glamorous lives we lead. Ok. So we have a free morning before your yoga—I mean cult—session. What do you want to do?"

Santokh smiled.

"No." Florence was adamant.

Santokh smiled again.

"Absolutely not." Florence shook her head madly.

Santokh tilted her head to the side, blushed, and smiled.

"Again?" Florence groaned.

Santokh smiled. And shrugged.

Ten minutes later, they were at the Bay Bridal salon, trying on wedding dresses.

Santokh looked heavenly in almost all of them.

"You are going to take off the turban for the wedding though, right?" Florence asked.

Santokh laughed.

"They're all white. They all go with it," she said.

"Your actual genuine *Indian* future mother-in-law will have a fit," Florence said. "And doesn't Michelle want some Hindi components in the ceremony? How does she feel about your weird Sikh yoga?"

Santokh smiled.

"She does occasionally ask me why I had to choose the only non-Hindi yoga around," she admitted. "And I would enjoy... I would very much enjoy horrifying my new mother-in-law."

And she smiled again.

And it was a wicked smile.

"Worst. Guru. Ever," Florence said, and pinned a veil to the side of Santokh's turban.

## Apology, But Not
### THURSDAY, FEBRUARY 22

*Saryang Park:* Dear Florence. I feel like I ought to apologize. Perhaps the tone of my note was over the top. Saryang Park.

**Florence Gunn:** Dear Mrs. Dr. When people fuck up, they usually say, 'I'm sorry. Forgive me.' 'I feel like I ought to apologize' doesn't cut it.

*Saryang Park:* I feel like you don't really want this job.

**Florence Gunn:** While scrubbing your grimy bathtubs was shaping up to be the highlight of my week, I'm pretty sure I can live without it. As you said, there are other cleaners. Go get one.

*Saryang Park:* I'm clearly not communicating very well here. Florence, I would like you to continue to clean my house.

**Florence Gunn:** Saryang, I'm still waiting for an apology to your assy note. And I am not interested in cleaning under your children's beds. Also, just because you know I'm coming in on Tuesdays is no reason to fail to unload and reload the dishwasher on Monday night or Tuesday morning.

## Routine, Responsibility, Regret
WEDNESDAY, MARCH 21

It was the longest, most horrible month of Florence's life.

Except it wasn't.

She knew it wasn't. Life unfolded as it had to. She got up in the mornings, bleary eyed, and thought about meditating—fucking Santokh, preaching enlightenment just by humming while cleaning—and maybe doing some yoga or going for a run, but just drank coffee and looked at Facebook instead. She kissed Isaac awake, and poked Sammy and Ethan until they crawled out of bed, teenage zombies. She watched them make lunches—argued half-heartedly with Ethan that he didn't really need to drink coffee, that if he had a proper breakfast—could she make him scrambled eggs?—he'd feel awake and energetic. But she gave up, as always, when he said, "Would you rather I buy a Red Bull at school?"

Sometimes, she'd drive Isaac and Sammy to school, but these days, even Isaac wanted to take the bus most of the time.

On Mondays, Wednesdays, and Fridays, she'd pick up

Santokh, and they'd do their morning cleans together. They'd talk—only and exclusively about the wedding, and how cute Michelle looked in her dress, and how cute Michelle was when she pretended to be jealous of this student, and how fucking annoying Michelle was about the turban, really, was it that big a deal?

"Yes," Florence said invariably, and Santokh would shrug, pat her head, and change the subject, but Florence would usually get in at least one more turban or cult dig before dropping her off at the yoga studio for her noon classes. Santokh took it all in good stride; Florence was occasionally ashamed of her teasing.

Monday, Wednesday, and Friday afternoons, she worked alone, smaller or irregular jobs. She was usually done by three or four, home when the boys arrived. Supper. Chauffeuring to indoor soccer for Sammy—her only athlete. Thank God, she often thought. Suppose she had to pay soccer fees for all three of them? Ethan's guitar lessons were, by comparison, almost free. And Isaac, for now, steadfastly refused to enrol in anything. She nagged him about it intermittently... was secretly grateful.

Tuesdays and Thursdays, now that she had fired Mrs. Dr., she had the days off, but worked three or so hours a night doing the banks; she also needed to pop in to do them on either Saturday night or Sunday. Santokh took the banks on Monday, Wednesday, and Friday nights, doing the cleaning after she finished teaching her evening yoga classes. Sometimes, they'd team up and work them together to give each other shorter nights, but that was challenging— they had to work around Santokh's increasingly demanding teaching schedule, and Florence's chauffeuring and domestic obligations.

"I know Martha will help," she told Santokh on the

times they struggled with their schedules. "But let's treat her as Plan Z, ok? I don't want to overuse her. You know?"

Santokh always nodded, agreed. Reminded Florence about the yoga students. She said Uttamroop was already shadowing her on Tuesday and Thursday nights.

"She should do a weekend with us, hey?" Florence said. "That's going to be my heaviest day."

Santokh agreed.

Saturdays and Sundays, they worked together to do the weekly deep clean on the local reproductive health clinic. The weekends were killer for Santokh—she taught three, sometimes four classes on each day, and the clinic was a minimum four-hour clean with the two of them working full out. They tried to do it in one go, on Saturday, but more often, they had to split it, have it spill-over into Sunday, around Santokh's teaching and before or after Florence's bank clean.

"You ever get tired of cleaning up after other people?" Florence asked Santokh as they were disinfecting keyboards and wiping down computer screens at the clinic. "Do you ever think, oh-my-fucking-god, this is so boring?"

Santokh paused and looked as if she was thinking about the question for the first time in her life.

"Do you?" she asked Florence.

Florence looked around the very sterile—and about to become more so—clinic.

"It should be, shouldn't it?" she said. "I mean, really. With the houses, at least, there's some change, right? People's personal lives are messy." She laughed suddenly, and updated Santokh on the latest text exchange she had with Mrs. Dr. "But this place, and the banks... even the contents of the garbage cans are the same."

"So are you tired of it? Do you think, oh-my-fucking-god, this is so boring?" Santokh asked Florence's question back at her.

And Florence paused and thought about the question hard. Perhaps for the first time in her life, she thought. Had she never thought about it? Maybe. Back when she started...

"No," she said finally. "I mean, yes. It is boring. Sometimes, it is fucking boring. But... I don't mind it."

She sprayed and wiped.

"It... soothes me," she said. "You know? It soothes me."

"I'm so going to get you to start meditating one of these days," Santokh said. Florence flicked her turban.

It was hard to not think about Will while she cleaned. After the first few weeks of fighting it, she gave up. And so she thought about him as she scrubbed toilets and took out garbage and vacuumed. She thought, at first, about his expensive table, the restaurant, the "I'm a financial planner —I knew you were an artist" conversation. She thought about what he'd think, if he saw her, at the bank—maybe his bank—taking out his colleagues'—maybe his—trash. Changing the garbage bags in the washrooms. Vacuuming the ATM foyer. Sweeping crumbs off the branch manager's computer keyboard—oh-my-fucking-god, why was this woman such a slob?

Then she thought about his hands. Eyes. Jawline. God, that jawline. Also, abs.

Penis.

Once, she took out her phone, and looked at the photo she had of him, from their second night together, leaning back against the pillows, looking at her quizzically. Naked.

But even shocked and appalled and flaccid, he looked too cute, so she never did that again.

She didn't delete the photo, though.

She should have.

But she didn't.

She made herself think—alcoholic. Dry for six years, he said, what did that matter? Jonathan—well, she never gave Jonathan a chance to quit. Not that she blamed herself for that. She didn't. She was too young to... and Ethan. Ethan was coming, and she wasn't going to raise Ethan... no fucking way.

She didn't blame her mother for much. But she did blame her for not leaving.

She had told Santokh that once, and Santokh listened very carefully and nodded.

She told Santokh how fucking happy she was the day her father died.

"Isn't that the most awful thing ever?" she asked her. Santokh shook her head.

"Fucking cultist," Florence said. And she kissed and hugged her.

And David—what did she blame herself for with David? Leaving? Staying as long as she did?

Falling in love with him in the first place?

Loving him so much she believed him—that it wasn't a big deal, that she was too uptight, that everyone deserved to have a little fun, party once in a while? "It's not like I'm passed out drunk on the couch every night, Florence," he said. "I work hard and provide for our family, right? All week. And I like to let loose on the weekends. What's the big deal?"

She loved him so much.

Fuck.

"Are you crying?" Santokh came up behind her.

"No," Florence lied. Scrubbed. Wiped.

Thought about Will and the hopelessness of it all. And the stupidity of chemistry and lust and desire.

The responsibilities of a mother. A parent.

She gritted her teeth.

Did not think about Will.

Then did.

*Fuck, Will.*

*Why? Why did you come into my life and why won't you just get the fuck out of my head?*

## No Manners



*Martha Gunn:* Florence, Dr. Park texted me. Again. She's really upset.

**Florence Gunn:** You don't say.

*Martha Gunn:* Florence, you are not going to keep clients by being rude to them.

**Florence Gunn:** Mom, I fired her rude ass, ok? Not the other way around.

*Martha Gunn:* Florence, she's a good, well-connected client.

*Martha Gunn:* Florence, are you ignoring me?

*Martha Gunn*: Florence, why don't you just text her and tell her you accept her apology?

**Florence Gunn:** Ha! So at least she told you mostly the truth.

*Martha Gunn*: You are so stubborn.

**Florence Gunn:** I know. Don't you love me?

*Martha Gunn*: Of course I love you. But I also worry about you. And firing clients is not a good idea. Not in this economy.

**Florence Gunn:** Mama dearest, you know there's always someone like Saryang Park looking for someone like me to do her dirty work for her. Don't stress. I'm not hurting financially.

*Martha Gunn*: She's a good client, Florence. I worked for her a few times over the years with Karla. And I was so happy to be able to connect you with her when she needed a new cleaner.

**Florence Gunn:** Mom, you've really got to let this go. Ok?

*Martha Gunn*: But she keeps on texting me!

**Florence Gunn:** Then tell her to fuck off!

*Martha Gunn*: Florence!

**Florence Gunn:** Seriously, Mom, what is she going to do to you? Neither one of us is working for her. I don't want to work for her. You don't need to work her. Can you just let it be?

*Martha Gunn:* Can't you just text her?

**Florence Gunn:** No.

*Martha Gunn:* If she texts you and apologizes, would you respond?

**Florence Gunn:** At the moment, today, in the mood you put me in? No.

*Martha Gunn:* You are the most frustrating child a woman could have. Are you starting menopause early?

**Florence Gunn:** You are the most amazing, supportive mother a woman could have. You sure you completely through your post-menopausal hormonal swings? Can we talk about something else? Please?

*Martha Gunn:* How's the planning for the yogic lesbian wedding coming along?

**Florence Gunn:** Just fine, Mom. The brides will be beautiful. Thanks for asking. I love you.

*Martha Gunn:* I love you too, Florence. So you'll text Dr. Park?

**Florence Gunn:** No.

*Martha Gunn:* Florence? Is there something else happening? Is something wrong?

**Florence Gunn:** No. I've got to go do shit, Mom. My glamorous life calls. I love you. Now shut up and go away. xo

*Martha Gunn:* I suppose it's all my fault. I didn't teach you any manners.

**Florence Gunn:** I said xo. That means we're done talking. Why do you always have to have the last word?

*Martha Gunn:* I don't. xo.

**Florence Gunn:** I saw what you did there. xx

*Martha Gunn:* Are you sure nothing's wrong, Florence? Mothers know these things.

**Florence Gunn:** OMG, Mom, I'm going away. STOP TEXTING ME.

*Martha Gunn:* Ok, darling. But think about texting Dr. Park, ok? xo

## A Full Confession



Florence did not text Saryang Park, nor did she think about Saryang Park, and she most definitely did not dream about Saryang Park.

Instead...

Jawline.

Neck.

Hands and fingers.

Jawline again.

Hipbone.

*That fucking hipbone, oh-my-fucking-god, how is that the sexiest part of his outrageously sexy body?*

Stop thinking!

Or was it a dream?

Hands. Fingers.

A really beautiful cock. And she didn't really think that much of penises, generally. Funny looking things.

Dreaming? Awake?

Awake.

Ah, fuck.

What time was it?

Florence rolled left. Right. Groped for her phone.

Unlocked the screen.

Fuck.

5 a.m.

Ugh.

She hated being up at 5 a.m. Sleep was precious: she had to be up at 7 a.m. anyway to do all things. Losing two hours of sleep to... why was she awake?

Fucking Will.

No.

Just... she closed her eyes. Forced sleep.

It didn't come.

"Fuck it." She jumped out of bed. The linoleum of her bedroom was cold—as always, when her feet hit it in the winter, she thought she should get a rug for the floor. Or, slippers.

She padded to living room to the ancient family computer that she now shared with Isaac, because Ethan had saved up for a gaming laptop of his own, and Sammy lived on the X-box Martha bought him for this last birthday.

Generous grandmother. Good mother.

She was just going to surf the Internet. Get frustrated by Facebook. Look at cat videos and shit.

She logged into OkCupid.

No.

Stop.

Don't do it.

But she was doing it, and, messages, and Will.

Will.

She looked at the messages, and the longing that hit her killed her. There was no other word for it—the feeling was so intense, she felt herself dying. Then, she was alive—but dead, too, and her head spun, and her eyes felt hot and wet.

She started typing.

She was incoherent.

She had no idea what she was saying. What was she saying?

She closed her eyes. Her fingers kept moving on the keyboard.

It hurt.

———

Will, I can't do this, I can't do this, I can't do this. I can't explain what happened, I can't explain what I'm thinking. I can't, I can't, I can't.

I can't stop thinking about you—and I can't stop thinking about how we can't work. At all.

You know?

You must understand.

Never mind the drinking—actually, fuck, you know, I know, we must mind it. It is THE problem. Right? I can say... well, ok, what set me off on Valentine's Day... Will, I live in a fucking trailer park. Ok? In a really nice trailer. But still. A trailer. A mobile home. In a trailer park. All my furniture is... well, let's just say that your *artisan* kitchen table is my entire year's housing spend. Ok? And I don't even want to think about how much your couch, which feels like it's made out of babies' butts—it really does, Will—how much that costs. Or your fucking suits. Or those roses. Or that dinner.

I can't afford you. Does that make sense? That night? I felt so small. And I felt... I couldn't afford you. I didn't want you to... What would you think, if you saw my house? My IKEA table, that I didn't even pay for, but reclaimed when a neighbour was tossing it out? My loud, puffy coach, covered with ten years of kid-made food stains?

What would you think if you saw me mopping the floors of your bank? Or scrubbing the toilets in your neighbours', friends' houses?

And don't say it doesn't matter. It matters. It always matters. People with money say money doesn't matter. It matters... It matters most to the people who don't have it. And it matters so much to the people who have it, they don't even notice how much it matters. So it matters, Will. That I'm a janitor and you're a fucking financial planner? It matters.

But we both know... Ok, Will, here's the deal. You want to know, right? You want to know how I knew you were an alcoholic. Don't get mad. I know you don't like the word—fuck, you have no idea how much I hate that word. What do you prefer? User? Addict? They're all awful, gross, disgusting words.

Well. I fucking knew. The first time, in the Cafe. When I said to go get your drink. And I said, do you remember? 'This is a fancy place—they serve beer and wine here.' The look. The awareness. I fucking know it intimately, Will. The entire body, the entire self *thinking* about *not* thinking about the availability of a drink. My father's body, at dinner, after dinner, during his bouts of sobriety. He had them. I don't know that they were better than his binges...

My mother... what would you think of my mother, Will? She's a cleaning lady too. See, not only am I a cleaning lady, I'm the daughter of a cleaning lady. And, an alcoholic carpenter. She started cleaning even before she had to become the primary supporter of the family because he lost two of this fingers on a saw—are you flinching? Grossed out? And yes. He was drunk when that happened—and yes, I was there. But frankly, it doesn't matter. That doesn't matter—there was never enough money, even before, because where do you think it all went?

I actually think you might like my mother.

I like her more now. I understand, better. But back then, Will, I fucking hated her as much as I hated him.

I moved out at sixteen.

The cliché is out of the frying pan into the fire. Does it offend you, bother you when I use clichés? I feel... when you speak... even when we speak. A gulf. Such a gulf. I never, I wouldn't have thought of myself as insecure. You make me so fucking insecure. With your suits and designer tables and your couch made of babies' butts and your three dozen roses.

Who gets a one night stand three dozen roses, Will?

Where was I? Fuck, I'm incoherent. I'm not drunk. I never drink. Not just because of my dad. He was just the beginning.

So, I moved out. I'll skip over the next couple of years. I travelled a bit. At eighteen, I ended up in Edmonton and I met Jonathan. He was... he wasn't the great love of my life. I wasn't even that much in love, or lust, you know? But he was smart and fun—so much fun. And, at twenty-four, already an addict and alcoholic. But so much fun. And I had never really had fun before, and so... we had so much fun together. Crazy wild days, nights, weekends. Life was one long party and one long hang-over and I didn't think about anything, except the next moment—the next party, the next drink, the next high, the next fuck.

We were together for three years. And I can't say it was bad, you know? Because... I didn't know any better, really. And we were young. And we had no responsibilities. And what did it matter...

My bucket of cold water, my awakening was my first baby.

I hate telling this story. I hate it. Typing it is no easier than telling you in person.

So what happened… I found out I was pregnant. I was twenty-one. I was well on my way to becoming a drunk too. It took me years to accept that, you know? That for those years that I was with Jonathan… I was just what he was. So I get it. When you don't want to call yourself an alcoholic. It's gross, foul. I don't want to own it either. I don't want to think about how much I drank, how many different pills we popped, what I snorted, what I smoked…

But I was stone cold sober when I took the pregnancy test. I didn't think. Really, Will, I didn't make any decisions. I took the test at work—I worked retail, at fucking West Edmonton Mall. I had had this thought— oh, it's been a while since my last period, what the fuck? And instead of worrying about it more, I ran to the drug store on my break to get a test. Peed.

Surprise!

But I didn't think. I just… I just was. I made no plans —I had no, 'How am I going to tell Jonathan?' Or, 'What am I going to do?' I just finished my shift and I went home.

We lived together in this tiny apartment off Whyte Avenue. So cute. I loved it. I loved it…

I got home after my shift—it was a Tuesday, I remember that. My shift ended at six, so it was seven, no later, when I got home. He was sleeping in the arm chair in the living room. Naked. Drunk.

I don't know how many cans of beer on the coffee table in front of him.

And I did have this thought, I remember—an overlay

of my father's body over his. I never saw my father passed out *naked* in our living room... but that image? Beer cans on the coffee table, a man's inert body in an arm chair? Those were the more *pleasant* memories of my childhood nights.

When he was unconscious he was contained... The ones when he wasn't unconscious were worse. But you might know this yourself. And I don't want to talk about that, anyway.

Jonathan. Drunk. Passed out. The father of my child.

And yet... do you know? That wasn't the thing. That wasn't why I packed up and left.

I went into our bedroom and there, in our bed, also naked and unconscious, was a girl. A mutual friend. Fellow partier.

And that was my... see? Looking back at it, I'm so ashamed. Does that make sense? Because... fuck. It should have been enough—that I didn't want to raise a child the way I was raised. That I didn't want to have a baby with a fucking alcoholic. That I didn't want my child to have a father who loved his beer more than he loved her.

But I'm not sure, if that woman hadn't been there... I'm not sure. So I'm ashamed. And I'm also grateful. I can't remember her name now—but I'm so fucking grateful she was there...

So, I wasn't thinking, Will. I just packed up my things and I left. I left. I took the bus back to Calgary, back home, and I arrived at my parents' house... and my father was passed out in the arm chair in the living room.

I ran to the bathroom and vomited.

I hugged my mother. I told her she was going to be a grandma. And I left again. I couldn't stay. How could I?

OMFG, I hate telling this story. It makes me sound

like a sob queen, a drama queen. I wasn't. I really wasn't. I got a job. I got an apartment. I had my baby. My mom helped. I think—I've told you, I understand her better now.

And then, David.

David... David, Will, was the great love of my life. I didn't think love was a thing until I met him. I drowned in him completely. Even after we had our babies—Will, this is an impossible thing for a woman, for a mother, to admit, but it is true—I love my children madly. So completely. I loved David more. I loved David more...

He was an artist. He was so fucking talented. Inspired. And also... so soft, empathetic. Human. He loved Ethan—that's my eldest son. Ethan was only two when I met David. And David just loved him. Let him use his paints, his most expensive tools. Didn't care.

I loved him... When I think back, how did I do it again? How did I not notice what I was getting into? The truth is that I noticed. Of course I noticed, I saw. But he was so fucking charming, Will. Sound familiar? So... even when he was drinking, using. He was so fucking charming. Except when he wasn't, but then afterwards, so apologetic.

And I suppose, in my defence, it was different. Jonathan... night after night. David was a binger. Hard worker. Fuck. He painted—he painted houses during the day, often on weekends, too. So there was steady money. And then he'd drown in his projects. He painted. Sculpted. So many ideas. So much talent, Will.

And then... no painting. Just...

And, another baby. And you'd think I'd start noticing, worrying more... but I fucking loved him so much. Fuck, Will—will you believe this of me? I used to go get him his pick-me-up shit at the C-train station.

When he was too hung over to function but needed to go to work. Or when he wanted to be up for days, painting.

I was his most enthusiastic enabler.

And, a third baby.

Women are so fucking stupid, Will. Are you thinking that? I am. Who does that? Who keeps on...

Well. I did.

And then, he almost killed us. I was pregnant with Isaac—that's my little—and Sammy was just three, the first time... well, except it wasn't even the first time. Sorry. Chaotic. I let him drive us while he was drunk. Because he said he wasn't. I let him do that repeatedly, with Ethan, with Sammy. Judge me, please—I judge myself, and I can't forgive... I was so lucky... so many times. And when the accident came... we were lucky still. We were all ok. He didn't kill anyone in the other car either.

And I stayed.

I stayed.

I wouldn't get into a car with him behind the wheel after that. I realized... I realized things. I pleaded.

He said I nagged. And we started fighting. And he was less charming less often.

But I still loved him so fucking much Will.

OMG. I'm so tired. Are you reading this still? Do you still want me?

I didn't think so...

I'll finish. We were fighting—we were supposed to go somewhere—he was in such a rage—he told me to get myself and the kids into the car or he'd beat me unconscious and drag me in. And I believed him—at that point... I knew, I believed that he would do it. And so. Car. My three children. My life.

His rage.

He drove us into that wall on purpose.

He told me that, later. Mad with contrition.

Me... trapped. So trapped, Will. Three kids. I wasn't working at that point, because, three kids. And my home —I couldn't take my kids home to my father, Will, right?

And then... miraculously, he died.

Not David. My father.

He died. And my mother... she called me, when she called me, she said, "He's dead, Florence. You can come home now."

She knew... I didn't tell her. Not everything. But she's a mother. She knew, enough.

And I came home.

And I became a cleaning lady, just like my mother.

And I got divorced.

And I still have to deal with my kids' raging drunken Daddy... who, when he is working and sober and happy, is loving and charming and tells me he adores them and wants me back but understands why I left and makes me remember how madly in love I was. And who, when he is drunk, wants me dead.

Don't worry. That doesn't happen that often.

And... I sound like a sob queen, drama queen, but I've built a pretty good life, you know? I love my trailer. It's cozy and funky and all my cheap-ass furniture and decoration that you might think kitschy and that my clients would turn their noses up at—they make a beautiful space. I have a garden.

I love my job—my business.

I love my children madly, and they are everything to me.

And I still have to deal with... my shame. My fears. So many fears, Will.

And so that's me, Will. My fucking past, my CV.

And why I can't love you.

I'd really like to, Will.

But I can't.

And if you think about it, if you get past the lust and sex and shit... you'll see you shouldn't love me either.

Ok?

Fucking life.

---

"Mom? Why are you crying?"

Isaac stood behind her, and then his arms were around her.

"I'm saying goodbye to someone," Florence said. She looked at the message. Essay. Confession. Paragraphs, and paragraphs, and paragraphs.

Closed her eyes.

What did it matter?

Wasn't silence better?

She kissed Isaac.

Looked at the screen. Hovered the mouse button over 'send.'

Could she do it?

## Breathing Helps
### WEDNESDAY, MARCH 28

She didn't.

She read the message over and over again... and deleted it.

She spent the next day, week, moving through life like a zombie. In a cloud of hopelessness so thick, Santokh made her do stupid culty breathing exercises.

"I'm not saying anything, I'm not asking anything," Santokh said. "But trust me. Breathing helps."

Breathing helped.

But fuck.

Naming to herself all the reason she couldn't, shouldn't, wouldn't see Will again felt like death.

Again, and again, and again.

And yet, in the middle of this death... life went on. Relentlessly.

## Now That's How You Apologize
### MONDAY, APRIL 2

*Saryang Park:* Florence, I'm hoping that you have now calmed down enough to accept my apology.

**Florence Gunn:** Mrs. Dr., I'm hoping you have realized you haven't actually offered me an apology.

*Saryang Park:* Clearly, you have not calmed down.

**Florence Gunn:** Clearly, you do not know how to apologize. You know what? I'll help you. This is how people generally do it: I'm sorry.

**Florence Gunn:** I am, by the way, ready to accept your apology. If you ever offer it.

*Saryang Park:* Great! Can you start cleaning again on Tuesday?

*Saryang Park:* This Tuesday. Tomorrow.

**Florence Gunn:** LOL. Oh, Mrs. Dr., you're adorable. And you still haven't apologized. Let's try it again when you've figured out how to do that, ok?

**Florence Gunn:** And remember—there are many, many cleaners out there. Many, many. And all of them deserve to be treated with respect.

*Saryang Park:* Why do I feel like you just called me a fucking bitch?

**Florence Gunn:** I probably thought it. I'm sorry. That was rude.

---

*Saryang Park:* I'm sorry.

**Florence Gunn:** For what?

*Saryang Park:* For writing you a rude, thoughtless note. And then a second rude, thoughtless note. And for expecting you for clean under my children's beds. And for not unloading the dishwasher on Monday nights. And for being a messy, hopeless housekeeper.

*Saryang Park:* And... anything else you need me to apologize

for. Florence, can you please come back to cleaning
my house?

**Florence Gunn:** I accept your apology.

**Florence Gunn:** This seems like a good time to double
my rates.

*Saryang Park:* Don't push it.

**Florence Gunn:** Make me an offer.

*Saryang Park:* Twenty percent increase.

**Florence Gunn:** Saryang? Seriously, there are lots of
other cleaners out there. Don't you just want to start fresh
with a new one?

*Saryang Park:* Florence... seriously, it makes no sense. I
know. But I want you. And also... I want you to like me.

**Florence Gunn:** Are you going to get your children to
tidy their rooms more? Because I'm not cleaning under their
fucking beds.

*Saryang Park:* Yes.

**Florence Gunn:** Ok. Also—I don't really mind that you
keep your vibrator under your pillow, but you should put it
in the nightstand drawer on my days. K?

**Florence Gunn:** Did you think 'fucking bitch'?

*Saryang Park:* Maybe. ;P

*Saryang Park:* So, Tuesday afternoon? I'll leave the keys at Santokh's yoga studio over the weekend?

**Florence Gunn:** Tuesday. Thanks, Mrs. Dr.

*Saryang Park:* Can you just call me Saryang?

**Florence Dunn:** I really like Mrs. Dr. ;P But I'll think about it.

---

Jump Down The Aisle
SATURDAY, APRIL 14

---

"I can't believe she took you back," Santokh said. They were in the change room of the yoga studio, which, for the day, was transformed into a bridal dressing room. Florence was helping Santokh into her dress. And updating her on life. In the last two weeks before the wedding, Santokh and Michelle ran around panicked and frantic looking for garlands, centrepieces, and other objects that would define and assure their perfection as a married couple. As a result, Florence had done most of the cleaning jobs alone, occasionally with Santokh's student Uttamroop helping her, and there hadn't been much time for chatting.

"Hey, be grateful. This means you're getting a wedding present."

Santokh giggled. Smoothed out the bodice of her wedding dress.

"I should put a mirror in here," she said. "I don't know what I look like. At all."

"So beautiful." Florence hugged her. And kissed the nape of her neck, and then her hair.

"You're just saying that because I'm not wearing the

turban." Santokh's hair was coiffed and braided, and embell-ished with flowers and pearls, in an elaborate creation that had taken Martha most of the morning to complete.

"I'm saying it because you are," Florence said. Hugged her tight. "Thank you for asking me to give you away."

Santokh flushed with pleasure.

"Are Isaac and Sammy really wearing those pink dress-es?" she asked.

Florence nodded. Laughed.

"Ethan is in a powder blue tux," she said. "His compromise."

"You've got some amazing kids, Florence," Santokh said. And started crying.

Florence held her.

"Thank god you're not wearing make-up," she said after a while.

"But now I think I need some," Santokh wailed.

"Thank god there's no mirror to confirm that. Come on, bride-to-be. Let's get this done."

"Florence?" Santokh took a few steps back and looked at Florence in panic. "Florence? Suppose I'm making a huge mistake? Suppose... suppose this is not the right thing to do? Suppose..."

"Suppose you do some breathing exercises and go get married?" Florence said.

"I'm going to cry again," Santokh said.

"That's fine. Everyone loves a crying bride. They'll think you're overwrought with emotion."

"Florence!"

Santokh's cry was loud and piercing. Florence fell silent. Looked at her friend carefully. Tears in her eyes and trembling hands. Pre-wedding jitters, the equivalent of first night stage fright? Or, genuine second thoughts, that moment before one jumps off a cliff when one realizes that the jump is actually a really horrible idea, that there is no soft landing? That no one will catch you, save you, if that darkness below is rock, not water? Or, worse, if there are rocks under the water?

*Nice metaphor, Florence. Shut your brain up.*

"Am I doing the right thing?"

*Don't ask me, don't ask me, don't ask me!*

Florence moved back to fold Santokh into her arms.

"Scared?" she whispered into her neck.

"Terrified," Santokh whispered back. "Florence, the last week, the last month. All we've been doing is fighting. Fighting over... everything. Stupid details. The colour of the napkins for today. The colour of the napkins! Who cares, Florence, really, who cares?"

Florence was going to say—every bride and her mother. She and Martha, planning her and David's wedding, had the worst fight of their lives, ever, over whether the flower vases at the wedding reception should be white... or clear.

But Santokh didn't need, wait for a response.

"And big things too, Florence. My students. I had to pare down the wedding list to nothing. And Uttamroop— she's like my number one student. My second-in-command, you know? She's totally saving my ass for the honeymoon. But she's not at my wedding. Because Michelle thinks she's too beautiful. And she doesn't like the way I look at her. Or she at me. It's fucking driving me crazy!"

"Uttamroop is so ridiculously beautiful I don't even mock her ridiculous name," Florence said. Babbled, really. She wanted to talk to stop Santokh from talking. "Don't bridle and call me a racist. A white woman named Santokh is funny and so is a Ghana-born woman named Uttamroop. Although I wouldn't know a genuine Ghanian name if it hit me between the eyes. Ears? And I'm trailer park trash, so I get to say so. Santokh, listen..."

But Santokh didn't want to listen, only talk.

"But I can deal with the jealousy. I can. I even—ok, it's sexy, right? Because it comes from love. She loves me so much, that's why she's jealous. But the turban... you know, Florence, of course—I can take it off for her for the day. I don't have to wear it everywhere, all the time. I just choose to, you know? Because it's important to me. It's such an important part of me. And if she really loved me, if she really loved me as I am—would she not... would she not understand that?"

Florence thought about Michelle. Whom she did not really like—the only likeable, loveable thing about whom, for Florence, was that she loved Santokh and Santokh loved her, and was there such a thing as a functional couple anyway?

"Would she not understand that?" Santokh wept. "I've given way on everything. The napkins. Uttamroop. The turban. I've asked your boys to wear the stupid dresses— honestly, Florence, I don't care about that either. I really don't. I just want to be... I just want to be happy. And married. Actually, honestly, I don't even want to be married. I don't care. She wants to be married. It's important to her. And... I want to give her that. I want her to feel secure and safe with me... And... and..."

Her voice disappeared in her sobs.

"Do you love her?" Florence whispered into her ear.

"So, so much," Santokh sobbed out.

*Then jump.*

"Then let's wash your face. And walk you down the aisle. Or, hallway, rather."

Cutting Corners, Not Sharing
Secrets

SUNDAY, APRIL 22

Martha insisted on helping Florence clean, every day, on every job, during the time that Santokh and Michelle took off for their honeymoon. Uttamroop and a couple of Santokh's yoga students pitched in as well, alternating teaching classes and covering Santokh's shifts. But Uttamroop was the only one who really carried her weight.

"You're fucking amazing," Florence said on their first day working together. "And if you end up joining Santokh's cult full on and wearing white clothes and a turban, I'll only make fun of you a little."

"You're a fucking bitch, Florence," Uttamroop said. "But I can handle you."

Florence laughed.

"No one can handle me, little girl," she said. But she liked Santokh's student. She moved gracefully, she worked fast, she shared Florence's taste in music, and she could dance.

Still, even with Uttamroop and Martha's help, Florence had to be there for every job, and by the time she and

Martha were doing the clinic on the weekend—Uttamroop was teaching all of Santokh's classes on the weekends—she was bone-tired.

Working alongside her mother was both soothing and infuriating.

"I cleaned the washroom mirrors, properly," Martha said, coming out of the washrooms with the garbage. "I know you said you did them already, Florence, but really."

"Thanks, Mom."

"Florence, I know we're cutting some corners this week, but professionals do not leave fingerprint marks, anywhere. I redid the ultrasound monitor screens."

"Thanks, Mom."

"Florence, you know you don't get corners clean with the mop. Where is the cloth?"

"Oh-my-fucking-god, Mom, we need to get this place done in three hours—at this rate, we will be here for six, and I still have to do the fucking banks!"

"No need to be snappy with me, Florence. I'm sorry that I'm old and slow and useless. I'm sure you'd be much happier with one of Santokh's young girls helping you."

"Yes, I would. Because they'd be doing a half-ass, as-quick-as-we-can job, and not redoing my perfectly good-enough work!"

"You should go out tonight," Martha said after a pause. "How about I do the banks myself tonight, Florence, and you go out?"

Florence laughed.

Hugged the infuriating woman.

"I love you," she said. "But at this pace, it would take you eight hours to clean the banks. And, as you are so old, you might die while you were at it. And I have no plans, no one to..." She stopped talking abruptly. Her hand slipped over her phone.

She hadn't logged into OKC for... how long?

So long.

But she knew the message, the last message she had seen, off by heart.

*iwillornot*: Florence? I'm still here. Anytime you want to message. You don't even have to explain, ok? Just—fuck, I don't know. Send me a happy face or something.

Except that was... two months ago. One week and two months ago.

And, of course he wasn't there.

Other people, though, were.

She could just... Do what she did before, always.

Ask for a quick and easy hook-up, a fun night dancing and fucking and laughing. A mini-vacation from...

"Well, you are getting older, my dear," Martha said. "I guess the pickings aren't as good anymore." She looked at Florence critically. "Still. With a good night cream and some better foundation, you could still pass for thirty-five. In the right light."

"Oh-my-god, Mom, why do I love you?"

But she was laughing as she said it.

"Because I'm sixty-five, and I've spent this week helping you work every single day." Martha didn't pause. "And I stay the night with the boys any night you ask me to. And I don't ask you any questions about who or why, or if it's the same person or six."

"You didn't on Christmas Eve," Florence said. Immediately wished she hadn't.

Christmas Eve.

The text.

"Help me."

Will.

Fuck.

"I do have a tiny life of my own, Florence," Martha said. "That you don't ask about. Did you ever wonder what I was doing on Christmas Eve, that I couldn't help you?"

And Florence realized she didn't.

"Oh-my-god, Mom, are you dating?"

And Martha flushed—and although she had Florence's white-and-freckled complexion, and the redness suffused her paleness in spotty patches, Florence had never seen her mother look more beautiful.

"Are you going to tell me about him?" Florence asked.

Martha looked at Florence sharply.

"Are you going to tell me why you haven't had a date in two months?" she asked. "And only once since Christmas?"

Florence shook her head.

They finished cleaning the clinic in silence, and didn't speak much at the bank either. But the kiss and hug Martha gave Florence after Florence dropped her off home felt like an electric blanket.

And Florence let herself cry all the way home.

## A Good Love-Hate Thing


*Saryang Park:* Florence, thank you, thank you, thank you, you're amazing.

**Florence Gunn:** Just doing my job, Saryang.

*Saryang Park:* Seriously, Florence. I don't know what you do. Everything shines.

**Florence Gunn:** Mrs. Dr., not that I don't appreciate being appreciated, but I almost liked it better when you were a fucking bitch.

*Saryang Park:* What?

**Florence Gunn:** We had this good adversarial, love-hate thing going. You'd leave me a nasty note. I'd leave you a nasty note. And now just all this boring complimentary texting.

*Saryang Park:* Are you kidding?

**Florence Gunn:** Maybe. ;P

*Saryang Park:* I'm so not going to empty the dishwasher Monday night.

**Florence Gunn:** Good. I'll pile all the dirty dishes on the dining room table while I clean the sinks and counters. Maybe I'll even leave them there.

*Saryang Park:* You're a little weird, Florence.

**Florence Gunn:** Good thing I'm so good at my job, huh?

*Saryang Park:* :) <3

# A Terrible Guru

## TUESDAY, MAY 1

Cleaning Saryang Park's house was now one of Florence's favourite parts of her weekly routine. And having Santokh there on this particular Tuesday was a bonus.

She was tanned and glowing and full of stories of the honeymoon, which, she said, had been a fourteen-day-long love-in during which nothing went wrong.

And Florence listened to her with joy, except when she faded out, and thought about...

> *iwillornot*: Florence? I'm still here. Anytime you want to message. You don't even have to explain, ok? Just—fuck, I don't know. Send me a happy face or something.

...Except she fucking well knew that there were rocks at the bottom of the cliff, they weren't even hidden by water, how could she, why would she jump?

"You don't have to talk about it," Santokh said suddenly.

"What?" Florence stopped. They were effectively done, and, sitting at Saryang's large kitchen table—which reminded Florence a little of Will's kitchen table, fuck, why was she doing this to herself—drinking disgustingly healthy and just generally *disgusting* herbal fake coffee out of Santokh's thermos and eating disgustingly healthy—but delicious—raw food energy balls.

"You don't have to talk about it," Santokh repeated. "But I can tell you *want* to talk about it."

"Talk about what?" Florence demanded. Bit into a chewy ball. "These are different today. What's the secret ingredient?"

"Rose water," Santokh said. "You're changing the subject."

"I thought you said I don't have to talk about it!"

"You don't. But you want to."

Florence didn't say anything. Chewed.

"You know I don't... You know I'll let you be, right?" Santokh said after a long silence. Florence nodded. "But Florence. It's been... how long? Two and half months. And I know you. And I love you. And I don't know what happened on Valentine's Day..."

"Nothing," Florence said.

"Ok, nothing happened on Valentine's Day," Santokh said. "Whatever didn't happen—it's been two and a half months, Florence. And in that time—ok, so when was the last time you went on a date?"

Florence chewed.

Santokh said nothing.

"Have you been talking to my mother?" Florence asked.

Santokh evaded her eyes, then turned them on her almost violently.

"When was the last time you told me a story about a funny message you got on one of the dating sites?"

Florence chewed.

"When was the last time you mentioned his name?"

Florence chewed.

"How long have we been friends?" Santokh asked.

"Us?" Florence smiled. "A lifetime. Ten years. A fucking decade. Oh-my-god, Santokh, we need to have an anniversary party!" She suddenly felt very happy. "Fuck. Ten years, Santokh! Since before you joined the cult. When your name was Emily."

"It is not a cult, it's a very unique and beautiful school of yoga," Santokh said, as she always did. Readjusted her turban. "Ten years. Do you think I know you well?"

Florence thought about this too. Very seriously.

She and Santokh knew each other only a few months before they teamed up as Karma Klean. But since then... almost every day, working side-by-side. Sunday dinners and potlucks. So many conversations. So many moments of silence.

More than a few nights spent sleeping on Santokh's couch after meh dates.

More than a few nights of Santokh at her house, helping her cope with the boys. With the havoc wrecked by David's occasional reappearances.

Every Christmas, Thanksgiving, Easter—birthday— spent together.

And yet...

So many silences.

"I don't actually know if you know me that well," Florence said. "I mean... what do you know about me? Really?"

Santokh did not know much about Jonathan, for example. She knew too much, unfortunately, about David, but that was unavoidable. In the small but necessary disclosures Florence had given her over the years—did she ever share her terrifying realization that her husbands were her father—a repeat of a horror tape from her childhood?

"What do you know about me?" Florence repeated. "Really?"

"Everything," Santokh said and embraced her. "I know everything that matters, Florence."

And stupidly, Florence burst into tears.

"I don't know what to say." She snotted into Santokh's shoulder.

"Let's start with his name," Santokh suggested.

"You want me to talk about Will," Florence sighed.

"No." Santokh shook her head. "You want to talk bout Will. You haven't mentioned his name in two months. You fucking wouldn't shut up about him for six weeks. So impressed he hadn't texted you, you'd say. When we both knew you couldn't believe he hadn't messaged. You didn't think he'd last. Well, he lasted. He got his date—which, by that time you wanted as much as he did. Maybe more? Did you want it more than he did, Florence?"

Florence shook her head.

"We both wanted it," she said. "God. We both wanted it. So much."

"Then what?" Santokh asked.

"I don't think I can tell you," Florence said.

"Can you tell yourself?" Santokh asked.

And Florence found herself crying and crying and crying.

"Probably not," she said finally.

"Maybe," she said a few minutes later. "I tried the other day. Sort of."

"Fuck," she said as she and Santokh got up, together, and started cleaning the energy ball crumbs off Saryang's shining table.

Santokh laughed.

"Do you want to tell me something?" Florence demanded.

Santokh laughed again.

"No, never," she said. "I don't give advice. I wouldn't dare. Just... I don't know, Florence. I don't want to be trite, ok, or cliché? But I've known you for almost ten years. And in those ten years, you've been—happy, mostly. Right? And... very self-assured. All good things. And you've enjoyed—I know you've enjoyed your lovers. And you've enjoyed... you've enjoyed keeping things... you know..."

"Casual," Florence supplied.

"Sure, casual," Santokh agreed. "But you've never..."

Florence waited.

Santokh put on her coat. Florence sighed and put on hers.

"You've never missed anyone. Or looked forward to anyone," Santokh said, in the car. "You miss this guy. Whatever happened on Valentine's Day... or whatever didn't happen. Whatever you think... I don't know. I'd just... you miss this guy. That's all. You've missed him, with your whole being, for the past two months. And the six weeks before that."

"What are you saying?" Florence asked.

"I don't know," Santokh shrugged. "Maybe he just popped into your life so you could miss him and be miserable about him. Or maybe he popped into your life so you could, you know. Fall in love."

"You said you didn't want to be trite or cliché," Florence said.

"Sorry," Santokh shrugged again. "Love is trite. And cliché. Because everyone wants it. I just think... if it's knocking... you know. You should... I don't know."

"You're a terrible guru," Florence said. "Aren't you supposed to offer, like, clearcut, insightful advice?"

"I'm not your guru," Santokh laughed. "And I'm not

giving you advice. I'm just... trying to get you to talk. To yourself. Not even me."

Florence drove in silence.

*I don't want to think about you, I can't stop thinking about you. What does this mean? What do I do with that?*

"Santokh?" she asked as she pulled up in front of the yoga studio.

Santokh waited.

*I don't want him to be my third mistake.*

*Oh-my-god, I miss him.*

"I haven't... I haven't acknowledged him in two months," Florence said. "Because... well, that doesn't matter. Ok. It matters, but I don't want to talk bout it."

Santokh waited.

Florence didn't say anything.

Santokh pulled out her phone and looked at the time.

"I'm going to be late," she said. "You want advice, Florence. Ask for it. I might give it."

Florence breathed. Groped around for words.

Found inadequate ones.

"I'm afraid of... I don't want... I don't want. Except all I want is... all I want is... Fuck. I don't know."

Santokh laughed.

"Do you remember, when Michelle and I started dating, and I was having my freak-out sessions, what you told me?"

Florence shook her head.

"You said, you said something like, 'How about you don't act as if this is the make-it-or-break-it event of your life. How about you think—this is just a coffee. This is just a date. This just... a night.'"

"That was pretty good advice, actually," Florence said. "Except that now you're married."

"Do you think my marriage was a mistake?" The panic

in Santokh's voice was so acute that Florence grabbed both of her hands.

"God, no," she said. Which might have been a lie, but it was what Santokh needed to hear.

"What I'm saying, Florence," Santokh said, "is that I think you're panicking over... something that could happen —but maybe not—sometime in the very far off future. And as a result... you're not enjoying the present. At all."

"I knew you'd turn this into a fucking yoga cult lecture at some point."

Santokh swatted her hand, then kissed her cheek.

"What's the worst that will happen if you see him again, Florence?" she said.

Florence said nothing. Shower. Table. Floor. Elevator. Lobby. Hood of car.

She was a flame of lust and desire.

*I'm going to fall in love with him. And make a third mistake.*

*I possibly already love him, Santokh. Because... I don't even know why. And I can't trust my judgement. Do you not know that?*

But she said nothing.

"And what's the worst thing that will happen if you don't see him again, Florence?" Santokh said.

And Florence died. Again. Her breath left her completely, and she felt herself...

"Florence!" Santokh's voice felt like a slap or a bucket of cold water. "What the fuck is going on?"

"I'm a stupid teenager who can't control her hormones," Florence managed to say. "Maybe my mother is right. Maybe this is early menopause."

Santokh laughed, but Florence didn't. She was trying... she was trying, really, really hard to...

"What should I do?" she said, grabbing Santokh's hands again. "Be the fucking guru. Tell me."

Santokh shrugged.

"Do you think I should see him again? I mean, message him, see if he even wants to see me again? Because suppose he doesn't?" Florence said. "Don't fucking shrug again. I swear, if you shrug again, I'm going to pull off your turban and stomp on it."

Santokh laughed.

"Do you want to see him again? Message him again?"

Florence felt tears well up in her eyes again.

"I don't even know what I would say. What I would explain. I don't want to..." She swallowed hard. "I don't want to explain. Why I left and why I was upset. And I don't want... I don't want to explain why I haven't messaged him for two months. And I don't want..."

She felt rather than saw Santokh getting exasperated. And then, she felt her reach for more patience.

"Ok," Santokh said. "Can you, like, let go of my hands, so I can go to class? Ok, Florence. You don't know what you want. Ask yourself... no, wait—yes or no question. Do you want to see him again? Don't think—just answer."

The, "Fuck, yes," came out of her mouth before her mind formed a thought.

And Santokh wiggled her hands out of Florence's grip and flicked her nose. Opened the car door and stepped into the early May sunshine.

"Florence? You miss him. So very much. And I think... I think all you have to do? All you have to do, if you want to see him again, all you have to do is say... 'Hi.'"

"You are a terrible, terrible guru!" Florence yelled after Santokh as she walked up the stairs to the yoga studio.

Santokh turned around. Gave her a smile. And shrugged.

## Silence, Interrupted
### WEDNESDAY, MAY 2

**notanightingale:** Hi.

...

...

...

# One Night Stand Times Three
## And a Half?
### THURSDAY, MAY 3

*iwillornot*: Hi. How are you?

**notanightingale:** Feeling awkward.

*iwillornot*: Don't.

**notanightingale:** LOL. Ok.

*iwillornot*: Coffee?

**notanightingale:** One more one night stand?

*iwillornot*: You got it. Tonight?

**notanightingale:** I can't tonight. Saturday night?

*iwillornot*: You got it. My place—at... 7 p.m.?

**notanightingale:** See you then.

## No Talking Allowed
### SATURDAY, MAY 5

He met her downstairs, in the apartment lobby, a finger on his lips.

"What?" she said. He put a finger on her lips, and then pulled her through the door. Held her against him, lips touching but not kissing, while he pushed the elevator button.

"Don't say anything." He breathed into her lips, talking without taking his lips off hers—but still not kissing. "Today —we don't say anything. Ok?"

She nodded, and pressed her lips against his. Her chest against his. Her pelvis... oh, fuck, yes!

"Hello, Mrs. Zie... Mrs. Z," Will said as the elevator door opened.

"Mr. Ornot," the woman—Florence remembered her vaguely, from when? Christmas Eve, she remembered and felt laughter rise up in her throat—"Is this the way we are going to keep on meeting?"

Florence exploded with laughter as soon as they were in the elevator and the door closed behind them. Will joined her—moving his lips off hers onto her neck, then forehead... hairline...

"How many women has she caught you fucking in the elevator?" she whispered into Will's neck when she could breathe.

"Ssssh," he said. "No talking today. Remember?"

She nodded.

He scooped her into his arms as the elevator door opened. Then groaned.

She laughed.

"You're just a little heavier than you look," he muttered. "Or I'm weaker than I think."

"Did you just call me fat?" she demanded.

He kissed her mouth.

"See, this is why we don't talk," he said. "No. Talking. Only kissing." He kissed. "And fucking."

And oh.

This time, they didn't begin until they were on the bed, fully clothed. He kissed her through fabrics and layers and she explored his lines, curves, and bulges through his shirt and pants, with her hands, her feet, her chin... they drew their bodies up and down and all around each other, and the clothes sometimes existed and sometimes didn't, and then they were partly naked, and Will stopped.

"I have," he groaned because she didn't, "this fantasy."

"We're not supposed to," she said, and bit his lip, "talk."

"Instructions are ok," he said, and kissed and tumbled her off the bed, and onto the floor, through the living room, into the dining room.

"On the table," he said, lifting her up. "I was wondering... oh, yes, fuck yes. The perfect height." He knelt down, and disappeared between her legs, into the folds of her lips and pussy.

"Oh-my-fucking-god," she moaned.

"Dessert," he said, words round and muffled. "My... just... dessert..."

She soaked him and the table and when he pulled her off down under it—and finally tore off her bra to devour her breasts—she soaked the floor, repeatedly, before he suddenly cried, "The fucking condoms are in the bedroom, run!" and they ran to the bedroom like ridiculous laughing children, and sank into the next round of sex greedily and selfishly, Florence chasing one more, one more orgasm, while Will, regardless of her desire now, chased his.

"Fuck," he moaned eventually. Then laughed. "Fuck, that's such a ridiculous thing to say after sex, isn't it? Why isn't there another word?"

"Because if you fuck properly, you should be out of words after you fuck. Except for fuck," Florence whispered lazily. Will laughed. Nuzzled her shoulder. Moved one of her legs up, the other down.

"If you give me a little bit of time," he said, shifting her hips and arms now, "I will..."

"What are you doing?"

"Putting you in the perfect cuddling position," he said. "I'm owed cuddles. Sorry. Scratch that. No talking. I didn't say that. I'm just doing as I will with your gorgeous body. Fuck."

She wasn't quite sure what he put where—left, right, under, over—but the feeling was fabulous. She felt molded. Melded. Melting.

"As I was saying," he murmured, "a little bit of time... and I will... regain... both words... and the ability to fuck more. I feel... I feel I neglected your ass. There are a number of... really awful things I want to do..." he struggled against a yawn... "to... your ass, and you are not to tempt me with your pussy until I do."

"All right," she murmured back. Melting. In utter heaven.

"How much time..." he yawned... "Do I have?"

"Till morning," she said. Yawned. "Till morning."

"Fuck," he said again. "Florence. Thank you."

His eyes closed as Florence fought against another yawn. Then surrendered to it.

Heaven.

---

## Safe Distance

SUNDAY, MAY 6

---

Florence woke up before her alarm went off. There was a moment of disorientation before she realized she was in Will's arms, in Will's bed. And, oh. She was wet. And happy. And... she kissed his chin and then his lips and he, still mostly asleep, squeezed her harder and then, without any attempt at foreplay and somehow without letting her out of his arms or opening his eyes, he found a condom, and they rocked together in lazy morning pleasure.

"Dammit," he said suddenly. "I told you not to tempt me with your pussy." And he slid out of her quickly and unceremoniously, without teasing or lubing, thrust into her ass. She gasped in surprise and then she gasped in shock, and then she just stopped breathing.

"Only time I believe in God," he told her after he came. She stroked herself lazily... or was he stroking her? It was hard to tell; it was heaven.

"I have to go," she said, finally. Her phone, in her purse, in the hallway, was quacking like a duck. He nodded, but didn't let her go. "I have to go," she repeated. "Children. And, so much work today. So much work." He nodded and released her, rolling away just a little bit. She slid out of the bed reluctantly. Leggings. Skirt. Sweater.

"Are you going to leave me another bra?" he asked, voice thick and lazy. "Is that your thing?" They both laughed. "I think it's under the dining room table," he said. "I'm so helpful."

"You could go get it for me," she suggested.

"I'm not that helpful, I guess," he said. "And, I like you braless."

She stood in the doorway of the bedroom and looked at him... with... what? Longing? Affection?

Love?

*Shut up, brain. Don't think.*

Why was she here?

Because... not being here, not seeing him again... felt like death.

So what was this? What had she asked for?

*One more one night stand.*

And now... what?

*Don't think.*

Florence thought.

She saw Will looking at her. With... she shuddered.

It was delicious. And awful.

*Don't run.*

"Is something wrong?" he asked, forehead creasing, eyes crinkling.

He was...

She shook her head very slowly.

"I'm glad I came," she said.

"I'm so glad you came too," he said. "Again, and again, and again..." He laughed. And looked at her, again, with... what?

It was something and it made her heart pound and her eyes water.

And he wasn't going to say anything.

She knew that, too.

She thought, *Today, if I walk out the door, he's going to let me go.*

She couldn't bear it.

She couldn't... not see him again.

But she was afraid... and she didn't want... and all the reasons that loving him—she did not think that, yes she did, *Shut the fuck up brain!*—was a bad idea, they all existed. Still.

She wished he'd say something.

But he was silent, leaning against pillows of his bed. Watching her. With...

Fuck.

"Fuck?" he said.

She blushed. "Did I say that out loud?"

He nodded.

She laughed, and so did he, and she was fucking going to... she was going to...

This was not—Santokh had said it, echoing advice Florence believed, because it was her own—the make it or break it event of her life. It was just... a night.

But it felt momentous, and terrifying.

And she was so scared.

But she was going to do it.

She wanted another one.

She did.

So...

She was going to jump.

"Will?" she said.

He waited. Still and silent on the bed.

One more night.

That's all.

And then after that... another one?

Maybe?

"Will?" she said again.

"Florence?" he said, with a smile.

She stood. Still. Searched for words.

And courage.

*Jump.*

"I guess... Will? I guess... I don't want you to make a big deal out of it. Or I will freak out. But I would like to see you. Again, I mean. Just, you know. Like one more time, maybe."

She did it.

She said the words and the world didn't end, except that Will leapt out of the bed and she was pressed against the frame of the door and somehow inside his throat.

"Me too," he said after he let her mouth go. "Do I have to even say it? Like, seriously, Florence, have you ever been chased by a man with as little pride as me?" He bit her neck and ear and disappeared into her hair and she moaned.

"I really have to go now, though," she said, as his fingers dove into her pussy again.

"I know," he said. "But we will see each other again—and I am not making a big deal out of it. Ok, I totally am, because fuck, I want you. Right now. And again... seriously, how much time do you have right now? Cause we could totally..."

"I have to go." She laughed. And wiggled away.

"I'll let you go in a second," he promised. Held her tight. "So... but... so... there's a complication."

He stepped away.

"I'm being seconded—I took this temporary position in our Toronto office," he said.

"Toronto?" she said. "You're moving to Toronto?"

Something rose in her. Anger? Disappointment? Relief? She couldn't tell. A confused messy feeling.

"Toronto is very far away," she said.

And closed her eyes. Felt... foolish.

Will kissed them.

"It's just for four months," he said. "Until September. Well, end of August. Still. Almost four months."

What?

"Four months?" she said.

He nodded.

She strained and tried to pull away. Will pressed into her and kissed her hair.

"It's just 3,400 kilometres," he joked. "It's—my kids are going to see their grandparents. Amanda's parents. For the entire summer, from June on. They have this cottage, in Ontario. Not super close to Toronto, but close enough that I can get out there most weekends. I couldn't bear, right now, to be away from them for almost three whole months. You know?"

"Toronto," she repeated. "When do you leave?"

He half-turned towards the nightstand, equipped with an old-school alarm clock.

"Yesterday, about now," he said.

"What?"

Arms around her. Face in her hair.

"I'll rebook for later today," he said. "Unless you can spend more of today with me. In which case, I'll rebook it for Monday. Unless you can spend some of Monday with me. In which case I'll fly on the red-eye that gets me in Tuesday morning, because I have a Tuesday 8 a.m. meeting with my new team."

"You missed your flight to see me?" she said.

He didn't say anything for a while.

"Are you going to freak out about it?" he asked finally.

She laughed. "No."

"Then yes. I missed my flight to see you."

She burrowed her face into his shoulder.

"Will you come out to visit me? For a weekend? Or midweek? At least once or twice?"

She started to pull away but he kept her contained.

"Talk to me, don't fucking run off," he said.

"No," she said. "I can't."

"Don't run off and don't freak out," he said again. "A weekend. It's just a weekend, Florence. It's just a 'I'd like to see you again,' except it's in Toronto and not in my apartment. It's like... our fourth—fifth—one night stand. In Toronto."

She swallowed. It felt like she was swallowing her pride.

"I can't possibly afford it," she said.

"I'd pay for it. I'd be so fucking happy to buy your ticket." He squeezed her harder. "Don't run off and don't freak out."

"I could not possibly accept it," Florence said. Sad. Not angry. She was sad and not angry.

And she was not feeling defensive.

At all. A little panicked, maybe? Just a little.

In a manageable way. Disappointed but also relieved, and, suddenly, happy, and she liked the feeling—was scared by it—burrowed her face into Will's shoulder again.

"Can you not get the time off?" he murmured. Into her hair.

"If I take time off, I don't get paid," she murmured back.

He held her and stroked her hair.

"And you won't let me take care of that," he said. Statement of fact. She stayed still, and waited for her hackles to rise.

They prickled. But they didn't peak.

"Not even remotely negotiable," she said. Kissed his cheek.

She wondered if she should say other things.

"And my kids. I can't leave them," she added.

"No part-time daddy around?" he asked. "Fuck, Florence, sorry, I shouldn't have said that. None of my business. I suppose offering to fly you and your kids to Toronto..."

"Don't even go there," she said. But she wasn't running. Her hackles weren't rising. And he was still holding her.

And this felt... it felt a lot like happy.

"I won't." He kissed her neck. Squeezed her hard.

"I'll see you when you get back," she said. "We'll have our... fifth one night stand."

"If that's what you want to call it," he said, loosening his embrace but not letting her go. "But... you'll text me while I'm gone, right?"

"Only if you're not obnoxious," she said. "And not every day," she added.

"God, not every day, what would people think." He let her go, then pulled her in again. She went limp in his arms.

"Ok. I really, really have to go," she said. "Children. Work."

She wondered if she should offer to drive him to the airport. She wondered if he would ask her... and if he did, what she would do.

But he let go of her this time, completely.

"Go," he said. "I'll text you from Toronto."

"Ok," she said.

She was in the elevator before she remembered she never retrieved her bra from under the kitchen table.

*iwillornot*: About to board. Florence—one more thing. Can I have your phone number now? Please?

**notanightingale:** Don't you like messaging me through the OKC app? And checking out all the other women who want you?

*iwillornot*: You mean all the women I could have instead? I love it. It's my favourite thing in the world. Give me your fucking phone number.

**notanightingale:** 587.555.0987. Fly safe.

*iwillornot*: ttyl xo

**notanightingale:** Aren't you going to give me your number?

**notanightingale:** Will? Aren't you going to... Ah fuck.
Never mind.

---

*iwillornot:* Patience, woman. I'll text you. From Toronto.

# BITTERSWEET HALLOWEEN

*For Sean,*
*because Halloween and Hot Mess*

---

## It Might Kill Me
### MONDAY, AUGUST 20

---

**Florence Gunn:** Tomorrow?

*Will Ornot:* Tomorrow. Excited?

**Florence Gunn:** Maybe.

*Will Ornot:* You're such a bitch. Admit you're excited.

**Florence Gunn:** I said, maybe.

*Will Ornot:* Tell me you missed me.

**Florence Gunn:** How could I miss you? We texted every single day.

*Will Ornot:* not every single day

**Florence Gunn:** Every. Single. Day.

*Will Ornot:* Florence?

**Florence Gunn:** Will?

*Will Ornot:* Would it kill you to admit that a) this is a relationship and b) you missed me and c) you're excited that I'm coming home tomorrow?

**Florence Gunn:** Suppose it does? Is that a risk you're willing to take?

*Will Ornot:* WTF?

**Florence Gunn:** Suppose it does kill me to admit that a) this is a relationship and b) I missed you and c) I'm excited that you're coming home tomorrow? Is that a risk you're willing to take?

*Will Ornot:* :)

*Will Ornot:* I saw what you did there. Thank you.

**Florence Gunn:** ;P

**Florence Gunn:** When does your flight land?

*Will Ornot:* Have I not told you?

**Florence Gunn:** No.

*Will Ornot:* Do you want me to tell you?

**Florence Gunn:** For fuck's sake. This again?

*Will Ornot*: Ok, I'm going to be the mature, emotionally secure partner again. Florence. Would you pick me up from the airport tomorrow? I would like that. Very much.

---

*Will Ornot*: But of course you don't have to if this is one of the things that makes you freak out and think that I'm going to walk off the plane carrying a wedding ring.

**Florence Gunn:** This again?

*Will Ornot*: This is terrible. We're getting very predictable.

**Florence Gunn:** Will? What time is your flight landing? I would like to pick you up from the airport.
Very much.

*Will Ornot*: :)

*Will Ornot*: I know you have a challenging schedule. What time would be good for you to pick me up?

**Florence Gunn:** LOL. I know you're a BIG DEAL but flights don't work that way.

*Will Ornot*: Look, I can pick a flight that lands at a specific time, right? There's one every hour, practically. And I want you to meet me at the airport.

*Will Ornot*: Because I missed you and I'm excited to see you. And also, I have this airport washroom sex fantasy. It involves pushing your dress up around your throat and using it like a leash.

**Florence Gunn:** Down, boy.

*Will Ornot:* Down, girl. I might say that. In my fantasy, you're so excited when you see me come off the plane, you start to hump my leg. Like a bitch in heat.

**Florence Gunn:** ...

*Will Ornot:* Fantasy. And I told you. I fucking miss you. What time am I going to see you tomorrow?

**Florence Gunn:** Have you not booked your flight yet?

*Will Ornot:* Answer my damn question.

**Florence Gunn:** It would be best between 12:30 and 4. Or after 10 p.m.

*Will Ornot:* Ok. Hold on...

**Florence Gunn:** What are you doing?

*Will Ornot:* Just hold on. I'm getting into yyc on flight WS671 at 21:59. So... probably 10:15 at earliest before I land. Ok?

**Florence Gunn:** Did you book your flight just now?

*Will Ornot:* Rebooked.

**Florence Gunn:** You're insane.

*Will Ornot:* I miss you.

*Will Ornot:* So, this dress—it needs to be fairly thin and stretchy. Skip the bra and panties—you'll just leave the bra behind in the airport washroom anyway. And—do you have any fuck-me heels? I'm sort of seeing you in fuck-me heels in this fantasy.

**Florence Gunn:** We are not having sex in an airport washroom.

*Will Ornot:* We so are, Florence. Fuck-me heels?

**Florence Gunn:** Don't you want any surprises for tomorrow?

*Will Ornot:* No, not really.

**Florence Gunn:** LOL. See you tomorrow, Will.

*Will Ornot:* Tell me you miss me.

**Florence Gunn:** You know I do.

*Will Ornot:* God, what are you going to be like when I say, "I love you"?

**Florence Gunn:** Let's not find out, ok? See you tomorrow, Will.

*Will Ornot*: See you tomorrow. Songbird. Dig up some fuck-
me heels for me.

## Fantasies And Expectations
### TUESDAY, AUGUST 21

He didn't expect her to wear fuck-me heels. Not really—not at all, actually. He couldn't visualize her in heels. He scrunched his eyes up to remember—the first night, in December, she was wearing... boots. Winter boots. Sexy winter boots, but functional rather than fuck-me. Heel on them? Maybe, a bit of a wedge. When they met at Weeds Cafe for the bra-return-gone-wrong, she was wearing sneakers. Battered, well-worn sneakers. But her socks—he thought her socks were pink. Or was he thinking that just because the bra she was wearing—that she had flashed and taken off so brazenly (so much hotter in retrospect than it had been in life, when it was a little terrifying and embarrassing)—was pink?

And on Christmas Eve... he couldn't remember. No, he could. There they were. Fucking Sorels. She showed up at the liquor store in white Sorels. She must have pulled them on as she ran out the door, not thinking how out of place they looked with the hot—fuck, it was so ridiculously hot—pink Santa dress she was wearing. He remembered its white fur.

His cock smiled. He shifted *WestJet*'s inflight magazine a little to cover it.

Valentine's Day... she was wearing patent leather flats. Ballet flats. So cute. He remembered how they reflected the light of the washroom of the restaurant... Fuck, yeah. And the last time... he couldn't remember. He thought maybe those ballet flats again. Definitely not heels though. Of that he was sure.

It didn't matter.

Freckles mattered. And red hair. And those hands. And that smile, slightly crooked teeth. Eyes and eyebrows—he was going to tattoo her eyelids with... Oh, fuck...

"Can I get you anything else, sir? Before the captain calls for tables up and seatbelt on and all that?" The flight attendant materialized at his elbow. Will shook his head. "Anything at all?" she repeated.

"All good, thank you," he said. Fucking cock. Think of... Amanda and Ranveer. Think of... his mother-in-law—*ex* mother-in-law in the Wal-Mart bathing suit she should have replaced three sizes ago stepping into the hot tub at the cottage. Think of...

"I would be very happy," the flight attendant said, again, "to help you. With anything."

She looked rather pointedly at the magazine, and Will looked down at his covered-up discomfort and then up at her—discomfited, but also amused.

Pretty enough.

Willing.

Will felt flattered—aroused—self-righteous—then mean. He wanted to say, "I'm going to see someone, soon, who will take care of all that."

Then, he wanted to say, "Um, and where would you do that? Take care of me, I mean?"

And then he was genuinely curious as to where...

And then he thought of Amanda. And their six-year-long conversations about slippery slopes and cheating-not-cheating. And the consequences of cheating-not-cheating-fuck-yes-it-was-cheating while under the influence. Shuddered.

Then thought about Florence's insistence that he date in Toronto.

"We're texting. This is not a relationship," she said. Well, texted.

*I don't want anyone else,* he thought. But he knew her well enough not to tell her that.

"Sure," he said. Texted. "Do you want me to tell you about each of them? In detail?"

"God, no," she responded. "Not my kink."

"Good," he typed, smiling. "Not mine, either. Unless they're really terrible in bed and you want to tell me I'm a sex god. No, wait. I take it back. I really don't want you to sleep with anyone else while I'm gone. But, you know, of course you're free to."

"Thank you," she typed, and he tried to picture her face as she did that. Happy? Cynical? Taut? A kind of "Who the fuck are you to give me permission" look?

A near four-month-long texting relationship was... challenging.

There had been some phone calls too. But those were more difficult to arrange. Children, privacy. Time zones.

He had suggested Skype. She just said, "No."

She was infuriating.

He was in love.

"Thank you." He smiled at the flight attendant. Who was very pretty and lovely, and whom he would ravage in a fantasy one night very, very soon. But who was not Florence. "I've got everything I need."

Or I will, very soon, he thought as his cock relaxed a

little, and his mind, perversely, served up an image of Florence in fuck-me heels and nothing else, the black dress she was wearing coiled around her neck.

Oh, fuck.

Homecoming



Oh... fuck.

She was wearing four inch stilettos with straps that wound around and above her ankles, and a thin, almost sheer black dress.

And she...

"What happened to your hair?" he demanded, sinking his fingers into short tight curls. "Is this why you wouldn't send me any selfies? Oh-my-god. It's all gone!"

"It's not all gone," she said. "It's just... short."

"All gone," Will said mournfully. "And I so loved having all those hairs to pull out of my mouth. And I was looking forward to..." he kissed her earlobe, then neck, "pulling them out of my shower drain. You've only been in my shower once, right? There was like an entire red cat in there the next day."

"I'm happy to see you too," Florence said. "You don't like it?"

"I love it," he said. "I can see more of your face. And, oh, fuck, those shoes. The dress. Where's the washroom?"

"Where's your luggage?"

"Fuck my luggage. I can buy new clothes. Washroom?"

"Luggage. Car. Apartment."

"Have you lost all your adventurous spirit with the hair? Look, right there. A handicapped washroom, no less. Just made for..."

"Will? Let's go get your fucking luggage."

"OK, fine. I've got a present for you in there, by the way. But as soon as we get the luggage, we find a washroom."

They didn't—or rather, they weren't able to find one that they could enter with anything resembling privacy.

"You'll have to wait until we get to the car," Florence teased.

He smacked her ass, then squeezed it.

"You hope," he murmured.

They didn't make it to the car. He dropped his suitcase and laptop bag inside the airport parkade stairwell.

"You are going to keep on saying, 'I missed you, I missed you, I missed you,'" he told her, pressing her against the wall.

"And what are you going to do?" she asked.

He unzipped his pants very quickly and pulled a condom out of his pocket.

"Come," he said. "Very, very selfishly. And you'll love it."

She smiled.

"I will," she said.

He pushed her dress—so fucking flimsy—up above her breasts. Relished her glorious, freckled nakedness.

"Go," he said, and thrust.

"I missed you," she said. "I missed you. Oh, fuck, Will, I missed you so much..."

## Not For You

### WEDNESDAY, AUGUST 22



Will woke up alone, but with Florence's smell all around him. When did she creep out? How did he not notice? How did he let her go? He traced his fingers along the shape he imagined she left in the mattress. Then shocked himself by getting another erection.

"Seriously, boy?" he asked his penis. He masturbated slowly and lazily, thinking of the airport parkade—the ride home, his hands on her naked thighs, fuck yes, the make-out session in his lobby—interrupted, yet again, by Mrs. Ziernicka. The slower sex in the apartment. On the couch at first—but she didn't want to stay on the couch.

"I once thought of it as made of babies' butts," she said. "It's a terrible thought. And a total turn-off."

He laughed as he carried her to the bedroom.

"Did you get stronger?" she said, as he said, "Did you lose weight?" And then she hit him with a pillow, and they had a pillow fight, and he pinned her on the bed, and kissed her eyes, and chewed on her eyebrows, and yes, tattooed those eyelids the way he had imagined he would...

Oh-fuck-yes!

*Ping.*

"Are you home, Daddy?"

"I'm home, Munchkin."

It was, in many ways, a difficult summer. His assignment in Toronto was challenging. His team not quite up to the task, and not responsive to a Calgary-sourced "expert." Still. He managed. Dealing with in-laws who were now ex-in-laws—but forever grandparents of his kids—that sucked ass. And not just a little. Amanda's parents were always a little overbearing. Now, they were—Will searched for the word—*unbearable.* Utterly unbearable. Especially her mother. At whom Will looked frequently as a harbinger of what his future might have been if Amanda had stayed with him. If she had chosen to stay with him.

It almost made him glad to be divorcing. Almost.

The kids... the kids were not ok. Well, they were and they weren't. They seemed more high-strung and volatile than he remembered them being back home—before the divorce. But also after. Polly seemed two years younger. Whiny. Clingy. Matthew seemed two years older, a full-blown teenager at not-quite ten. How did that happen? He was with them almost every weekend through the summer, fighting the excruciating Highway 11 to Magentawan traffic for four hours one way and sometimes near five hours on the way back, to be nagged by his *ex* mother-in-law and patronized by his *ex* father-in-law.

Who seemed to think that he was the cheating bastard.

"Amanda's so lucky to have found Ranveer so quickly," his mother-in-law said once. He had been helping clear the table and had his hands full of dishes. He dumped them into the sink roughly, hoping some would break.

He wished Ranveer had been there, so that he could punch him in his this-wasn't-really-cheating-because-you-cheated-on-your-wife-first-six-years-ago-everything-has-consequences smug psychiatrist face.

Breathe, Will.

And do not call your wife a fucking cunt.

Don't think it.

Breathe.

"Daddy? Are you there?"

"I'm here, kitten. Just getting ready for work. What else happened?"

It was worst when the kids mentioned him, actually. So casually. "Mom and Ranveer." "We all went... us, and Mom, and Ranveer." "No, Mom didn't drive us to the game, she had a meeting. Ranveer did."

He was so angry about that. "Why didn't your Mom ask me to drive you?" escaped his mouth before he could choke it down. How could they know? But he texted Amanda immediately. "My children. My responsibility!"

"He was here, Will. It was easier."

Fucking asshole. Stealing Will's time with his kids.

Fucking cunt. Letting him.

And why was he even thinking this shit anyway?

Florence.

Sex.

Scent.

Happy.

Where did his happy go?

"Will!" Rosie jumped up when he walked into the office. "Oh, Will, I missed you so much!"

Her arms wrapped around his head and his around her waist. He kissed both her cheeks. He adored the width of her cheekbones and the set of her eyes.

"West African genes for the win," she told him the first time he complimented her on them. Six years ago. "By the way, Mr. Ornot, you're not supposed to say things like that to your employees."

He felt admonished and embarrassed and put in his place. He told her so.

"Good," she said. Then smiled. "Totally inappropriate, Mr. Ornot, but I love the compliment."

He could tell her how much he loved them now, and she'd accept it with a dismissive smile.

But he didn't say anything, just looked at her lovely face and enjoyed it.

"Was the Big Kahuna a big pain in the ass while I was gone?" he asked.

Rosie shook her head.

"I just... I just missed you," she said.

"I missed you too, sweetheart," he said. "Fuck. I promised not to call you sweetheart too, right? What am I supposed to call you?"

"She who keeps my shit together," Rosie said. "She who keeps me from getting fired. She who keeps all my secrets."

*That* still made him blush.

"I got you something."

She got up quickly, smiling, and he reached into his pocket.

A box.

"I should warn you, it's not a wedding ring," he joked. He had said the same thing to Florence when he gave her her box. Which had just been a box of chocolates. A large box of chocolates.

"That would have been some wedding ring," Florence joked back. "How big do you think my fingers are?"

"Huge," he said, biting them. "That's where all your weight is." She smacked him, playfully and he caught her hand, and they wrestled and they flattened the box, and...

Oh-fuck. Down, boy.

"Oh, Will, it's beautiful!" Rosie hugged him again. Kissed his cheeks. And then his lips.

"So beautiful!"

"Oh, good," he said. "I'm glad you like it." He watched her run the chain and beads through her fingers. Started telling her how he bought it and from whom—Kensington market, street seller, one of a kind—then realized she wasn't listening. She was putting on the necklace.

"It's perfect. Perfect!" she said.

"Good." Will smiled. Fuck, he loved Rosie. He was so happy to be back. Home. "God, I missed you," he said. "Next time—if I ever do something like that again, you have to come with me. I'm apparently too old and too demanding to work with a new assistant."

She smiled. Said, "I'd go to Toronto for you." He hugged her again, and enjoyed the way her body fit into his. Almost like Florence's.

Memories. He didn't remember—he didn't really remember that night six years ago. How could he?

But he remembered last night. Florence.

His cock twitched.

What the fuck? Stop.

Rosie pressed herself closer to him.

He made distance, awkwardly.

Down. Boy.

"Well, let's see what they did to my office while I was gone," he said, too loud, and almost ran to his office.

Rosie followed him.

"Will? I love it," she said. She came across the threshold. Expectant.

Oh fuck.

"I'll email you if I need anything," he said, sitting down. "Give me a couple of hours to get my bearings, and then we can go over the stuff you have for me."

She nodded... and withdrew. Yes, that was the word. She backed out—withdrew—from the room.

Will felt like an ass.

Rosie.

He emailed her.

"Was I an ass?"

"Yes."

"I'm sorry."

"It's ok."

He stared at the screen. How did you tell your amazing, hot, mostly gay-but-I-make-exceptions-and-I'll-make-one-for-you—that was what she said that night, didn't she? Fuck. Stop thinking about it!—executive assistant... she was more than his assistant, she was his friend and fucking lifeline! But how did you tell someone like that... that she wasn't the reason for your erection?

Politely?

## Perspective, Not Wanted


"I guess you don't," Niko said. "I mean, you and Rosie have always had a bit of a fire going, right? You think she's hot, she thinks you're cute. You like it."

He and Niko were sitting on the patio of the James Joyce, enjoying a warm late summer afternoon before heading out for their weekly Thursday meeting.

Will was confessing. Niko was listening.

"You've been married and hands-off and..." Niko paused. "Well, and you've handled it, right? You even recovered from..." He paused. It was difficult, even for the chill Niko, to talk about. Will appreciated the reticence. It was difficult to even think about. "Anyway. You managed to recover. World's best boss, world's best assistant bla bla bla. And you're married... and oh. Oh. And now you're not married. Does that change things?"

"Not for me," Will said. Paused. "Well, not anymore."

Niko waited.

Will tried to figure out what to tell him about Florence.

"Will?" Niko said. "I don't give advice, right? Well, only one kind of advice." They both laughed awkwardly. "But you're not even properly divorced yet. Don't fucking fall in love."

*Too late, Niko,* Will thought.

"And definitely not with your secretary," Niko added.

"She's not my secretary. She's my executive assistant," Will said.

"Don't fucking fall in love with your executive assistant."

"I am definitely not in love with my executive assistant." Will was pleased that he could say that and feel it as a total truth.

*I'm in love with Florence.* Why was that so hard to say to Niko?

Well.

Because. "You've not even properly divorced yet. Don't fucking fall in love."

And... "She's been married to two alcoholics. What the fuck would have to be wrong with her to give a third one a chance?"

And... "So you've essentially seen this woman, what, three or four times? And the rest of your great love story consists of texting? Get a grip, Will."

And... "How about some perspective, Will?"

Will didn't want perspective.

He wanted Florence.

This was very, very clear.

But he wouldn't talk to Niko about her.

He'd talk to Rosie.

That would fix, clarify things.

# Bad, Bad Idea
## MONDAY, AUGUST 27

It didn't.

She sat opposite him at Charcut, poking at her parmesan fries with a fork, not drinking her wine, and not looking at him.

Will felt stupid and awkward.

"I guess I shouldn't have said anything?" he asked. "I just thought... I wanted you to know. What was going on with me."

She said nothing. Stabbed a fry. Viciously?

"Rosie..." Will reached for a small hand. She withdrew it.

"Rosie, I didn't say any of this to make things weird and awkward between us," Will said.

"No?" she raised her eyes to meet his, and now he wished she wasn't looking at him. "What did you think this would accomplish?"

"I wanted... I just wanted to clarify things," Will said.

"You wanted to make it eminently clear to your stupid secretary that, married or divorced, you were not available," Rosie said.

"That's not fair."

He was going to call her on calling herself a secretary—she rode his ass about it for the entire first year that he worked at the bank—but decided now was not the right time.

"Don't deny it, Will. Why today? Why didn't you tell me about her... oh, anytime before I rubbed myself against your fucking dick in the office?"

Did she really say that?

That loudly?

In the restaurant potentially full of their co-workers and clients?

"Am I embarrassing you, Will?" Rosie demanded.

"A little," he said. "Just, you know... a little."

"Good."

He laughed. Stopped himself immediately.

"I'm not laughing at you," he said, very quickly. "Rosie. Listen. I met this woman just before Christmas. She—did not want to see me again after our first date. Even though it was fucking—it was phenomenal, Rosie. And I'm... I'm not saying this to upset you, ok? It was just... I had had, what, six, nine months of mediocre sex. Awkward dates and awkward sex, and nothing but... and then this woman... And she infuriates me and annoys me and keeps on trying to repel me. And I adore her. I adore everything about her. She plays my Christmas Angel in my darkest hour—I won't tell you about that, not today, but Rosie, she came to me and... And I love her. I know it doesn't make sense—I hardly know her. Well, except for the last four months of daily texting. Can you really get to know a person through texting? I don't know. Rosie, am I rambling?"

"Yes," she said. "And you're being an idiot. And you shouldn't have told me—you shouldn't have told me about any of this. Why would you do that, Will? How stupid and blind are you?"

"Neither stupid nor blind." He took her hands again. "Rosie..."

"I've loved you since the day I started working for you," she said, letting him keep them this time. "And I would have gone on... I didn't expect anything. Ever. Or plan. And that night—six years ago? I never... I never minded. I mean, I realize now... but I never minded that it was one time, because if that was all I could have... I didn't expect. Anything. Or even fucking hope, Will! Until the other day... you were so happy to see me, and my beautiful present, and then..."

She stopped. There were giant tears rolling down her cheeks.

"I thought it was for me," she said. "Stupid, stupid me."

"Rosie..." He squeezed her hands. "Oh, fuck, Rosie. Come here, you idiot." He got up and crossed over to her chair. Knelt down beside it. Stretched his torso up to her face and kissed her tears. "You idiot," he said gently. "Rosie." She slipped from her chair into his arms, sobbing. He held her and rocked her.

"Do I need to find another job?" she asked in a few minutes.

Will shook his head. He was kneeling in the middle of his colleagues' and clients' favourite restaurant, his crying assistant in his arms. The president of his bank was at his usual table by the window and Steven from accounting was sitting at the bar. Will nodded to them both. Turned his attention back to Rosie.

"Don't you dare leave me," he told her. "Ok? Just... go do more yoga. I'll run and box. You do... whatever the fuck people do in yoga. We're gonna be ok. Ok?"

She smiled wanly.

He suspected she'd start working on her resume that afternoon.

He wondered if he should text, tell Florence what happened.

Stupid thought. Why should he? Why would he?

He just wanted to, because... Florence.

But he didn't think Rosie would want him to. So. He didn't.

## Routine, Enjoyed, Then Thwarted
### TUESDAY, SEPTEMBER 18

If Rosie was looking for another job she was doing it on the QT, and Will started to relax. They recovered from the biggest fuck-up ever six years ago, he thought, they'd get over this awkward moment. They would. He was sure.

Meanwhile, the days and weeks that followed started to fall into a comfortable routine. Will woke up, texted with Polly—exchanged poop emojis or smiley faces with Matthew. Occasionally texted, tersely, with Amanda, to make "arrangements." Went to work. Smiled too brightly and happily at Rosie. Brought her coffee and donuts in the morning. She accepted the offerings. Not coldly. But not warmly either. And not... naturally.

She'd get over it. They'd get over it.

He worked, did what had to be done. Sent Florence a text mid-day and received an answer mid-afternoon. His texts tended to be dirty. Hers dry and snarky.

It felt like love.

Florence came to his apartment most Tuesday or Wednesday nights, late on Tuesdays, after 9 or 10 p.m., but, when she managed a Wednesday, usually around 8. They fucked. Everywhere. Deliciously. Insanely. Even on the couch made out of babies' butts, which was the way Will thought of it now too, irrevocably. He had the refractive period of an eighteen-year-old and the staying power of his age, and she was... well. She was. Delicious. Insane.

Every second weekend, he was Disneyland Dad. Except he was running out of Disneyland things to do, so he was turning into more ordinary, boring Dad. The kids didn't seem to mind. They were playing a lot of board games. He was learning to cook, from blogs and YouTube videos.

One day, he would work up the nerve to cook for Florence. He'd make her... um. Something quick and easy. But sophisticated. Like... quiche.

It seemed only a step up from an omelet, and he made killer omelettes now.

Every other second weekend, he got Florence for a full night. And an almost-lazy morning. Long enough to devour her one more time. Make her breakfast. Shower with her.

Once they had a jacuzzi and flooded the bathroom. Mrs. Ziernicka came to pound on his door and tell him he was causing ceiling damage to the unit below him.

"Shall I tell her it's all your fault?" Will whispered to Florence. She bit him.

The day they flooded the bathroom was also the day Amanda started planning a wedding. *Her* wedding. With Ranveer.

"Fucking seriously?" Will demanded. "We're not even fully divorced yet."

"We will be. In two weeks. Unless you accidentally forget so sign something," she snapped. He looked at the words on his phone screen. They snapped. Screamed. He hurt.

He hurt enough that Florence noticed when he saw her.

But he didn't want to tell her. He wondered if he hurt enough that Rosie noticed. In the past, she'd tell him...

...but this time, she didn't.

He ran it out on the treadmill. Did not think about drinking. At all.

But he thought about Florence, in his bed.

Rosie, wanting him in hers. And about how he was shallow enough that he liked that, even though she suffered.

He felt really bad when he had that thought, so that morning, he brought her a mocha slathered with whipped cream and shaved chocolate instead of the regular old Tim Horton's double-double.

She laughed at the offering, naturally. And he was happy.

"My cock has filthy plans for you tonight," he texted Florence, watching Rosie drink her mocha, not thinking of Amanda and Ranveer's impending wedding at all.

"I'm so sorry, Will, I won't be able to make it tonight," she wrote back, immediately. "Family emergency."

"Can I help?"

"No. Everyone's ok—don't worry—I just can't leave the kids tonight."

"Tomorrow?"

"This week's not good. I've got to hustle and scrub shit. Talk later, ok?"

The entire week was not good. For Florence. Rosie, however, perked up, and accepted the next day's—and the next day's—coffee with jokes and laughter.

"Where's my mocha, Mr. Ornot?" she demanded. "You've raised expectations."

"You don't get a 20 percent bonus every year, Ms. Safo," he shot back.

It felt good.

Like old times.

## Always Clean Up After A Mid-Day Quickie



"Can you just call me?" Will typed. He was tired of the texting exchange that was going nowhere.

"Are you going to yell at me?" Florence typed back.

"No. Florence, come on. Call. Talk to me and tell me what's going on."

"Nothing's going on. Timing is just more difficult for me right now."

"Florence. We're doing the circle again. Fucking pick up the phone and call me. We go from seeing each other, pretty predictably, twice a week, to barely any contact for two weeks. Even your texts. Talk to me, woman. Call."

"Why don't you call?"

"Will you pick up?"

She didn't text back. He dialled.

"Oh-my-god, Florence, are you crying?"

"No." Her voice was odd. "I am really happy to hear your voice."

"Good. I miss you."

"I miss you too."

"Come see me, then. Anytime, Florence."

"I can do a lunch quickie. Do you want to do that?"

"Florence? I want anything you can give."

That, he was pretty sure, was love. Did she know that?

He cancelled a lunch meeting and rescheduled an early afternoon consult to have her in his bed, and in his arms. And lying on his bed with her in his arms, snuggled tight against him, he knew it was love. And he thought maybe she did too.

But she looked stressed. Tired.

He wasn't allowed to ask questions.

He tried to give her all the release in his power.

"So unselfish today," she said finally. "I must really look like shit."

"A little," he said, coming up for air. "My time will come. Are you going to tell me anything?"

She shook her head.

Kissed him.

"I miss you. Very much. It's not you."

"It's never me," Will said. Kissed her. Watched her dress, pulled on his pants and straightened his tie and walked her to her car before running back to work.

His face smelled like her pussy and so did his hands, and he didn't think anything of it until he came face to face to Rosie in the hallway.

"You should..." she said, her voice tight, "wash your face."

Fuck.

In the washroom, he got a text from Amanda.

"The kids would really like you to come to wedding."

Fuck.

This, he thought, was why people drink.

He ran half a marathon on the treadmill before going home that day. Slept hard. Alone.

Thought about Florence. Not just with pleasure.

## I'll Take Anything
### THURSDAY, OCTOBER 4

*Will Ornot*: Florence, I miss you. And this is getting ridiculous. This is not a fucking relationship. I'm not in Toronto. I'm in Calgary. I want to see you.

**Florence Gunn:** Will, I want to see you too. Really. I miss you. Things are just difficult right now. I don't have reliable child care. I can't leave my kids.

*Will Ornot*: Then let me come to see you.

*Will Ornot*: I'm not suggesting we fuck at your house the way we fuck at my apartment. Ok? I'm a parent too. You don't come over on my kids' weekends. I get that. Can't I just come over as a... friend? You've got those, right? We can watch a movie on Netflix.

*Will Ornot*: Or play a board game. I miss you, Florence. So much I'm willing to endure Settlers of Catan or some other shit like that with your children.

------

*Will Ornot:* Florence?

**Florence Gunn:** I really miss you too. Yes. I would love for you to come and watch a bad movie with me on Netflix. But if you make me play Settlers of Catan, we're never having sex again.

*Will Ornot:* Good to know. Now I know what to do if I ever do want to stop fucking your lusciousness.

**Florence Gunn:** Jerk.

*Will Ornot:* Hey, it could happen. Tonight?

**Florence Gunn:** I work tonight, and late. Friday?

*Will Ornot:* Daddy weekend. Sunday night?

**Florence Gunn:** I work Sun... no, ok. I'll clean earlier in the day. Sunday.

*Will Ornot:* Sunday. Thank you, Florence.

**Florence Gunn:** Oh, Will. You have no idea how much... Sunday.

# Demons, 1



"And you complain I don't tell you things?" Florence demanded. They were sitting on a crazy-patterned couch—definitely not made of babies' butts, she told him when he touched the fabric—in her living room, and Florence's boys had all disappeared into their rooms, so Will now had Florence in his arms, or perhaps was in her arms—it felt more as if she was cuddling him than that he was embracing her. It felt good. And head on her chest, he told her about Amanda's wedding plans.

Also, about Rosie. Just a little. Awkwardly and badly, but it seemed important that she know... just a little. She listened. Kissed him gently. Then reprimanded him for accusing her of not sharing.

"When was I supposed to tell you?" he countered. Then felt ashamed. She looked exhausted and stressed, even more so than during their quickie. "Florence?" he asked, caressing her hair. "Are you sick? Is someone sick? Your mom?"

Florence shook her head. Kissed him.

"I'm glad you're here," she said, and now she put her head on his chest. He waited.

But no words followed.

He patted her hair, and was stroking it, very gently, when her eldest son came into the room.

Florence jumped.

"Chill, Mom, I think I figured out this was your boyfriend," the boy-man—fuck, he was tall, Will thought— said. Gave Will the same measured looked he gave him when Florence introduced them, awkwardly, earlier.

"Women my age don't have boyfriends." Florence sighed dramatically. "Well, I suppose we do. But what an awful word."

Will thought about kissing her to shut her up, but— what was this boy's name again? Ethan?—made him shy.

"Heading out?" Florence asked.

The boy nodded.

"Be good," Florence said. Will watched her get up—the fluidity of her movements still made his breath stop—and kiss her son on his forehead.

The boy was as tall as she was. Maybe taller.

"How old is he?" he asked.

"Ethan? Sixteen," Florence said. "Well, almost seventeen, but I'm in denial. Sammy is thirteen now, and Isaac almost eleven."

"And you can't leave them home alone, without a babysitter, to come see me for a couple of hours?" Will said, forehead creasing, and anger rising in him, hot and sharp.

"Do you think I'm lying to you about something?" Florence asked. Not sitting down next to him. He felt her anger, too.

"No," he said. "Just carefully not telling me. Much at all. As always."

Her eyes narrowed. She was about to counter. He could

see it coming, and he tightened up to brace for her onslaught.

Instead, they both jumped as they heard Ethan shout, "Fuck!" A slammed door resounded. And then, "Mom! He's here! He's fucking here again!"

Panic. A child's panic in the young man's voice.

Will was on his feet in an instant.

Florence was halfway out of the room.

"Stay there," she called. "Will, for god's sake, just stay there!"

Ethan ran into the room and stopped and stared at Will.

"I have to go be with my brothers," he said. "We have... we have a drill for these situations. Stay here."

Will sat on the couch. Felt like an idiot.

He heard Florence's voice at the door.

Pounding.

Screaming.

Pounding.

Was she crying?

He was not going to just sit there.

He went to the front door.

Florence was slumped against it, hands around her knees. Crying.

On the other hand of the door, a man's voice.

Angry. Slurred.

"Fucking bitch!"

"Fucking cunt!"

"Keeping me away from my kids! I'm their fucking daddy, bitch! When was the last time you let me see them, you goddamn whore? Do they even know who their fucking daddy is!"

Florence. In tears.

Her pain hit him across the face like a slap.

He dropped to his knees.

"Florence, you don't need to listen to this," he said. "Come on. Let's go."

He pulled at her.

She stared at him, glassy-eyed.

"Call the police," he said.

"I called them as soon as Ethan said he was here," she said. Voice wooden, exhausted. "I just need to make sure he doesn't get in."

"Fucking bitch, I'm going to rip you into shreds when I get in there, turning my boys against me!"

"How often does this happen?" Will asked. He sat down beside her. Put an arm around her rigid, unresponsive shoulders.

"Not that often," she said. Her voice was horrible. "Not that often. He just... He's just... when this happens. He's not himself. He's... There's a cycle. It's usually fine. It's usually fine. And then there is... this. But it passes. It passes. And then it's all fine for a while. For a long time. The last time was... two years ago. More than two years ago. Not that often..."

"Jesus fucking Christ Florence."

The drunk's foul, angry voice. Will felt another surge of... hate. Rage.

"Go to the back of the house. You don't have to listen to this. Ever."

She looked at him, her giant eyes sunken, exhausted.

"Ever," he said. "Just go. I'll watch the door. I promise. He won't get in."

Florence nodded and got up, slowly, like an old woman. Shuffled out of the room.

"Is there a man with you in there? Are you cheating on me, you fucking whore? Do your children know that their mother is a fucking whore?"

Will clenched his fists.

Covered his ears.

*The police would be here soon.*

"When I get at you, you worthless bitch, I will..."

Breathe, Will.

He felt the door shake as the man on the other side threw his body at it.

He wasn't sure, afterwards, if he had heard the police siren as well. He must have.

He opened the door as the flashing red-white-and-blue pulled up to the curb. And as the cops were getting out of the cruiser, he punched Florence's ex-husband with his boxer's right hook straight to the jaw and watched him crumple on the doorstep, feeling nothing but satisfaction.

---

# Demons, 2
## SUNDAY, OCTOBER 7

---

"You realize, sir, that was a stupid and irresponsible thing to do?" the officer who took his statement in the back of the police car said. He said it... with kindness, Will thought.

"Yes, sir," he said. "I was... angry."

An understatement.

"You understand that you could be charged for that?"

"Yes, sir."

Although Will didn't really understand that. Fuck. The asshole had it coming. For years probably.

"You are very lucky that he didn't hit his head. And die."

Fucking seriously?

Worthless piece of shit. If he had died, Florence's life would probably be easier.

"And when he comes to, he may insist on laying charges. We will try to dissuade him, sir, but there's nothing we can do if he insists. Do you understand that?"

"Yes, sir."

"What is your relationship with the lady of the house?" the cop said, his voice less kind.

"I'm her friend," Will said.

Lover.

Soulmate.

Protector.

*I have no status*, Will realized.

The cop was still saying something. Will wasn't inputting. Processing. Suddenly, he felt as exhausted as Florence looked and felt ashamed of the comparison.

He watched the ambulance pull away from the curb, and he watched the other police officer exit Florence's house.

"Can I go now?" he asked.

The cop looked at his partner. Who nodded.

"Free as a bird," he told Will. "At least until your victim wakes up."

Will walked up to the front door. Turned the knob. Locked. Of course.

He rang, then tried the doorbell.

Ethan opened the door a crack.

"She doesn't want to see you," he said.

"What?"

"She said to not let you in. She doesn't want to see you." The boy gave him a peculiar look, shrugged, and shut the door.

Will stood on the doorstep for a few minutes.

Then shuffled—like an old man—to his car. Pulled away from the curb slowly, looking at Florence's house with... what? Longing? Fear?

A little grey Fiat pulled into the spot he vacated. In the rearview mirror, he saw three people, three women, slide out of the car, walk up to Florence's house. Sisters? Friends?

He didn't know.

Well. At least she wouldn't be alone. He should be happy about that.

He wasn't—he wanted to be the one she wasn't alone with.

The resentment burned, rose. Fuelled the rage not fully extinguished by the punch.

He wanted to turn around and pound on the door and...

Holy fuck.

He would have slapped himself if he hadn't been driving. Instead, he pulled over. Got out of the car and did ten push-ups. Then twenty. One hundred.

Drove home.

Called Niko en route to make sure he had help in fending off his demons.

# She'd Need Him



*Will Ornot:* Hey, Florence, want to talk?

## Or, Not



She didn't.

He knew her well enough now, though, that he didn't freak out. She needed time. Also—he was there. And it was... well. Messy. In one night, and not entirely out of her volition, she let him into the... what was he going to say? Drama? Tragedy?

One or the other. Both.

The secret suffering of her life.

Will knew that even inviting him into her home was a big deal. The Florence he knew last December, in February —the Florence who came to his bed for "one last one night stand" before he left for Toronto—even the Florence who struggled to meet him at the airport the last week of August, wouldn't have invited him to her home. That Florence didn't want him to know where she lived. That Florence, he now suspected, although he'd never tell her, felt ashamed and insecure. About her "interesting" neighbourhood, the mobile home in the trailer park ("It's really nice," he said, the surprise in his voice evident, and he saw a variety of emotions play on her face, and was ashamed of his surprise).

That Florence—he now understood—left on Valentine's Day because he took her to a restaurant she couldn't afford, and bought her three dozen roses, and blathered on about the cost of his fucking dining room table.

Which he still loved.

But fuck. *Shut up about it, Will.*

He came across as an overly privileged upper class snob. And she ran.

This Florence... he was pretty sure this Florence loved him. This Florence, who texted with him every day while he was in Toronto, who came to his bed twice a week since he returned, who told him she missed him—who wanted to protect this secret, this part of her life from him—this Florence, he was pretty sure, loved him.

And he understood... if he had *that* in his life? Would he want her to know?

Amanda was enough to have in the closet. And she wasn't really in the closet, anyway. She was poking her head out, always.

What would it be like for Florence and Amanda to meet?

How much would they hate each other?

And Rosie.

He frowned.

Why was he thinking about Rosie?

A touch of guilt there.

Also, desire.

To talk to her about Florence. Her ex-husband. The shit show. His near-arrest for assault.

He thought about calling Niko and asking him if he thought talking to Rosie about Florence, again, was a good idea. He knew the impulse to call Niko was one of self-protection. Which probably meant he shouldn't call Rosie.

Florence would calm down, process. Recover.

Text him.

Maybe thank him for punching out her loser of an ex-husband.

# She'd Reach Out, Any Time Now

TUESDAY, OCTOBER 16

She didn't.

# I Need to Hurt You


She didn't for a week. He had texted, after the first few days of silence: "Just checking in. Giving you the space you need if you need it. But I'm here. Anytime."

He waited a week, not anxious. It would take her time.

He wasn't anxious on day eight, either. A week was an arbitrary period of time.

On day ten, he texted, "Florence? Are you all right?"

Silence.

So on day fourteen, after running ten kilometres in the morning, boxing for two hours at lunch, and running another ten kilometres in the middle of the afternoon, he asked Rosie if he could hurt her again.

Literally.

"Rosie? I'm an ass, and I need to talk to someone, and I want to talk to you about things that will cause you pain."

"Fuck, Will," she said, and Steven from accounting, who was walking down the hallway, stopped and stared. Will and Rosie both turned and glared at him. "Don't you have any other friends?"

He turned red.

He had Niko.

And...

Well, that was actually about it. Because all of his other friends were his and Amanda's friends. And now they were mostly Amanda's friends. He wasn't quite sure how that happened. Wasn't the left person supposed to get the friends?

Wasn't that one of the rules?

"Not really," he said. "My sponsor at AA. You. My ex-wife, and she's even less appropriate a person to talk to about this than you. You think I should call her?"

"You think I want to hear anything about you and your lover?" Rosie said. "Fuck, Will. We were almost back at normal."

"Ok," Will said. "Ok. I'm sorry. Stupid idea. I'm gonna go..." he felt his knees give... well, not box or run... "I'm gonna go home and watch Netflix."

"And not drink?" Rosie said.

He turned red.

"And not drink," he said. "I am not guilting you into hanging out with me like that. It's not that bad."

"Come on, you jerk," she said. "Let's go get a virgin something or other. And you can break my heart. Again."

He fucking loved her. And he told her so, thoughtlessly.

"I know," she sighed. "Just not quite enough. You love this other woman, though. Yeah? You're filthy with it. So what's wrong?"

He told her slowly and badly. The story didn't flow as he had expected it to flow. It was supposed to be, Will thought, an almost heroic narrative. He was there to protect his woman, right? She was so worn, so tired—so fucking abused. He was so incensed. And he... he didn't regret it. The punch. Fuck, it felt good. Watching that asshole drop to the ground made him feel good.

And he wasn't mad or upset. He didn't expect Florence to thank him or anything. He knew she needed her space. That it was so hard for her. That it would so hard for her to accept that he saw...

"Fuck, Will, you are such an idiot," Rosie said at this point.

He blinked.

"Think about it," Rosie said.

He thought about it.

"You seriously don't see it?" Rosie said. "So, you're upset—no, you're not upset, exactly. You think she's upset, and processing, that you saw her... what did you call it? Secret tragedy? That she's ashamed or something?"

Will nodded.

"Fuck, Will, you are stupid," Rosie said. "Think. Think. Think."

"I don't get it," he said after a long pause. "At all. What am I missing here?"

"Jesus, Will." Rosie rolled her eyes. "This woman—the first time, or second time you met, right? She told you, she typed you as an alcoholic. I know you don't like that—I know you will protest, ok, I know... I was there, remember, the one time you did drink in all the years I've known you?"

Will flinched. He remembered. Pain.

The pain in Rosie's voice, on her face was almost as pronounced.

He covered her hands with his, and touched his forehead to the table.

"She then told you—she's been there, done that. Twice. Which was stupid enough and she's not going to do it a third time."

Will nodded without lifting his head.

The light bulb begun to spark.

"But for whatever reason—your good looks or your

prowess in bed or whatever the fuck it is about men like you that makes women like..." she was going to say *women like me*, he knew, but she swallowed it, she didn't, "that makes women suspend their better judgement, she fell for you. And continued this... one night stand of yours. Into a relationship."

Will moaned.

"And then, her baby daddy comes out of the woodwork or prison or halfway house or wherever it is that he hangs out intermittently. And starts to turn her life into hell again. Not the first time, right? Part of a cycle?"

He lifted his head up and nodded again, mouth dry. Throat raw.

"Do you see it yet?"

He nodded.

"Shall I say it anyway so you hear it?"

He nodded.

"First, I think she was just pissed. That you—you interfered. It's a cycle. It's an awful cycle, but she probably has some sort of system. Right? Keep the boys safe and out of it. Minimize the damage. She wouldn't come see you because she didn't want them home alone, or with her mother, right? Or to overtax her mother—maybe her mother is there every other night, when she works, and she wants to give her some respite. She sounds... I fucking hate her, Will, but she sounds like she... takes care of her people. So... Anyway. She's got her priorities set, clear. And maybe that hell, maybe that thing doesn't happen every night. Of course it doesn't. But she's aware it might. She knows what she has to do. But you're there, and she's stupid, she loves you, she misses you. So she lets you come—and the worst happens. Her ex shows up, out of his mind."

Will closed his eyes.

"Did you say she loves me? Do you think she loves?" he

said. It was the only thing he really heard. He didn't want to hear anything else.

"Fuck, Will are you listening to me? It doesn't matter. It doesn't matter if she loves you." Rosie's voice was... angry. But also kind. And sad. So fucking sad.

"Will, you shouldn't have opened the door, and you shouldn't have punched him. Got that?"

Eyes still closed, he nodded.

"But the reason she's not texting you right now... you know what that is?"

Will felt tears under his eyelids. God. He was going to cry.

"She's not going to take a chance on another alcoholic, Will. She fucking can't."

Will folded into her arms. And cried.

He was pretty sure Steven from accounting was somewhere in the audience, watching.

Because that would make the moment even more pathetic, awful.

_________________________

## Love's Not Selfish
WEDNESDAY, OCTOBER 17
_________________________

Rosie walked him home, and because he was grasping convulsively at her arm, went up the elevator with him. Mrs. Ziernicka came out of the elevator, of course, as they came into the lobby. Gave Will a look that under other circumstances would have made him laugh. But under these circumstances, it made him want to cry again, and he felt like a wuss and loser and oh-my-fucking-god, he was never, ever going to make out with Florence in this lobby, in this elevator, in this lifetime, again.

"When do you see your kids next?" Rosie asked. "This weekend?"

He nodded dumbly.

"Good," she said.

"Would you come in?" he said as he unlocked the door.

She hesitated.

She wouldn't.

She did.

"What do you want to do?" she asked him, standing stiff in his hallway. Looking up at him with... what? What was it? Longing? Pity? Desire?

How stupid and selfish was he?

"Go to bed," he said. Looked at her sadly. "Alone. Sleep. Without any fucking dreams. Wake up. Feel... well, maybe feel nothing."

"Ok," she said. "Go to bed. I'll tuck you in and let myself out."

He felt... longing. Pity. Desire.

But he was not that stupid and selfish. Not anymore.

She pulled his comforter up all the way to his neck, and kissed him on the forehead.

"I love you," she said. Her voice was so sad.

"I love you too," he said. His voice was sadder. Maybe. "Thank you," he added. A surge of shame.

"I'm so sorry, Will," she said. She was going to kiss him again, and he would reach up for her, and fuck everything up—again.

But she just smiled, sadly, and left the room. Left him, alone.

---

# Fuck You, Mick Jagger
## THURSDAY, OCTOBER 25

---

Routine.

Wake up. Don't think about Florence. Shower. Don't think about Florence. Text Polly.

"I love you, Munchkin, you are the sunshine of my life."

"Your so mushy Daddy. I luv u 2."

Call Matthew—fuck the poop emoji exchanges.

"I want to hear your voice, son. You can grunt or say shit-shit-shit, I don't care. I just want to hear it."

"Shit-shit-shit. Happy, Dad?"

"Yes, Matt. Have a good day at school. I love you."

"Have a good day at work. I love you too."

Don't think about Florence. Pick up a mocha on the way to work for Rosie.

"You're going to ruin me, woman. If I had only known..."

"I guess I'm never, ever going to a mocha *and* a, I don't know, bagel, now?"

"Is there no end to your expectations?"

"Hope springs eternal, Will."

Don't. Think. About. Florence.

Work. Boring as shit. Dialling it in. Thinking way too much about Florence.

Gym. Treadmill. *Run faster, asshole, run faster, run faster, exhaust your muscles, lose your breath, and don't think...*

Meeting. So checked out. Clients. Focus. Jesus. Job. Do it. Move money around, shift assets, make decisions. Pain. Don't think...

Boxing ring.

"God, Will, what's with you today? Trying to kill me?"

"Sorry. Tense."

"Loosen up, man. I'm your trainer, not a punching bag. The punching bag, dude, is over there. But if you bust it, you're buying us a new one."

"Sorry."

Food. Did he eat today? Yesterday? A smoothie with a shot of protein powder and some ginseng-wheat grass-energy voodoo shit. "Actually, maybe make it all the things." The girl behind the counter. Gorgeous. Too young. Too pierced and tattooed. Did she slip him her number?

She fucking did.

A smile. Smugness. Not a shot, but a touch of... desire.

Longing.

Florence.

Fucking don't think about Florence!

"Will?" Niko.

"Don't say you're worried about me. I'm fine."

"I think you've lost like twenty pounds in a week. And aged a decade."

"I'm dealing. And sober."

"I never suggested you weren't, friend. Want to talk about it?"

No.

Don't. Think. About...

"Dadda?"

"Yes, Princess?"

"Why are you so sad? Are you upset about the wedding? Did Mom tell you I'm going to be flower girl? But Matthew doesn't want to be the ringer bearer?"

"Well, he's a little old to be a ring bearer."

"But it would make Mom so happy if he was."

"You can't always get what you want, Munchkin."

Mick Jagger screaming in his head.

Amanda's wedding plans. Seriously who the fuck cared?

"Will you come to the wedding, Will? I think it will be good for the children if you are there."

"Is that playing fair, Amanda?"

"It's not a game, Will."

No. Nothing's a game. Everything's a game. Nothing matters—it's over.

"Will you, Will? For me, Will. It will mean a lot to me."

Don't think about...

"Whatever. It means nothing to me."

Almost the truth.

Would he be more upset about the wedding, Amanda and Ranveer's projected happily ever after—would she wear a white dress, he wondered? Or a traditional Korean wedding dress again? Maybe a sari this time? And why the fuck wouldn't they just get married in fucking India with her new in-laws' entire extended family acting out a scene from the Bollywood movies she'd been inflicting on him for the last three years of their married life—oh-my-fucking-god, is that when it all started? Three years ago—would he be more upset about the wedding if he weren't...

Don't. Think. About. Florence.

"I wish she was just a girl. A woman. A..." four letter word, unspoken. This, to Niko, over their pre-meeting wings and no-beer. Two guys, in a pub, not drinking. "Just... someone. Someone I could exchange for someone new."

Niko chewed. Silently, thoughtfully.

"I don't want to think about her. Talk about her. I want to get over her. Really, Niko, don't look at me like that. I do. I mean—I know it's possible, right? I hardly ever want to strangle Amanda anymore. I've even told her I'm going to their stupid wedding. For the kids. And I really don't care that much."

Niko coughed.

"Honestly. I don't. I would... Truthfully, Niko? One-hundred-percent unadorned truth? I think I'd care more about Amanda and my ex-marriage if I weren't constantly obsessing about Flo..."

Niko nodded.

"Do you think I'm obsessing about Florence as a coping mechanism?"

Niko put another wing in his mouth.

"Fuck." Will paused. Grabbed a celery stick and broke it in half just to hear the sound. "Fuck. Maybe. That would make sense, right? Would not that make more sense... I mean, what should I be upset about here, more, in the grand scheme of things? My ex-wife's wedding, which is probably part of her overall strategy to maintain full custody of the kids by showing that she's offering them a more stable home... oh-that-calculating-manipulative..." One should not call the mother of one's children a fucking bitch, Will reminded himself. "...viper," he substituted. "Or the end of this ridiculous, dysfunctional relationship? That's not really a relationship, but sex. All we did was fuck. It always went wrong when we started to talk."

Sex.

Phenomenal sex.

Florence.

Fuck.

Four months of texting, too. Was that not a relationship?

It felt like a relationship.

It felt like love.

Don't... think...

"Will?" Niko swallowed the meat and washed it down with a swig of Coke. "Remember how I told you it was a bad idea to talk to Rosie about this shit? Go talk to Rosie."

"Why?"

"Because my balls shrink every time we have one of these conversations."

Thursday night meetings. Tuesday nights driving Matthew to soccer.

"I know Ranveer can do it, Amanda. He's my fucking son. I want to do it."

Wednesday nights without Florence. Don't. Think. About...

Take-out for dinner.

Big grocery shop every second Friday afternoon.

"Daddy, this actually tasted good!"

Victory.

Routine.

He was going to be fine.

## BFFs, M-F style
### FRIDAY, OCTOBER 26

"You look like shit," Rosie said.

"You, on the other hand, look gorgeous. As always." He put the mocha on her desk.

"You're not even looking at me, Will," she sighed.

"I don't have to." He raised his eyes and looked at her. "You always look gorgeous."

"Fucking hell, you're going to cry," she said.

He flinched. "I am not."

And cried.

Rosie herded him into his office and shut the door.

"Wiping your nose is definitely not in my job description," she said. Handed him a tissue.

Will tried to laugh.

"Jesus, what's wrong with me?"

"Love hurts," Rosie said. Shrugged.

"Jesus. Do you remember when I was all, like, suave and cool, Rosie?"

She laughed.

"You were never that cool. But, yeah, you were a little

tougher. More of the alpha male than the weeping princess."

"Thanks. Gender-stereotype much?"

"Always," she said. She was sitting on the corner of his desk. She had amazingly fabulous legs. She noticed him looking at them.

"How you didn't end up getting accused of sexual harassment at any point during your career is a mystery to me," she said.

He looked up at her eyes. Then pointedly dropped his eyes to her breasts.

"Feeling better?" she asked.

"Great legs and breasts make a lot of things better," he said. "However, making myself feel better with your breasts and legs generally makes me feel worse. Because..." He paused. She waited. He didn't dare finish.

"Jesus. How did we end up in this relationship? What am I going to do when you leave me?"

"Maybe you'll go and get some real friends." Rosie patted his head. "But, you know, there has been a silver lining to all of this."

"There has?" He couldn't think for the life of him what it would be.

"The more you whine and slobber, the less I want you," she said. "A few more weeks of this, and I'll be completely cured."

"I fucking love you," he said.

"And then you go and say shit like that." She swatted his head. "Come on, Will. Pull yourself together a little. Go have some fun. She's still not responding?"

He nodded.

"Go play with someone else."

He closed his eyes. Shook his head. How could he

explain to Rosie that "someone else" just wasn't an option? That he only wanted...

Red hair, freckles, crooked teeth, a pink tongue that... and nipples that... and a voice that...

Fuck.

"Fuck, Will, are you thinking about her?" Rosie was staring at his crotch.

"It doesn't take much," he said. Put his hands over his lap.

"Loser," she said.

He didn't protest.

In fact, he agreed.

"Loser," he said. "And, Jesus, Rosie, I know it's hopeless and I know... but I can't stop feeling. And... Fuck, I don't want to spend another night moping alone at home, too depressed to even masturbate. I really don't. But I also don't want to inflict this—myself. On anyone else. Well, except apparently you. I'm sorry. Fuck."

"Loser," he repeated.

Rosie flicked his nose. With such affection, his eyes teared up again.

"Want to go to yoga with me?" she asked.

He laughed.

"I think I'd rather stay home and not masturbate," he said. "When I go to yoga with you, we will know I've reached the point of no return."

"Ok. Then come play with me."

He flinched and she laughed.

But it was a good laugh. An unforced, natural laugh.

"I didn't mean—we've settled that, right?" she said.

He nodded.

"Right. So. Come dancing with me. You don't have the kids this weekend, right? And it's Halloweenish. There are so many great parties happening. I'll take you to a good one."

"You're sort of my best friend, you know," he said.

She sighed.

"I feel like you said that just so I wouldn't ask for a raise," she said.

"It's a big deal. Don't you think?"

She thought about it.

Moved into his arms in a move so like Florence's he flinched again before embracing her.

"Don't take advantage of it, Will," she said into his ear. "I love you and I want you in a way that you don't love or want me. And that's fine. I'm dealing with that. Just don't... damage me more, ok?"

He held her tight. And felt like an utter asshole.

And also, loved. And so fucking grateful, he could barely breathe.

## Like An Invisibility Cloak
### SATURDAY, OCTOBER 27

"You look better," Rosie said.

"I'm wearing a fucking morph suit and you can't see my face," he retorted.

"Ah, that must be it," she laughed. She was wearing a...

"Are you a walrus?" he asked.

"I'm a beautiful magical griffin. Are you blind?"

"A little," he admitted. "Everything's a bit... well, not fuzzy, exactly. Sort of like looking at the world through a dirty glass. Or a dusty window screen."

"Well, come on, let's go." Rosie took his hand. Dragged him into the line-up. "God, Will, what's the matter?"

"Nothing." He followed slowly. Tried to remember the last time he went to a Halloween costume party. A decade? Fuck, no, more. It would have been in college. Maybe the year, two after. A vague memory of being somewhere crowded with Amanda. She was wearing a slutty nurse outfit. He was a... Zombie?

He was still drinking then. Alcohol. Fog. Ugh.

Alcohol on the breath, in the pores of the man in the line-up in front of them. Alcohol saturating the club.

"I feel old!" he yelled at Rosie over the music.

"You are old!" she yelled back. "That's why you're wearing a morph suit. To pass!" He slapped her padded ass. She laughed and waddled towards the dance floor.

He followed her through a swarm of superheroes and circus freaks, cowboys and construction workers—what the fuck, nice Village People theme, he thought—a gaggle of Pokemon onesies—was that Whitney Houston? It was totally Whitney Houston, arms around a very burly Madonna—vampires and harlequins, and fairies and...

"Hey, do you see that? Is that Justin Trudeau? That's totally Justin Trudeau!" he yelled at Rosie, pointing at a man sporting boxing gloves and shorts. "Great costume, man!" he yelled in his ear. Got a smile and a light punch in the gut.

Grinned as three very hairy, very fat men wearing nothing but jock straps, their hair tied up in Samurai knots on their heads, conga-danced by.

He wished, suddenly, that he wasn't too lame, too uptight—too sober—to join them.

*Remember what it was like to have fun?*

*Shut the fuck up, brain. Now.*

A slap on his ass. From a cowboy.

"Don't see much, but fuck, I like the outlines," into his ear. In a deep throaty voice, from the burly Madonna.

Night clubs have changed from his time, Will thought.

He wasn't sure he liked it.

"Wanna dance?" a svelte, tall brunette, wrapped in gauze and nothing else rubbed against him. Will smiled automatically... then...

"Um, I'm just looking for my friend right now," he called in the very male ear that leaned into his cheek.

"Want to look together?" The boy slipped an arm

around his waist. "I'm open to all sorts of possibilities tonight. What does he look like?"

Oh-my-fucking-god, Rosie!

"Oh-my-fucking-god, Rosie, where have you brought me?" he yelled into her ear when he managed to extricate himself from the boy and found her shaking her padded-clawed-and-tailed griffin booty in a crowd of morph-suited Power Rangers—he adjusted his eyes to watch their feminine, definitely feminine shapes with more pleasure—anime characters, and shapeless bodies in onesies and pyjamas.

"A Hot Mess party," she yelled back. "I told you!"

"How was I supposed to know what that meant?"

"How was I supposed to know you didn't?"

"Rosie!"

"You said you didn't want to spend another Saturday night moping alone at home too depressed, and I quote, to even masturbate," she screamed. The music fell silent as if on cue, and the people around them laughed. A Power Ranger—the red one—high-fived Rosie.

"What's the matter, Will? Out of your comfort zone?" she mocked.

He looked around.

"Yes. And not just a little," he said. Too old. Too straight. Too... boring.

Too sober.

*Not going there. Stop those thoughts. Now.*

Another drunk child stumbled into his path, his arms. He righted him, turned his attention to Rosie, who was looking, with a big smile, at a... what the fuck? A mime in a turban?

Fucking weird.

This place was fucking weird.

"What am I supposed to do here?" he asked her.

"Dance," she laughed. "You chose a great costume to do

it all *incognito*." She sidled up to him and yell-whispered into this ear. "You can grind ass with eighteen-year-old boys to find out what it feels like, and nobody will ever know!"

"Is this some kind of revenge on me?" he asked before moving away.

She just laughed.

Will looked around. Costumes. People. Music.

*Fucking dance, loser.*

He started to dance.

He was a black ghost, he was invisible, he was hidden, he wasn't really there—yes he was, he was free. He was dancing, nobody was looking, nobody cared.

Sweat trickled down his back.

It was hot.

He was hot.

Oh, fuck, she *was* hot.

He saw her from behind, a slim figure curved in all the right places, wearing sparkling blue tights, a white tutu and rainbow fairy wings. Hair dyed green—actually, it was probably a wig. How could someone look this fucking gorgeous, this fucking desirable in a green wig... from behind?

It was probably, Will thought, her ass. It was a deliciously perfect ass, perfectly designed for caressing and patting and spanking and fucking, like Florence's perfectly designed, delicious ass, and *Oh-my-god, do not think about Florence and do not get an erection while wearing a morph suit.*

He dropped his hands down to his crotch, and the green-haired fairy spun around.

Her nose and cheeks were covered with a thousand freckles and he wanted to kiss every single one.

She smiled and swayed her hips and returned to her dance partners.

The turbaned mime beside her slipped an arm around

her waist and spun her in a circle. A Zombie Marie Antoinette, her white wig illuminated by flashing fluorescent lights, joined them.

Will watched.

Florence.

"What's up?"

Rosie, beside him.

Her eyes, he thought, couldn't really follow his, hidden as they were by the black morph suit. But they did.

"Oh," she said. "Oh-my-god. Oh. Will? Is that her?" He felt her wilt. Drew her close to him. She pulled away—then surrendered to the embrace.

"I think I'm going to cry, Will," she said. "Because I'm stupid. Can we please leave?"

Florence.

He wanted to just stand there and watch her and... if this was as close as he could get to her then...

Rosie clung to him, shaking. And he just wanted to be selfish. So very much.

"Ok," he said.

He drove Rosie home in silence. Shook his head when she asked him if he wanted to come in. She gave him a strange look. As if she wanted to say something, then thought better of it. He was glad. He was pretty sure... he didn't want to know. He wouldn't make it better.

He watched her walk to her front door slowly. Suspected she was hoping he'd change his mind—knew he never could. Suspected he should... something. He didn't know what. Tell her... what?

He was an asshole, and he loved that she loved him, but all he wanted was...

Florence.

He drove home first and actually entered the parkade before finding himself driving straight out again. Back towards the nightclub. Where was it, exactly? Eighth avenue? Tenth? He circled around the block four times before finding a parking spot almost as close to his house as it was to the club.

What was he doing?

Not thinking.

Walking.

Getting back into the line...

Back into the fray...

Was she still here?

He didn't hear the music anymore. See the men. Smell the booze in the air. The world consisted of not-Florence and Florence. And he needed to find... Florence.

He saw Marie Antoinette first. Were they together, or did they just happen to be dancing beside each other when he saw them? He stalked. Not, he hoped, in a creepy way...

Fuck, totally in a creepy way. Not only was he stalking, but he was stalking a woman who didn't want to have anything to do with him... while wearing a morph suit.

*Loser.*

He accepted the thought. Classless loser, creepy stalker, obsessed male animal with only one purpose.

Florence.

And there she was, the green-haired fairy. Standing next to the mime she had been dancing with earlier, and the bare-chested Justin Trudeau. Who had taken off one of his boxing gloves to hold Florence's elbow. Wrist.

A wave of jealousy, madness washed over Will. Then pain. Sickness. Jesus.

Florence.

He stood, frozen.

What the fuck was he supposed to do?

What did he want to do?

Just to... watch. That's all. He wouldn't... he just

wanted... watching her dance with Trudeau would kill him. He'd want to punch him.

He needed anger management counselling.

Breathe, Will. Fucking breathe.

Florence.

Safe and hidden in his morph suit, he just wanted to...

Watch.

That's all.

It would be enough.

She could, she should, be happy with someone else.

He was poison, rage, her third mistake.

He would just stand there. And watch.

"Excuse me." Marie Antoinette's wide skirt bumped into him.

"No problem," he said, stepping to the side. He watched her approach Florence, Trudeau, and the mime. He watched Florence laugh as she took her friend's—lover's? stranger's? who the fuck knew? none of his business—hand. And then he watched her look over Marie Antoinette's shoulder... straight at him.

Oh-god, she was looking straight at him and he existed and it felt so good and he was so happy he was wearing his morph suit...

Her face shimmered and changed expression and her mouth shifted from a smile to a surprised "oh" and he could swear she was forming his name with her mouth and that she knew him.

And that was the point at which he realized that after driving Rosie home, he never put the head of the morph suit back on.

# To Club A Baby Seal
## SATURDAY, OCTOBER 27

Will stood perfectly still. Actually, the whole world stood still. The bodies dancing and milling around him weren't really there—they were in some other dimension. They formed a still, almost irrelevant background to... Florence. Who was also standing still—but in this dimension—and who was doing nothing except looking at him. Her whole being was looking at him.

His whole being wanted nothing more than to experience this: her eyes on him.

Oh-my-fucking-god.

Was this love?

Bliss?

Delusion?

Another kind of addiction?

He pulsated with... everything. Longing. Desire. Madness.

He willed himself to be still.

He would not... force it. Go to her. Ask for more.

He would just stand here.

Still. Pulsating.

Thinking, of nothing but Florence.

Her face expressed... he didn't know. Feeling. Feelings. Waves of them, washing over each freckle, each line. He would remember her like this, he thought. Always. Her lips forming his name. Her eyes melded to his.

This would be enough.

It wouldn't.

Of course it wouldn't.

But if that's all he got, it would have to be.

He stood still.

His entire being wanted to run to her and pick her up and carry her out of the throng and just have her. Possess her. Completely.

He stood still.

This was probably going to kill him.

She stood still too... except for those waves of everything on her face.

Then—no. It was his imagination.

Fuck. Yes. A step. Half a step. A hesitation.

And then, she was walking towards him and the fucking archangels were singing Hallelujah at the top of their lungs in his head—or maybe all around him, in real life, did the DJ put that song on, at that precise moment, just for him?—and then, her face was pressed against his chest and her arms were around his waist and his were wrapping around her back and the front of his morph suit was wet with her tears and this was bliss and suffering and... love.

And the world stood still.

Until it started to swirl around them. Weirdly and perversely, like in a drug-addled hallucination or a Baz Luhrmann film, and Will tightened his hold on Florence to keep her from being swept away in the surrounding whirl.

Her face was still crushed against his chest.

He gently inserted a finger between the green wig and her ear. Wiggled it loose, then off... sunk his hand into her red hair. Still so short. But longer then the last time he touched it.

She felt his cock respond before he was aware it did. Looked up at him.

"And here we go again?" she said. And her voice was suddenly so sad, he wanted to cry.

He shook his head.

He kissed her, very gently on the lips.

He was going to let her ago.

Any moment now, he would drop his arms, and let her go, and...

She hid her face on his chest again.

The world whirled.

Justin Trudeau, Marie Antoinette, and the mime in a turban looked on. Will met their eyes over the dancing throng. Wanted to say... what? What the fuck did he want to say? "Don't worry, I'll be good to her?"

"I love her," he shot at them with his eyes. Squeezed her harder.

"Let's get out of here," he whispered into her forehead. Then cheek. "Let's go talk."

He felt what could have been a nod against his chest.

He moved his arms.

And she laughed.

"Will?" she said. "I know you really want to scoop me up and carry me off the dance floor. Perhaps even to your car. As if I was a fucking princess. But..."

"I was thinking more over my shoulder. Caveman style," he said. "Maybe I could club a baby seal or two on my way out. I think I've seen some seals around."

"But I think we should just walk out of here holding hands," she finished. "Because a hernia is a real buzz kill."

He laughed and very slowly let go of her. He felt her hand slip into and around his. Squeezed it.

They walked off the dance floor hand in hand, the rest of the world spinning like mad around them.

## Words



"Are we walking to your car or your house?" she said after the first three blocks. He laughed. Squeezed her hand. And said nothing until they got to the Audi.

"I never noticed your car was yellow," she said.

He put his finger on her lips. Words, any words, were very dangerous. They needed to come. But not yet. Not yet.

They drove to the apartment in silence. In the parkade, he squeezed her hand again before getting out of the car and walking over to her side. He opened the door in silence. Took her hand as she came out.

It seemed like an important gesture.

He held her hand as they walked to the elevator. While they waited for the elevator. In the elevator.

"Is this the first time we're not doing the nasty in the elevator?" he whispered as they neared his floor. She drew closer to him. But neither kissed nor fondled him. It was intensely intimate anyway. "And the one time there's no chance of bumping into Mrs. Z," he sighed.

And Florence laughed, loudly, and was still laughing when they exited the elevator into the hallway.

The door to apartment opposite the elevator opened.

"Mr. Ornot, do you know what time it is?" Mrs. Ziernicka, in a bathrobe and curlers, providing a cameo from a 1960s movie, demanded.

They were laughing so hard as they finally came through the door of his apartment, Will could barely breathe.

"I'm going to make coffee. Or tea?" he said when he could form words, then changed it to a question. She had taken off her wings and put them by the door with her wig.

"That depends," she said. "Are we going to sleep... or do things that require... energy?" She smiled.

He smiled back.

"We're going to talk," he said. "Don't you think?"

She shivered. Closed her eyes and the waves of feelings he watched on her face on the dance floor came flying again.

She nodded very slowly and unenthusiastically.

He made coffee while she stood behind him, still. Close. Not touching.

He was aware of every minute movement. Every restrained stillness.

"Put your arms around my waist," he said finally. "I want that. So much."

The pressure of her palms on his belly, slight, caused fire to shoot up his spine.

Coffee.

She stayed behind him, arms wrapped around him, while he reached for mugs. Poured coffee into them.

"I don't have milk for you," he murmured.

"I don't care," she murmured back.

They walked from the kitchen to the living room very slowly, Will holding a mug of coffee in each hand, Florence still behind him, arms around him.

"Where's the babies' butts couch?" she exclaimed.

"I had to sell it," he said, putting the mugs down on the coffee table, and sitting down on the oversize sofa bed from IKEA. "First, because every time I sat down on it, I felt like something akin to a cannibal. And that, very squarely, is your fault, woman." She laughed. "And second," his voice softened, "because my son no longer wants to share a room with his sister when they sleep over here. So, while I search for a three-bedroom apartment, he gets to sleep in the living room on the most uncomfortable sofa bed I could afford."

"Is it so very uncomfortable?" she asked, sitting down beside him.

"Have you ever slept in a comfortable sofa bed?" Will asked, wrapping an arm around her shoulders but not... not pulling her in tight. Or onto his lap. God. He wanted to. He wouldn't. "You know they are all designed with the idea that you don't want your guests to stay too long, right?" She laughed again, and nuzzled closer into him. She smelled like sweat and tears and the madness of the nightclub, and it should have been repulsive, but he wanted her. Immediately, intensely. Always.

"This particular model is so fucking uncomfortable, my son refuses to sleep on it," Will made himself say. "So, he sleeps in my bed instead. And I—thus—have first-hand, painful experience of just how uncomfortable this sofa bed is. Really. It hates people."

She laughed again and wrapped an arm around his head and moved her entire body towards for a kiss that he knew would be the end of...

"Florence," he said, evading, for the first time and, he hoped, the last time in his life, her lips. "We need to talk. You know this."

She nodded.

So. They did.

---

## More Words, Even Those Three

SLIGHTLY LATER,BUT STILL TOO FUCKING
EARLY IN THE MORNING, SUNDAY,
OCTOBER 28

---

After, naked next to each other in bed, the nightclub scents washed off them in the shower, they had more words still. But these came easily and lazily. Will talked about boxing. Not to evade, but to explain. Rage. Release. Focused violence. She didn't like it, she said. But she could see... she could see why.

He apologized for the punch on her doorstep.

Also admitted a part of him enjoyed it. Fucking gloried in it, still.

She accepted the apology but did not issue forgiveness. That was ok too.

He asked if he could ask where her ex-husband was now, what was happening. "Husbands?" he corrected himself—did she want to talk about the other one too? Her history? She thought about it for a while. Told him, a little. Rough sketches. He listened.

"I loved him so much," she said about David. The one he punched. "I often—there is a part of me that loves him still."

He found that appalling and painful, and horrible and beautiful, incomprehensible and yet inevitable, and he held her tighter.

Told her Matthew didn't want to be a ring bearer at Amanda and Ranveer's wedding, and how happy that made him. She looked as if she understood.

She told him she liked to sing and dance while she worked. How it was the best part of cleaning the clinic on weekends. She and Santokh—her business partner, she explained, the mime in the turban at the night club, she added as an afterthought—could turn up their tunes to blast over the sound of two vacuum cleaners and just gun it. It was glorious. The banks, at night, they couldn't do that, because people sometimes worked late. So those were solo dance performances. Whether they worked alone or together, they worked in headphones. Santokh—"she belongs to a weird yoga cult, I'll tell you about it some other time," Florence said—often listened to mantras and other holy music. Florence rolled her eyes as she said "holy" but then looked ashamed. "It's quite beautiful, really," she added. "Just not my thing, you know?" He nodded. Florence listened to stuff that "possessed" her feet. The decade, the style of music didn't really matter—so long as she could dance to it.

"I like dancing when I mop the most," she said and he could see her, dancing in the lobby of his bank, wielding a mop.

In his vision, she had bare feet. He told her that. She laughed. Kissed him.

He told her about Rosie. Not everything... then, as he fell silent and she didn't say anything, and he felt her breathing stay calm and steady, everything.

He invited a comment, but she didn't say anything.

"I suppose... I know, now, that was the beginning of

the end of my marriage to Amanda," he said. And it was a confession to himself as much as to Florence. Probably more so, because, laying still in his arms, she looked untouched and undamaged and unharmed. "It wasn't... for Amanda, it wasn't that I fell off the wagon. That I..." the word was awful to get out, but he did it... "that I drank, that I was drunk. It wasn't even that Rosie and I... it wasn't even that. It was that I... kept—*her* word, Amanda's word, not mine—kept Rosie after. I mean, as my assistant. Do you understand? She said, that I, in that moment, unchose *her*."

"Do you think she's right?" Florence asked. Voice quiet, gentle.

"I didn't," Will said. "Six years ago? I denied it. Completely. And—we're so fucking civilized, Florence, Amanda and I. She didn't demand or ask... she didn't ask me to choose. And it didn't occur to me. Why would I punish Rosie for my stupidity? If she was willing to stay, to forgive... Right now? Today? Yes. I think Amanda was right. But I didn't know. I didn't know then."

"You love her very much," Florence said. And they both knew she was talking about Rosie.

"I do," he said. "She's my best friend."

Florence nuzzled him. "She sounds lovely," she said. Yawned. "Will? I know we have more to say. And I am happy... well, not happy. But grateful. Yes. That's the word. Grateful for this conversation. But I am also so very, very sleepy."

He kissed her yawning lips. Cheeks. Nose. Eyes.

"Can you stay till morning?" he asked.

She nodded.

"My mom's staying at the house," she said. "I was going to crash at Santokh and Michelle's house today." Michelle, he now knew, was Marie Antoinette. "They have a very comfortable couch," she added. "It's not, mind you, a sofa bed."

"And therein is the secret of its comfort," Will said. Cradled her closer to him.

He felt sleep coming.

He fought it off. He didn't want to lose any of these moments.

What had they not talked about? What had they not settled?

So much.

How the fuck do you cover everything that needs to be said, clarified—promised and not promised—in a single night?

They did cover, Will thought, sleep coming closer and closer, the important things.

"I do not want to be your third mistake," he told her.

"I don't want you to be my third mistake either," she replied.

"I don't want to make promises you'll think I can't keep." He said that, too.

She nodded.

"I can't promise I will stay," she said.

He nodded. Kissed her hand.

"I can't expect you to."

"I'm so fucking afraid," she said. She didn't add, "Don't damage me, Will. For fuck's sake, don't damage me." But he heard it.

Her eyes were closed now, he thought. He kissed them. Fought a yawn.

Surrendered to it.

Felt one last moment of clarity and consciousness.

"Florence? I love you."

She rolled in the nook of his arm from cheek onto forehead.

Her breath was deep and steady.

He closed his eyes and let sleep come.

But he thought he heard her muffled, "I love you," before he sank into oblivion.

*For Lisa,*
*who made it better*

## So... About That Dating Site Profile



*iwillornot*: Hey there, Songbird. What's cooking?

**notanightingale:** Why are you messaging me on OKC?

*iwillornot*: Why is your OKC profile still up?

**notanightingale:** Why is yours and why are you on it?

*iwillornot*: Jealous?

**notanightingale:** Are you?

*iwillornot*: Fucking livid. I'm not having sex with you for six weeks as punishment. FYI.

*iwillornot*: But seriously, why is your OKC profile still up?

**notanightingale:** But seriously, why is someone whose OKC profile still up asking me this question?

*iwillornot:* I went on the app to disable it, actually. So I'm not one of those assholes not responding to messages from gorgeous but desperate women. Because I'm in a relation-ship. With a gorgeous-not-desperate woman I adore.

*iwillornot:* And then I thought if you hadn't de-activated yours, I'd send you a message through it... because—do you know what today is?

**notanightingale:** Oh, fuck. Oh, Will. I do—now. But I forgot. Our first text-anniversary. That's so sweet.

*iwillornot:* It was supposed to be sweet. And now we're fighting over why we're leaving our options open.

**notanightingale:** Is that what we're doing?

*iwillornot:* Yes.

**notanightingale:** Don't worry. We'll have sex and make up.

*iwillornot:* I told you, no sex for six weeks.

**notanightingale:** You won't make it.

*iwillornot:* Fucking watch me. Will of Iron, that's what they call me.

**notanightingale:** Will of Iron, does that mean I should

bring a puzzle or a board game or something to amuse myself Wednesday night?

*iwillornot*: I was thinking, I'm gonna tie you up, and watch terrible porn, and jack off while you lie there, not having sex.

**notanightingale:** You are the most romantic man in the whole entire world.

*iwillornot*: I try.

**notanightingale:** See you Wednesday. Don't forget to pick up some rope after work.

*iwillornot*: Aren't you going to provide that?

**notanightingale:** I'm bringing the board game. As Plan B. In case you don't know how to tie knots.

*iwillornot*: Oh, baby. You should see the things I can do with knots.

**notanightingale:** LOL. See you Wednesday. Doofus.

*iwillornot*: See you Wednesday. Songbird.

---

*iwillornot*: But seriously, Florence, are you going to disable your profile?

# Suffering, Indulged
## MONDAY, DECEMBER 3

Santokh was still sleeping on the couch when Florence ran back into the house after dropping Isaac off at school.

The blanket was pulled up over her head and she was breathing the breath that years of parenting tweens and teenagers led Florence to label as awake-but-lazy-and-will-not-get-out-of-bed-fuck-you-mom breath.

"Come on, Guru, get moving," she said, pulling the blanket off Santokh. "We're gonna be late. Today, we do the Mansion, top-to-bottom, remember?"

Santokh moaned.

"I don't want to," she said. "I can't. Can't you please, please do it yourself? Just one more time? Or... ask one of my students? But not Uttamroop."

Florence looked at Santokh. Curled up. Mewling. Heartbroken. Pathetic. She thought of the nights she had spent curled up on Santokh and Michelle's couch. Curled up. Mewling. Heartbroken. Pathetic.

"I fucking can't and you know it," she said. "Uttamroop is the only one who can work at a decent pace, and she has a fucking day job, and... you can't pull any of the rest of them into this, you know that. Santokh, I gave you all of last week. I gave you last weekend, and I gave you this fucking weekend—do you know how long it takes to clean that clinic all by myself? You guessed it, twice as much time as it does with you. It almost killed me, and I didn't have any time for the kids or any downtime, period. And what did you do? You didn't even feed them supper."

"I ordered pizza! And gave them money for burgers for lunch!" Santokh protested.

"I can't afford to feed three boys pizza twice in a weekend. Never mind the burgers. And neither can you. Now get your ass off the couch, skip the shower and just pull on some clothes, and let's go."

"You're so..." Santokh said. Then stopped. Sobbed.

Florence shoved her off the couch.

"Ow!"

"This is called tough love," she said. "Santokh, honey. You can cry in the car. You can cry while we mop. But we have to go."

Santokh cried in the car. She cried while they cleaned the Mansion's six bathrooms.

"How many people live here? Why do they need six bathrooms?" Florence asked, as she asked every day that they cleaned the Mansion since Saryang Park referred Karma Klean to the client—her fiancé's brother's wife's uncle or someone like that—a few weeks ago.

Santokh didn't say anything. She cried. She cried as she dusted its countless mahogany bannisters and surfaces. She cried while she vacuumed. She cried while Florence made them tea, and she cried while drinking the tea.

Florence watched and her heart turned, and she wanted to cry too. And she also wanted to slap Santokh. Hard.

"Are you going to cry while you teach yoga, too?" she finally asked.

Santokh looked at her.

"How do you not understand this?" she asked finally.

Florence flushed.

"I understand... I understand you're suffering," she said. "Santokh. Emily." She knelt down beside her friend. Looked up at her. "Santokh, I understand suffering." She thought about the nights she had spent breathless in pain last February, March. April. This past October. Not thinking about Will—thinking only about Will. The horrible, almost life-ending suffering that preceded and followed her decision to leave David. The pain in her belly, her heart, her throat—pounding through every nerve of her body—as she walked out of Ethan's father's life.

Pain so all-consuming you think you want to die—but you need to live...

"I understand suffering," she said again. Took Santokh's face in her hands. "I don't understand..." she paused. What was this? What was this that Santokh was doing? "I don't understand... indulging it like this. Wallowing in it. And honestly," Florence got up in one quick motion and now towered over Santokh, "isn't the whole point of your cult that you're supposed to have techniques to cope with this kind of shit?"

"It's not a cult," Santokh protested. Weakly.

"It's a cult and it's a damn lame cult," Florence attacked. Would that work? "I mean, you've talked to me about this before. Positive mind, neutral mind, negative mind. Accept the emotion... let it go. Are you letting it go, Santokh?"

"I don't fucking want to!" Santokh exploded. "I don't want to let it go! I don't want to let *her* go!"

"I know," Florence said, more gently now. "I know. Come on. I've got to drive you to yoga and you've got to pretend to be a guru for an hour."

This time, in the car, Santokh breathed more than she

wept, and by the time Florence dropped her off at the studio, her eyes were dry.

"I love you," she said as she hugged Florence. "But you're a mean mom."

"I love you too." Florence hugged her back. "But you're a terrible guru."

Santokh snorted.

"I am not a guru," she said. "I am..." She sighed. "What am I, Florence? Other than a dumped, unworthy wife? And dumped, exiled for what? What am I?"

She left the car, the question unanswered.

Florence tried not to cry as she drove to the next house. This one was easy—a two-bedroom apartment occupied by a part-time dad. Who hardly ever used the kitchen—it was virtually immaculate. The garbage consisted of take-out containers. Her big task here was the sheets. Which almost always smelled like sex and cum.

"Enjoying your divorce, Daddy?" she muttered at the bed as she pulled them off. A picture of two cute kids looked at her from the nightstand table. She winked at them. Had a sudden thought of Will. Did Will have a cleaning lady? Probably. How did she feel when she washed his cum-soaked sheets? Did she roll her eyes at the wastebasket in the bathroom, filled with condoms and wrappers? Did Will wash his own sheets, empty his own garbage?

She had a pang. Of... Santokh had once called it defensiveness, not insecurity. Florence named it, now, for what it was. Insecurity. Fear. Fear of being found... unworthy.

It was an interesting and also awful feeling.

When he finally shook off their fog of lust and looked at her—at them—realistically and rationally, what would he decide?

How would she feel when he found her... unworthy? Uneducated, uninteresting, un... unloveable.

Florence cried while she scrubbed the bathroom—more used than the kitchen, and less maintained, *Fuck, did some men never learn how to aim in the fucking toilet?*—and blamed Santokh and Michelle.

Lesbian wedded bliss my ass, she thought viciously as she polished the mirror. How long did this grand love affair last?

Florence remembered dancing at their wedding, less than eight months ago. Her two younger sons wearing the pink dresses Michelle insisted on. Ethan flirting with Santokh's yoga students. Michelle frowning every time one of the female or femme students came to give Santokh a congratulatory hug.

Banning the outrageously beautiful Uttamroop from the wedding—Florence thought with unalloyed and un-jealous pleasure of the woman's beauty, all the shades of black and brown one could imagine molded into a dancer's body—didn't bring Michelle peace of mind.

Would anything, ever?

Stupid, jealous bitch, Florence let herself think and snarled at the unreasonable, irrational, erratic Michelle, the architect of the marriage and now of Santokh's suffering.

She didn't even know—she didn't ask—what the final fight was about. Maybe it was about Uttamroop. Maybe another student. Maybe, a stranger who happened to smile at Santokh and at whom she smiled back. It didn't matter to Florence—all that mattered was that it sent Santokh running out of her house, barefoot, in the middle of a November night.

"I'm at the 7-Eleven on 17th," the text read. "Can you come get me?"

Santokh didn't explain. Just cried.

Cried and cried and cried.

Florence carefully did not think about the fact that Michelle and Santokh had met two years ago this December. Just as she and Will had met one year ago this December.

There was no parallel.

None at all.

# One-Track Mind



*iwillornot:* So, seriously, Florence, are you going to disable this account?

Chrone, Uncensored
WEDNESDAY, DECEMBER 5

"I'm not better and I don't want to talk about it," Santokh
told Martha pre-emptively as Florence's mother hugged her.

"When have I ever made anyone talk about anything?"
Martha asked, with a pointed look at Florence. Florence
rolled her eyes, then kissed the increasingly wizened cheek.
Creased her forehead. She always hated this about her
mother. Her aged, used-up look. It filled her... with pity.
And with fear. Is this what she was going to look like? She
remembered first having this thought at, what? Twenty,
twenty-one. Living with Jonathan. Drinking and getting
high and riding his ups and downs and watching his crashes
and...

She didn't have a lot of memories from that time of her
life. Just that awful end scene, really. And she tried not to
think about that too much.

But this memory, this one, so vivid—it came upon her
often. A year, two years in? She wasn't, yet, conscious of just
how self-destructive Jonathan was and how much his self-
destruction was affecting her. But she remembered—looking
at herself in the bathroom mirror the morning after a night

of partying and fucking and drinking and fighting and screaming and crying—a night that started in pleasure and ended in such suffering—and seeing her mother's face look back at her.

She remembered flinching.

Her father's ghost shimmered across the mirror too.

She saw him—her father—every time she saw her mother's face. He was imprinted in every line. Every expression.

One day, she might ask her mother... she might. Or, she might not.

Today, she just kissed one cheek, so much older than the cheeks of other women Martha's age, and then the other.

"Shall we call Michelle a fucking bitch and tell you how we never liked her?" Florence asked. "Sammy! Come set the table! Grandma's here."

"You never liked her?" Santokh asked. She looked horrified.

Florence wanted to laugh, then felt shame.

"I liked her—I like her—a lot," she lied. "Almost as much as you."

She didn't really like... she didn't really like Michelle *with* Santokh. But there was no need to say it.

"I like her too," Martha said. "Very nice. And not at all ugly. For a lesbian."

Florence coughed and grasped at the kitchen counter.

Santokh's mouth fell open.

"I'm not saying you're ugly, my dear," Martha said, patting Santokh's hand. "You're quite attractive. Especially when you take off that turban. But I don't really think of you as... well. One of them."

"My mother, being open-minded," Florence said. "You're welcome."

"Oh-my-god. Martha," Santokh said. "What am I supposed to say? Thank you?"

"No need to thank me, my dear," Martha said. "One must move with the times. Now. Speaking of moving with the times. Am I allowed to tell my grandsons when it's time to go to bed, or are they just going to bed whenever they feel like it?"

"It's Saturday night. They can stay up till morning if they want to," Florence said. "Isaac! Ethan! Supper!"

"Well. A meal anyway," Martha said, looking at the Indian dishes on the table. "Santokh? Honey? Just because you're starving yourself on this crazy yoga diet does not mean the rest of us shouldn't get to eat meat."

"I guess I know where you get those less endearing traits of yours from," Santokh said to Florence as she scooped an obscene amount of dahl onto Martha's plate.

"Too much!" Martha cried.

"I expect you to eat every last fucking bite," Florence said. "Because that's good manners. Santokh worked very hard to make this."

Ethan laughed and Martha yelled and Florence laughed, and Santokh didn't cry, so it was ok.

"Is your mother... I don't know... off her meds or on new meds or something today?" Santokh whispered to Florence at the kitchen sink as they cleared up after supper. "Is she always like this and I'm just noticing now? Is today worse?"

"Honestly?" Florence looked at Martha being affable but also annoying with Isaac. "She read this article a couple of weeks ago about how changes in the brain as it ages reduce inhibition and self-censorship in the elderly and is now taking full advantage of that. She's told me, in the past two weeks, that she loves me even though I'm a promiscuous whore and she only hopes I get tested for STDs regularly. That I should change my brand of night cream, because she thinks I'm getting even more freckles, not that she thought that was possible. And also that she's heard that children of single mothers are four times more likely to die of an overdose and am I prepared for that."

"And you'd rather have her stay with the kids overnight than leave them with me?"

"I wasn't planning to have you here, remember?" Florence gave Santokh a hug then pushed her away. "Don't cry. Wash pots."

"I wasn't planning on being a dumped wife, either." Santokh sighed. "Don't tell me what you and Will are planning for tonight. It will only depress me."

"Heterosexual sex usually does," Florence said. And Santokh laughed, and Sammy wanted to know who said sex, and Martha demanded whether anyone was aware that there were children and seniors in the room, and Ethan asked her which one she considered herself to be, and when Florence left the house, her children and mother were yelling at each other, half-serious, half-joking, and Santokh was trying to bring them enlightenment but failing—but not crying—and that all made Florence almost as happy as going to see Will.

Will.

Fuck. Will.

She...

Was this love?

## Happy Anniversary
### WEDNESDAY, DECEMBER 5

"Happy," he said and kissed her lips, "anniversary," and kissed her nose, "of the best," he kissed her left eye, "one night stand," he kissed her right eye, "of my life," he kissed her lips again.

"But fuck," he said, after a deep dive into her mouth, "you were so annoying that night. Why on earth did I persevere?"

"I am outrageously cute," she said. Started unbuttoning his shirt.

"And unbelievably horny," he said, smacking her hands away. "I have things in the oven. Dinner."

She didn't tell him she ate. But she went back to the buttons.

"Will they burn?" she asked, kissing her way across his chest, then down.

And down.

"Probably," he said as she undid his pants. Zipper.

Christ. She loved his cock. It wasn't funny looking. At all.

Well, except when it was soft. But it didn't take much… she nuzzled it with her nose… to change that.

"Probably not very much," he said as she flicked a tongue over the head.

"Ah fuck, I like things crispy," he said as she worked her way down the shaft and he dropped his hands to her head.

She slid her mouth up and down it, delighting in his pleasure. And feeling her power. His hands held her head steady and then… impaled and gagged her.

She struggled. He pulled her, cock in her mouth and into her throat, on her knees into the kitchen.

"But not that crispy," he mumbled. "Don't come off. Stay right there… This is going to be awkward…"

It was. But Will opened the oven door and slid out the baking tray without burning either her or himself, and Florence found out it was possible to burst into laughter with a cock in your mouth.

"That did kill the mood a little," he reprimanded her after she stopped laughing and he went limp.

"You did want to eat," she said. Climbed into his lap as he sat at the dining room table she no longer loathed.

"I did," he said and lifted her off his lap onto the table. And ate.

"Happy anniversary of the worst-best one night stand of my life," she murmured somewhere between orgasm three and four.

"Say, 'Thank you,'" he said, coming up for air. Smug.

"Thank you," she said, caressing his hair.

"Say, 'I love you,'" he said. "Although, parenthetically, it would be great to hear you say it first. Unprompted. Sometime."

"I love you," she said. "Although, parenthetically, it would be great if you, you know, didn't keep on asking… Ow!" He bit her thigh. "Why?"

"For being mouthy," he said. "And gorgeous. And fucking delicious. And not letting me eat the incredibly impressive, almost gourmet dinner I prepared. Have I told you how hungry I am?"

"Eat," she invited, spreading her legs.

"Greedy bitch," he said, dragging a tongue along her slit. "I am temporarily full of that. And you interrupted my stream of thought... which was leading to..." He stood up abruptly and pulled her off the table and onto his lap. "Your OKC profile."

Florence stiffened. Also, and she found this fascinating, dried up—not just inside, but the juices that had just been trickling down her legs, disappeared. Or so it felt.

Cycles. Patterns.

"No," she said.

"No?" Will turned his head. And now she felt him go stiff. His spine, not his penis.

"No," she said and kissed him. "Tonight is the anniversary of our first one night stand. And we are going to eat..." she looked at the tray full of tarts... "what did you make?"

"It's this quiche-soufflé hybrid," he said. "Which, ungrateful woman, took me hours to find on the Internet."

"Don't call me ungrateful—I am nothing but awed—I am awe, how do you like to put it, I am awe incarnate. And don't interrupt. We are going to eat your soufflés—I can't believe you made that, by the way, Will, you are amazing. And we are going to fuck. And at some point, we're going to ride up and down the elevator half-naked until we see Mrs. Z. And we will fuck some more. And maybe have a shower or jacuzzi and flood your bathroom. And... let's see... did you buy the rope?"

"If I tie you up, you don't get sex," he muttered into her hair.

"If I don't get sex, you don't get sex," she muttered into

his neck. "Point: we are going to have a fucking fantabulous night. And we can fight in the morning."

"Are we going to fight about it?" he asked.

Florence looked at him. Then pulled off her dress.

"Fine. I'm willing to wait to find out," he said. "Now, let's go tie up your tiny titties."

It turned out that Will did indeed know many things about knots.

## That Conversation, Avoided
### THURSDAY, DECEMBER 6

*iwillornot*: You nasty, delicious, manipulative goddess/bitch —you left before we had a chance to talk about this. And your profile is still up.

**notanightingale:** You did not leave me—us—much room for conversation. I'm referring to the rope ball gag. Which you stuffed in my mouth as soon as we begun to fuck in the morning, and did not take out until my alarm went off. So— I think if we didn't talk—totally your fault.

**notanightingale:** Also, Will? If you wouldn't keep on logging into your OKC account, you'd never know whether or not my OKC profile was active, and it wouldn't be an issue. So I don't think this is my problem.

*iwillornot*: Florence? Next time—rope, no rope gag, and I don't untie you until we fucking talk about this.

**notanightingale:** Promises, promises.

*iwillornot:* :(

**notanightingale:** I love you.

*iwillornot:* :{

**notanightingale:** ?

*iwillornot:* :P

**notanightingale:** :*

*iwillornot:* :*

**notanightingale:** Say I love you too.

---

*iwillornot:* I love you too.

---

*iwillornot:* Manipulative bitch.

---

**notanightingale:** Will? I wasn't going to say anything about this, because I don't want to be a possessive, nagging girlfriend, but I think you're spending way too much time on OKC for someone who's supposed to be in a relationship.

*iwillornot:* I am going to throttle you.

**notanightingale:** I thought you were going to tie me up?

*iwillornot:* Tie you up. Then throttle you.

**notanightingale:** Will? Don't you ever work at work?
Cause, like, I have to go vacuum 2700 square feet in the
next hour. I love you. Go away. And stop stalking me
on OKC.

The text from Michelle made Florence's head hurt.

"I'm worried about Santokh. How is she doing?"

What the hell was she supposed to say to that?

"She's a fucking mess, because you left her. Kicked her out. Whatever."

Santokh would kill her.

"She's fine."

That was a lie.

Florence stared at the phone.

*Ping.*

"Are you mad at me, Florence?"

Well. That, she could answer.

"Fuck, yes."

"So she's really upset."

Fucking Michelle.

"What did you think she'd be? Happy?"

Florence turned off the phone. Met Santokh's red-rimmed, but so-wide eyes over the expanse of the clinic waiting room.

"What did she say?"

"Why do you think it was her?"

"Because I know you, Florence. And your face is the most telegraphic thing in the universe. What did she say?"

*Nothing worth repeating,* was what Florence wanted to say.

"She just wanted to know how you were doing," was what she said instead. And, oh-Jesus-Christ, Santokh's face lit up like a Christmas tree. Although that may have been because she was standing next to the clinic's Christmas tree and accidentally turned on the lights with her foot as she—literally—jumped up.

"She misses me," she said. "She's thinking about me."

And she turned back to the vacuum cleaner, her face so suffused with happiness, Florence was ashamed to be in the room to share the moment.

She turned her attention to the garbage cans.

You could tell a lot, she thought, about people by what they put in the garbage. Even here, in this clinical—hee hee hee, she laughed to herself—setting. She knew, without ever setting eyes on her, that the clinic director was on an eternal diet... that she kept on breaking. Also, taking fertility pills. Also, for some reason, frequently tossing pairs of laddered pantyhose into the trash. Why was that?

She thought about the one time she wore pantyhose—she hated them—over to Will's and what he did with them. Shuddered with pleasure.

Thought about their last night. Felt herself go gooey in the knees, and wet between the legs.

Thought about their texting exchange this morning. Frowned.

It was just texting. It didn't matter.

Looked at Santokh, moving the vacuum cleaner up and down the massive waiting room, in and around and then under the chairs—in a state of complete and total meditative bliss. *Because* of a text—not even a text she got. A second-hand text. A hearsay text.

She did not think about her reluctance to disable her OKC profile.

Instead, she thought about how she had just celebrated a one-year anniversary. In a relationship.

When was the last time she had been in this place? Such a place?

She couldn't remember. She had been with Jonathan for three years. Did they celebrate anniversaries? She couldn't remember a single one. She barely remembered what he looked like. She never thought about him really. A few years ago, he found her and tried to friend her on Facebook.

She shuddered at that memory. Accepted that one day, she would have to talk to Ethan about his father.

But not yet.

"Anytime you want to talk about it," she put the offer on the table to her son when he turned twelve, did the math, and realized David wasn't his father. "I will tell you everything."

He chose... not to ask then. Or since.

But he would. She knew he would.

She would start that conversation with, "I was with your father for three years."

And David. David... it was four years. No, almost five. She left before they could celebrate their five-year anniversary. But. It was almost five. Five years, two children? How could she, Florence asked herself, as she always did when she thought about David, make the same mistake twice?

Because, she answered herself as she always did, David was an amazing, charming human being. When he was sober.

She let the good memories come. It was easier now. To

remember them. To remember who he could be, to value what he could have been.

Leaving him was the right thing to do, too.

Leaving Will would kill her.

The thought, grandiose and hyperbolic, shot from her brain to her gut and made her shake. Santokh was next to her immediately.

"What's going on?" she asked.

Florence hugged her. Bliss, she thought, as she held onto Santokh in silence, is less selfish than suffering. Funny, that.

They stood still, holding each other. Florence felt calm returning to her. And she felt Santokh... she felt Santokh, she was sure—it was crazy, but she was so sure—she felt Santokh decide not to suffer.

"What just happened?" she asked her, leaning back.

"One of those stupid cult things you mock," Santokh said. And smiled. Kissed Florence on the cheek. "You know what, Florence? She loved me. She misses me. For now... that's enough."

They finished cleaning the clinic in a strange but welcome mood of tranquility.

## One-Track Mind, Continued
### THURSDAY, DECEMBER 13

*iwillornot*: So... about this profile...

**notanightingale:** Can't talk. Christmas shopping.

*iwillornot*: Also... I can't help but notice you are now a year older.

**notanightingale:** Happens to the best of us.

*iwillornot*: When was your birthday?

**notanightingale:** Does it matter? It came. It went.

*iwillornot*: It fucking matters. It's the sort of thing you share with the people you love.

**notanightingale:** It was this past Monday. Ok?

**notanightingale:** I didn't want you to make a big deal out of it. We had our anniversary. And it was beautiful.

**notanightingale:** And seriously. I'm Christmas shopping. Can't talk.

*iwillornot:* We will talk. Florence? Promise me? This is what I want for Christmas.

**notanightingale:** A stupid fight over my birthday?

*iwillornot:* No. A serious conversation about... us. And your OKC profile.

*iwillornot:* And how people in relationships share things, like birthdays, with each other.

*iwillornot:* Are you going to ask me when mine is?

**notanightingale:** Have. To. Go. To. Mall. With. My. Insane. Mother. And you're eating up my data. Why did I even respond?

*iwillornot:* Because you love me.

**notanightingale:** :)

*iwillornot:* Say it.

**notanightingale:** because I love you

*iwillornot:* And we're going to talk about this later?

**notanightingale:** I love you. I have to go. xo

*iwillornot*: You. Are. Infuriating.

# Everyone's At the Mall
## THURSDAY, DECEMBER 13

"Why am I doing this again?" Florence asked Santokh.

"Because she was in labour with you for seventy-two hours and she's going to die soon," Santokh said. "At least, that's why she said you should do it when she asked you."

"Oh-my-god," Florence sighed. "I love her. But why is she so infuriating?"

Santokh laughed. And Florence beamed, because it was, she thought, the first laugh she had seen on her friend's face since she moved in.

"Aren't all mothers? Go. Take her Christmas shopping. It can be your walking meditation. A chance to practice unconditional love and compassion and..."

"Stop trying to recruit me to your cult!" Florence swatted Santokh's turban. Very lightly. "You'll make supper?"

"I'll make supper," Santokh said. "And not order pizza. I promise. But I don't think the boys will like my rejuvenation dhal. Just so you know."

"You could, you know, make meatballs," Florence said. "Or... fuck, even grilled cheese sandwiches."

"I'm making rejuvenation dhal," Santokh said. "Or, ordering pizza."

Florence sighed.

Took her mother Christmas shopping. Which was... well, everything she expected it to be.

Arduous.

Annoying.

Amusing.

Exhausting.

Embarrassing.

"Look, there's that black girl that helped us clean during Santokh's honeymoon," Martha said suddenly. "Oh, isn't she pretty in that yellow dress. It's too bad you can never wear yellow, Florence. She and Santokh would make a lovely couple, don't you think? She's so much prettier than Michelle. Why don't you wave her over to join us? Do you remember her name? Hello! Hello!"

"Oh-my-god, Mom, can you be any louder?" Florence cringed. But she joined Martha in waving at Uttamroop. Who came over slowly.

Reluctantly, Florence thought.

Did she know, Florence wondered, about what was going on with Santokh and Michelle?

No.

Because as soon as Martha's attention was distracted by another shiny thing, Uttamroop awkwardly took Florence's arm and pulled her a little aside.

"It's none of my business," she said. "But is Santokh ok?"

Florence wasn't sure what to say.

"I'm not sure what to say," she said. Was strangely pleased with herself for that approach. "What do you mean?"

"You don't want to tell me," Uttamroop said.

"I do kind of think it's none of your business," Florence agreed. Aware, suddenly, of something else, unspoken, simmering between the two of them. What was going on? She looked at Uttamroop carefully.

The beautiful woman—fuck, no wonder Michelle was jealous, Florence thought again—did not meet her eyes.

"Ask her yourself, ok?" Florence said.

"She doesn't talk to me or look at me at yoga," Uttamroop said. "Florence, you have no fucking idea how hard it is for me to ask you about this..." her voice trailed off. "And not just because..." She stopped and looked as if she was about to cry.

And it was Florence's turn to look away.

"I don't know what to say," she said. "I don't want to be anyone's go-between, Uttamroop."

"Florence..." Uttamroop said, still holding onto her arm, and Florence braced herself for another plea.

Martha, to the rescue.

"Florence! Are you buying... what's your man's name again? Will? Are you buying Will a present? Of course, I'm only inferring he's your man. And that it's the same man. Because you never tell me anything. It's a good thing I get the chance to eavesdrop on your conversations with Santokh occasionally. But are you getting him a present? Because they have the sweetest socks here. Come see!"

"Who gets a lover socks for Christmas?" Florence said to Uttamroop, laughing. But Uttamroop was already walking away. And Florence felt like shit. But also relieved.

"Florence!"

Grand Central Station!

Saryang Park was standing in front of her. "Oh, thank god, Florence!" And before she knew what was happening, Florence found herself agreeing to do the Park house on Sunday. "I'll pay you a fortune, double, triple your rates, whatever you want, Florence, I just need it perfect for my in-laws."

"Of course she'll do it," Martha piped in.

"Sundays are hard for me," Florence protested. "Even Saturday is easier. Can we do Saturday?"

"Florence, you know what my children will do to the house in the space of a day," Saryang wailed. "Please. Sunday. They come at eight. I'll do my best before. I'll put things away. But you know I'm hopeless."

"Of course she'll help you out, Dr. Park," Martha said again.

"Are you volunteering to help out, Mother?" Florence hissed at Martha as Saryang rushed off.

"I can't," Martha said primly. "I have other plans."

And she strolled off too, leaving Florence feeling railroaded... and ridiculously grateful that she was going to be seeing Will on Saturday.

And she was not going to buy him socks for Christmas. Yuck.

But... was he expecting a Christmas present? Should she get him a Christmas present?

Were they at that stage of their relationship?

---

## Worst Guru Ever
### THURSDAY, DECEMBER 13
---

*Santokh:* OMFG, Florence, seriously?

**Florence Gunn:** Well, we haven't done any presents ever. Not for birthdays. I mean, I didn't even tell him about my birthday. Or... look, I'm asking for advice. Which is a rare thing. Fucking enjoy it and give it to me.

*Santokh:* No.

**Florence Gunn:** 'No, I shouldn't get him a Christmas present' or 'No, you're not giving me advice.'

*Santokh:* No. Fuck off.

**Florence Gunn:** You're the worst guru ever. Fuck.

**Florence Gunn:** Can you help me clean Mrs. Dr.'s house on Sunday?

*Santokh:* No.

**Florence Gunn:** Is something wrong?

*Santokh:* I miss her, Florence. That's all. I miss her. I'm in your kitchen, wishing I was in my kitchen. I'm on your couch, wishing I was in her bed. That's all.

**Florence Gunn:** I'm sorry. I love you.

*Santokh:* I know. I love you too.

**Florence Gunn:** But if I were going to get him a present —it shouldn't be something lame like socks, right?

*Santokh:* Florence? Go pay attention to your mother.

**Florence Gunn:** Worst guru ever. Just for that, I'm not going to tell you that I ran into Uttamroop. Or what she said.

*Santokh:* What? Tell me!

# Petty Revenge


But, she didn't.

---

# Hard Conversation, Evaded
### SATURDAY, DECEMBER 15

---

"Do you know when relationships die?" Will asked her. They were in his jacuzzi, not flooding the bathroom. There were candles. Incense. Romantic music.

"When?" Florence said, not really hearing his words, just leaning back into his body and loving his embrace.

"Well, maybe not die," he corrected. "Founder. Get into trouble. You know? When that happens?"

"Mmmm," she whispered, cuddling into his chest. More hairy than any chest she had ever cuddled into before. She wouldn't have thought she'd like that. She loved it.

"When you think you don't have to work on them anymore," Will said, stroking her head. "When you think— hell, it's been... whatever. A year. A decade. I've got this marriage thing down!"

"Are we talking about us or you and Amanda?" Florence asked, sitting up.

"Both," Will said. She frowned. "And this is a conversation you do not want to be having," he said, pulling her back towards his chest. She folded in, but felt her body stiffen and felt the rigid response in his torso and shoulders.

"No." She kissed the place on his chest where the hair thinned to let a nipple peek out. "No."

"What do you want, Florence?" he asked. Stroking her hair and relaxing, a little, into her kisses.

"This," she said. "I want this. I like this. I love this."

"And you want this... for a year? Another year?" he asked.

"Don't say a decade," she said, moving between his nipples. He grabbed her head, her hair and pulled it up to his face.

"Florence," he said.

"Will." She filled the syllable with love and longing. But also fear. "I want... a day after day. That is all. A good day—a good night—today. A good day, a loving day, the next time. One after the other. That is all."

His hand tightened on her hair. She caressed his cheeks. The nose she adored.

"There is nothing more," she said. She didn't want to—she didn't think she had to. Explain about the fragility of... the big R relationship. Did she have to point out—his failed marriage? Her two divorces—well, one formal, the other *de facto*?

She thought about Santokh and Michelle. Celebrating their engagement last Christmas. Their hyper-planned fairy tale wedding.

Santokh sleeping on her couch. Suffering.

Michelle sleeping in their dream home—alone. Suffering also.

Will's arms tightened around her.

"I want more," he said. "All I want for Christmas, Florence... is more."

She leaned against his chest.

This was love, and it was good. But also scary.

"All I want for Christmas, Will," she said—realized she

was humming, wanted to laugh, realized it would hurt him, muffled the sound—"all I want for Christmas is you. One day at a time."

He kissed her. And she put all of her love and passion into the kiss back.

But he was unconvinced, she knew.

It was not, Florence thought, going to be an easy Christmas.

She was right.

———————————

## It's A Small World After All
### SUNDAY, DECEMBER 16

———————————

"Stay." He wrapped his arms around her, hard. Florence loved it: she sank into them and wanted to stay there forever.

"I have to go," she said instead, kissing his bare shoulder.

"It's a Sunday morning in December," he whispered. "Your mom's with the kids. You're done Christmas shopping. Stay."

She stayed still for a few delicious seconds.

"I have to go," she said again. And kissed his bare shoulder again. "I have to clean the clinic, on my own, today. Again. I can't count on Santokh. I hope I'll be able to get her ass out of bed in time for her to make it to her cult yoga class. But I..." He started kissing her... "Will..." she moaned. "Will, I love this. You know that I want to stay. But I need to do the work of two people today, and then I'm doing a special clean for a client this afternoon..." His kisses worked his way down her body... "Oh-my-god, Will stop—I have to go... I have to do the work of two people today, and..."

"I'll help you," he said, disappearing below her belly—

the kisses only on her thighs, never anywhere else, but his hands getting closer and closer to her lower lips. "I'll help you and you won't have to do the work of two people, and it will go faster..."

"Oh-my-god-Will," she moaned. Then stiffened and wiggled away.

He pulled her back.

"No," he said. "None of this 'I can't accept it' bullshit. It's a fair trade. I want more time with you. Therefore, I am going to reduce the amount of time you're spending somewhere else. Now lay back, spread your legs, and let me..." his fingers spread her now and she felt herself melt into them... "do my work... and then we'll go do yours."

So they did.

<hr>

Will wasn't as awful at cleaning as she had expected. He was, actually, quite efficient. He followed instructions quickly. She thought he was cutting corners a bit with the vacuuming, and she had to point out to him that he needed to vacuum underneath the waiting room chairs, not just in large swaths down the middle. But once she told him, he did it.

He worked the mop hard, and she laughed.

"How do you do it?" he asked her.

She took it from his hands and danced with it.

"Not here, not now," she whispered as he grabbed her and pressed her against a wall.

"On a desk. Of your least favourite person here," he said. "Or... in one of the exam rooms. Your legs spread in those whatchamacallit things. Clearly designed for my kind of fucking."

"Everything's designed for your kind of fucking." She

laughed in between his kisses. "And no. No desk or couch or floor sex here."

They ended up fucking in the men's washroom instead. A focused, foreplay-free quickie that was clearly Will fulfilling a bucket list fantasy.

Florence watched his face in the mirror with pleasure. Then, after he came, she gave him detailed instructions on how to clean the toilet and urinal.

"This is disgusting," he said.

"Men are disgusting," she said. Laughed. She was so ridiculously happy, she wanted to fly.

Instead, she danced her way through the rest of the clinic chores. Checked in with her mom and kids while Will texted with his.

Martha complained that Ethan left home without telling her where he was going.

"It's the middle of the day on a Sunday in December, Mom!" Florence texted. "Mall. Christmas shopping. Right?"

"Or he's buying drugs, Florence. Do you ever think of that?"

Will laughed when she told him.

"Everything ok with yours?" she asked.

He nodded. Seemed perturbed, though. But she let it be.

They went through a Wendy's drive-through and ate Baconators in the car as Florence drove to Saryang Park's house.

Will put a hand on her knee and rubbed it.

"I'm exhausted," he said suddenly.

"From the cleaning or the fucking?" She laughed.

"The cleaning," he said. "My back fucking aches like an old man's. Jesus, Florence, you work hard."

And she felt... something. Squeezed his hand. It felt good... to be acknowledged.

"Where are we going now?" he asked suddenly.

"It's one of my regular mid-week clients," Florence explained. "I usually do her on Tuesdays. But she's entertaining her new in-laws for the first time today. Maybe even meeting them for the first time? She was super-frazzled. The house is apparently a disaster... which, you know, probably just means lived in. I was just there last Tuesday. And I didn't cut that many corners." She laughed. "But she's got kids, right? And they are kind of sloppy. She's not that neat herself, frankly. Although she tries. Now, anyway."

She thought about her own house. So much messier... but in many ways so much better organized, she made the thought more positive—than the houses of her clients. Although... less so now. Ethan's messes were mostly in the kitchen. Sammy's biggest issue was taking off his socks and leaving them wherever. She was going to break that habit before he moved out—she hoped his future roommates and partners appreciated the battle she was waging on their behalf. And Isaac... she smiled. Felt her body softened. She loved his messes. The Titanic made out of cardboard. Mr. Eggy—a six-foot tall sculpture made out of egg cartons.

"You look so happy," Will said suddenly.

She touched the hand he still had resting on her knee.

"I am," she said.

She pulled up in front of the Park house.

"What are you doing?" Will said.

"Parking," she said. Laughed. "Come on."

She pulled her cleaning caddy out of the Civic's trunk and handed it to him as he slowly came around.

"We're going to leave the bedrooms for last," she said once they were in the house. "We'll make the kitchen, dining room, and living room, and downstairs bathroom sparkle. That's where she'll be entertaining her in-laws. Everything else just needs to be clean enough. I'm going to start in the kitchen, and I'll get you vacuuming. They have a killer central vac system. The hose is stored right through here, in the pantry. Are you coming?"

Will walked towards her very slowly and rigidly. His walk looked painful.

She reached for him and hugged him. "Such a very sore back?" she murmured. He was stiff and unresponsive in her arms.

"How long have you been working here? Doing this house?" he asked.

"Since... January, I think," Florence said. "Yeah, coming up on a year. Beautiful layout, isn't it? She has some gorgeous furniture. You'll like it. Especially the dining room table. I even like it better than yours," she said, playfully. Still holding Will. Who was still stiff.

"As you vacuum, gather up the kids' toys and clothes and random shit and toss it towards the bottom of the stairs," she continued. Rubbing his belly. "Will? Are you too tired? Do you want to sit down?"

"No," he said. He shrugged her off him. Unkindly, she thought, and she felt her arms drop to her sides awkwardly. "No."

Florence shrugged. Went into the pantry and came out with the hose. Handed it to Will, who took it from her hands with a strange look.

Florence felt her happiness recede, replaced with anxiety. Why? What happened? Well. Will. Will was, suddenly... weird.

It was a mistake, Florence thought, to bring him. To show him...

She made the cleaning lady very real for him.

She felt unwell, and even more anxious, and so she

talked more. About how her mother connected her with Saryang. And the exchange of pissy notes. The subsequent texting exchanges. How now Saryang was probably her favourite client. Although still the messiest one too, and every once in a while...

"Saryang?" Will said. "That's her name?"

"Saryang Park," Florence said. "Isn't that a beautiful—yet sort of hilarious—name?"

"Yes," Will said. He fingered the hose.

Florence felt the need to fill the silence.

"I think she's Korean? I mean, she's Canadian," she said. "But she looks vaguely Asian. I think Park might be a Korean name? I don't know. We've only met twice. Honey? If you're unwell, sit down. But I've got to boogey. Dr. Park's in-laws descend in..." she looked at her watch... "three hours, and things gotta sparkle."

She kissed Will's cheek.

He kissed her back. Mechanically. Rigidly. But turned to the vacuum cleaner.

Florence started to work in silence and she felt her mind go to a hundred terrible places at once. "You work so hard" turned from a compliment to a judgement. Her agreeing to let Will help her transformed from a delicious surrender and intimacy into an act of idiocy. A way to remind him, so very forcefully, how separate their worlds were. At least, Florence thought, scrubbing Saryang Park's kitchen counters viciously, they weren't cleaning his bank. God. What would that make him feel like?

She imagined, suddenly, having sex with Will at his bank on his... no, not on his desk. On his manager's desk.

The thought cheered her up immediately.

"Tunes!" she called out. Popped her phone into one of the house's iPod docking stations—"These speakers are incredible, Will, they go all over the house!" she yelled over the sound of the vacuum cleaner—and selected her "Dance Yourself Happy" playlist.

And danced and sang herself into peace.

She caught up with Will as he started maneuvering the vacuum hose up the stairs.

"Perfect," she said. "I'm going to do the bathrooms first, and then a quick tidy of the bedrooms. When you finish the upstairs hallway, start with the master bedroom, ok? I'll leave the door open so you know which one it is."

He didn't say anything.

He was still not all right.

She decided not to say anything about it. If his back was hurting him and he didn't want to admit it... he'd have to pay the price for wanting to look to her as an indestructible he-man.

There. That was a good thought. She grabbed onto it. He was sore and challenged by what he might have dismissed yesterday as routine, light woman's work. So. It was all good.

She tore through the master bathroom very quickly. There was no hair in the drains or around the sinks, there never was anymore. "Train thy client," Florence sung out of sync with the music. Rinse of the shower and jacuzzi. Solid cleaning of the toilet, always—never, ever cut corners there, she mentally instructed Will. Quick wipe of the sinks and counters—oh for a bathroom with two sinks, she dreamt, as she often did. One for the boys. One for her...

Floor.

Mirror.

What else?

Right.

Bathroom garbage.

She was walking out of the bathroom holding the

garbage bag when Will entered the bedroom with the vacuum cleaner.

Stopped at the threshold.

"God, Will, you look like you're going to puke," Florence said. "Come on. No more he-man. Sit down."

He took a step backwards out of the bedroom.

"Florence, I've got to tell you," he said as she dropped the bathroom garbage—in a bag, it was ok to drop it, she had to tell herself—and moved to embrace him. He accepted her arms around him, but did not reciprocate for a moment. Then did, and squeezed her so tightly, she lost her breath.

"Florence, I've got to tell you," he repeated again.

"Will?" Saryang Park's voice shredded Florence's ears. "Will? Will? What the fuck are you doing here? Are you fucking making out with my cleaning lady?"

## Healing Massage, Ineffective
### SUNDAY, DECEMBER 16

"Shit show?" Santokh asked.

"Shit show," Florence agreed. They had locked themselves in Florence's bedroom after supper with a bottle of wine that neither particularly wanted to drink—but it seemed, Santokh said after Florence sketched out very quickly what happened—like the sort of situation that called for a bottle of wine. And one of Santokh's students had just given her a bottle of wine as a Christmas present.

"It was very sweet," Santokh said. About the gift of wine.

"Hypocritical or ignorant, no?" Florence challenged. "Doesn't your cult reject all stimulants? From caffeine on down?"

"Could you just call it yoga and not a cult?" Santokh sighed.

"No," Florence laughed. Point: they had wine.

They did not have a corkscrew and after they finished laughing about that, they set the unopened bottle on the bed between them.

"We're still doing this with wine present," Santokh said.

"See? When you tell the story, we locked ourselves in the bedroom with a bottle of wine to talk over... the..." She paused... "Shit show?"

"Shit show."

"Do you think we lost a client?" Santokh asked after a few minutes silence.

"Yup," Florence nodded. "It's quite possible she was still freaking out and yelling at him when her new in-laws came in. And her new husband. Or fiancé. Will told me she was planning a wedding. But he didn't mention—I'm sure he would tell me, if they actually got married. Oh-my-god, Santokh. What have I done? How could I have taken him to help me clean his ex-wife's house?"

"You didn't know." Santokh rubbed her shoulders. "How could you have known? You've never been to his house. I mean... you know what I mean. And..."

"But why wouldn't he tell me his wife's real name?" Florence asked. "He talks about her—not often. But sometimes. Amanda. Amanda this. Amanda that. Not fucking... Dr. Saryang Park."

"You didn't know." Santokh rubbed her arms and hands. "Lie down on your belly."

"No. You'll stick your elbows into sensitive spots on my spine, make me scream in pain, and tell me it's for my own good," Florence protested. But she lay down on her belly and submitted to Santokh's cultic torture.

"It's a form of healing massage," Santokh said patiently. "And so... you just left?"

"After the third time she screamed, 'Why are you sleeping with my cleaning lady? What the fuck is wrong with you?' I decided my presence there was... unhelpful. Ow!"

Santokh, Florence was sure, smiled. Not at what she said. At her cry of pain.

"Do you think I abandoned him?" she asked after a pause. "Should I have stayed? Or at least waited in the car outside?"

"He's a big boy," Santokh said, drilling an elbow and a thumb into Florence's back. "I'm sure he found his way home."

"Or, he and the ex-wife ended up fucking. In the master bedroom that I had just cleaned—in *their* master bedroom. And were still there, in bed, when her new guy came home with his parents. Oh-my-god. I might have ruined her new marriage. And put her and Will back together."

"Or," Santokh put all of her weight into an elbow and Florence let out an unmuffled scream, "they just had a massive big fight that reminded them why they're not together. Chill, Florence."

*Chill, Florence.*

Florence closed her eyes.

*Chill, Florence.*

*He'll text you soon, Florence.*

*It will all be ok, Florence.*

# But, No
## MONDAY, DECEMBER 17

It wasn't.
He didn't.

---

## Another Anniversary
### TUESDAY, DECEMBER 18

---

"You could text him," Santokh said. For the umpteenth time. She was doing the banks this week with Florence, to make up for "the two weeks I was a pile of goo," as she had put it.

Possibly, avoiding yoga. And Uttamroop? Michelle? Life?

Florence didn't ask. Accepted the help gratefully.

The advice, less so.

"You could text him," Santokh said five minutes later.

"I could," Florence agreed. *I won't*, she finished the sentence in her mind. *Why not?* she asked herself. Because...

*"Why are you fucking my cleaning lady, Will, what the fuck is wrong with you?"*

*Because I'm afraid.*

*Because I'm afraid he's back with his ex-wife.*

*Because I'm afraid he just doesn't want to be with me anymore. Because...*

Florence felt Santokh kiss the tears off her cheeks before they even fell.

"Come on," Santokh said. "Fucking December. We're moving at a snail's pace. And if we finish before 9 p.m., we can go experience the hell that is a mall at Christmas."

"No!" Florence cried out. In mock horror. Maybe real horror.

"Yes," Santokh said. She paused. "Fucking December," she said. "I need a few more things."

They finished cleaning the bank in silence and at a pace that elevated their heart rates and caused a few beads of perspiration to peek out from under Santokh's turban.

"You know, I'm pretty sure you just have to wear that thing when you teach yoga," Florence said.

"I'm pretty sure I know the rules of my cult better than you do," Santokh said.

"You admit it! You admit that it's a cult!" Florence exclaimed. They were laughing, and walking through the crowded mall hand-in-hand, very happy when Florence's phone pinged.

Will.

Oh, fuck, yes.

It was going to be Will, and...

"Get it," Santokh said. And Florence felt selfish and awful—and she remembered the tough love she had been administering to Santokh for the whole of December and she thought of Santokh's very gentle, completely compassionate love that she received after the shit show—and, really, always, anytime, and she felt so selfish and awful and grateful and lucky.

She kissed Santokh.

Reached for the phone.

No.

Not Will.

A text from Michelle.

"It's our anniversary today. Of our first kiss. What is Santokh doing?"

Anger. Oh-my-god, from where this anger at Michelle and why?

Anger, suddenly, at herself. An even worse anger. Because Santokh had been off all day... but Florence didn't ask why. Or offer... love, compassion, help.

And, Santokh wouldn't need love, compassion, and help —if Michelle hadn't been a jealous, possessive bitch who freaked out over every dance floor flirtation, smile, relationship, interaction...

"Not Will?" Santokh said, sadly, as Florence typed, angrily, "If you don't want to ask her yourself, then it's none of your business."

Then she wrapped her arm back Santokh's waist.

"Where to first?" she asked.

*Ping.*

Santokh's phone.

They both knew it was Michelle.

Florence didn't ask what Michelle texted. Or what Santokh typed in response.

They wandered through the mall with no apparent purpose, Santokh fingering this scarf and that dress, Florence smelling all the bath bombs at Lush, Santokh tracing her finger along a dozen book covers on display at the bookstore without—of this Florence was sure—seeing a single one.

When they bumped into Michelle on the third floor of Simon's department store, Florence was not surprised.

She started to ponder how to politely make her excuses —until Santokh convulsively clutched at her arm.

"Don't you fucking leave me!" she whispered into Florence's ear.

The three of them stood there, staring at each other—well, Michelle and Santokh staring at each other, Florence a third wheel, unwelcome by Michelle, tethered by Santokh.

"Do the two of you need to talk?" Florence said finally.

Santokh shivered. Michelle shuddered.

"Fucking children," Florence said. She grabbed a dress off a rack, and then grabbed each of them by the hand.

"I'm locking you in a fitting room," she said.

"There will be a horrible line-up!" Santokh cried out. Michelle, however, did not protest. And there was no line-up.

Florence shoved Santokh, then Michelle into the cubicle.

"Talk," she commanded. "I'll let you out in fifteen minutes."

She leaned against the door.

Thought about Will.

Listened to two... three... four... five... minutes of silence.

Then... not words. A kiss? A smack? A moan?

Oh-my-god. They were fucking in the fitting room.

Florence stepped away from the door to the mirror on the wall opposite. She leaned her forehead against the mirror. She heard Santokh gasp and Michelle laugh.

"Never mind me," she muttered. "I'll keep guard."

She looked back over her shoulder at the fitting room door. She could see Santokh's bare feet. But not Michelle's. Very briefly, she imagined Michelle wrapped around Santokh's waist.

Smiled.

Thought of Will.

Smiled more. Felt such a shot of drowning love—and then lust—that she felt her knees buckle.

Reached for her phone and caressed it. Imagined sending him a text. "Want to meet in the Holt Renfrew parkade for a quickie?"

Could she... would she?

"Never mind me," she said to the closed fitting room door. "I'll go home."

# Invitation, Refused
### TUESDAY, DECEMBER 18

**Florence Gunn:** Want to meet me in the Holt Renfrew parkade for a quickie?

*Will Ornot:* It's not a good time, Florence. Sorry.

_____________________

## It's Complicated

WEDNESDAY, DECEMBER 19

_____________________

Well. At least he didn't ghost her. That was something, wasn't it?

Santokh didn't come to sleep on Florence's couch that night and that was something too. But she was at the curb of her house, dressed—radiant—and ready to go when Florence pulled up to pick her up at 8:45.

They didn't talk about it at all as they cleaned the Mansion. And they didn't talk in the car at all either. But Florence felt infected with Santokh's happiness.

Which was ridiculous because she didn't have any of her own.

Will.

Fuck, Will.

*Do you want me?*

*Are you angry?*

*Are you ashamed?*

*Confused?*

*What am I supposed to do?*

Perhaps, she thought, as she fixed herself a solo lunch at

home and wrapped the boys' Christmas presents, these were questions she should be texting to Will.

Except... Well, where to start?

The invitation for a parkade quickie, clearly a bad idea.

*"I'm sorry I made you clean your ex-house."*

Um, no.

*"I didn't know she was your ex-wife."*

Well, self-evident, right? Did she need to say it?

What, really, was the misunderstanding here?

Was he angry? Was she ashamed?

Was *she* ashamed?

Florence closed her eyes.

Maybe. It was very hard to be proud of being someone's cleaning lady.

It was very hard not to be conscious of the fact that your lover's car payments were about the same size as your mortgage, or that his kitchen table cost as much as you spent on food... in a year.

It was very hard not to worry about... the future. A year of weirdness. And amazing sex. And growing intimacy. And... what next?

Florence did not want... she closed her eyes and briefly relived the shit show in Saryang Park's house. In the house that was Will's and Saryang's. Then she imagined a blended family that included her boys and Will's—Will and Saryang's kids. Slobby kids, who didn't clean up after themselves (they made progress this year, Florence admitted... but fuck. They would know. "Dad's new girlfriend is Mom's cleaning lady!"). Bizarre custody arrangements. Could she imagine living with Will? Will living with her and her kids? His kids there part-time?

His kids there when David dropped in for a drunken... or even sober... visit?

She couldn't.

She wouldn't.

And Will was probably imagining the same thing.

*"It's not a good time, Florence. Sorry."*

*"It's not a good match, Florence. Sorry."*

*It's been fun, Will,* she thought. Felt mournful. Tried very hard to shake it off.

*It's been a good year, Will. Well, it's had some hard and shitty parts too, right? But it's been such a good... I'm so happy I have had you, I'm so happy to have had the time I've had with you, this past year.*

Fucking December.

"What?" Ethan was behind her. "Oooh. Loot! Which ones are mine?"

"One third of them. Except for the ones that are for Grandma and Santokh." Florence laughed and spun around to hug her son. Who, she noticed, was now taller than she was. "Oh-my-god. When did this happen?" Ethan smiled. Smirked. Then...

"Have you been crying, Mom?"

"No!" Florence protested. Then realized her face was wet. "Apparently," she said. She went to the kitchen sink and splashed cold water over her face.

"Something with your guy?" Ethan said. Awkward.

Florence nodded. Awkward.

"So it doesn't get easier, hey?" he said. "Girl stuff, boy stuff? Love stuff?"

"No. It's a bitch, always," Florence said and started crying again. Oh-my-god. In front of Ethan.

"So why do we do it?" Ethan asked.

Florence tried to think about it but the words came without reflection.

"Because it's... magical. When it works, in-between the hard stuff? It's fucking magical, son."

He smiled—a smile that looked like paradise.

"I think you just saved my Christmas, Mom," he said. Kissed her on her cheek. "Do you want me to save yours?"

Florence nodded.

"Is there a gift for Will there?" Ethan pointed at the packages. Florence shook her head. "There should be."

Florence kissed his cheek.

When he left, she put bows and labels on all the packages.

Then logged into OkCupid.

# Whatever You Do, Don't
# Text Her

THURSDAY, DECEMBER 20

**Florence Gunn:** Mom? Have you heard from Saryang Park lately?

*Martha Gunn:* No. What happened? Oh my god, Florence, did you have a fight with Dr. Park again?

**Florence Gunn:** No, no. She just had… a lot going on and I was wondering if she was ok.

*Martha Gunn:* Ask her? Text her yourself? Is it better if I text? Do you want me to text her and tell her you're worried about her?

**Florence Gunn:** No! Absolutely not! I fucking forbid it.

*Martha Gunn:* Well, but now I'm worried about her.

**Florence Gunn:** Mom, I swear to you, if you text Saryang, I will disinherit and disown you.

*Martha Gunn:* Florence, respect your elders.

**Florence Gunn:** And put you in the worst, cheapest nursing home I can find. Before you have Alzheimer's. So that you're aware of your suffering.

*Martha Gunn:* Florence, did you break up with that Will person you never tell me anything about?

**Florence Gunn:** No! Stop texting me! And don't text Saryang!

---

## Unnoticed



---

Did he notice what she had done?

No.

He didn't notice. Or, if he didn't, he didn't text.

Florence composed a dozen texts that she didn't send.

*"Will, I don't know what to apologize for—but I'm sorry for everything."*

Fuck, why? No. What did she do wrong?

*"Check OKC."*

No.

That felt... well, she couldn't explain it. It just felt wrong.

Saryang Park didn't call or text either, which made Florence assume she was no longer cleaning her house. Will's ex-house. Fuck. She had been cleaning Will's ex-house for almost as long as she had been fucking him. What sort of joke, message from the universe was that?

She asked Santokh.

"Are you asking me to be your guru?" Santokh teased. "I don't know, Florence. You get mad if I tell you things were meant to be. Or everything happens for a reason."

Florence got mad, and Santokh laughed. Santokh went back to the mop and Florence went back to composing texts to Will in her head while pretending to dust computer screens and desks.

*"I love you, Will and I miss you."*

That hurt her pride.

Enough that she wouldn't send it?

Her stomach churning with fear, her heart pounding, she took out her phone and typed the eight words.

Pressed send with a shaking finger.

She noticed Santokh looking at her from the bank lobby. Stuck out her tongue at her.

Santokh laughed, and Florence, suddenly, felt better. Lighter.

She remembered holding Santokh, in this bank, in her arms, a couple of weeks ago, and she remembered the moment when Santokh decided not to suffer.

So Florence took a deep breath.

*Will. I love you. I miss you.*

And decided not to suffer.

She stood there with the feeling... she didn't know how to put it into words. It was just... not bliss. Not happiness. It wasn't like it was suddenly ok that Will hadn't been in touch all week or that going to that house was not a big deal or that Saryang Park's voice, "What the fuck are you doing Will, making out with my cleaning lady? OMFG, are you fucking my cleaning lady? What's wrong with you, Will?" wasn't hurtful. All of that mattered, hurt.

But Florence was...

Not blissful... but... tranquil.

She felt tranquil.

She smiled.

"This has nothing to do with your cult practices," she

told Santokh when they reconvened in the janitorial room and Santokh, unprompted and silent, hugged and kissed her.

Santokh laughed.

________________________________

## The Plot Thickens
### SUNDAY, DECEMBER 23
________________________________


*Uttamroop*: Hey, Santokh invited me over to your house for Christmas Day dinner. I just wanted to check that it was really ok with you?

**Florence Gunn:** For sure. I'm happy to hear from you and I'd love to have you. Um—are you sure you want to be there?

*Uttamroop*: Honestly? I'd rather be in my apartment alone contemplating suicide. I love Santokh, you know. I can't stand her wife. And you... Well, it's hard for me to be around you, Florence. But Santokh was very insistent. Apparently it has something to do with not inviting me to her wedding and feeling bad about it.

**Florence Gunn:** Ok, I know I can be a bitch sometimes, but seriously? I really like you. I liked working with you. You're one of Santokh's least weird cult friends! Is it that I make fun of the cult? I mean, yoga? It's just this thing I have with Santokh. She doesn't mind, much. I'm sorry if it offends you.

*Uttamroop*: It's nothing you've done or said. Actually, it's something I ought to explain to you. Sometime. And I will, ok?

**Florence Gunn:** Ok. I like you, Uttamroop, and I'd love to have you over for Christmas. I should warn you, my mother will be there.

*Uttamroop*: Is she going to teach me how to load the dishwasher properly?

**Florence Gunn:** She might also lecture you on the proper use of utensils.

*Uttamroop*: I'll just chant 'Wahe Guru' under my breath a lot.

**Florence Gunn:** No, do it out loud. It will unsettle her and make for a more interesting night.

*Uttamroop*: You are sort of a bitch.

**Florence Gunn:** Yup.

*Uttamroop*: Will anyone else be there?

**Florence Gunn:** My three boys. Santokh and her jealous wife. My insane mother. You and me. But no presents.

*Uttamroop*: Wine?

**Florence Gunn:** Juice? Or, like, cake or fruit or something?

*Uttamroop:* Right. Ok. Thanks. I'll see you at Christmas.

**Florence Gunn:** Looking forward to it.

*Uttamroop:* I'm not sure I am. But, Florence? You're... you're not a fucking bitch. You're ok.

**Florence Gunn:** LOL. Damn me with faint praise and call me 'quite nice,' why don't you? See you on Christmas, and good luck surviving my mother and Santokh's crazy-ass wife.

## It's About Boundaries
### SUNDAY, DECEMBER 23

Florence texted Santokh as soon as she was finished texting with Uttamroop.

"Anything I should know?" she asked.

"I'm asserting myself. My boundaries," Santokh typed back. "It's ok that I invited her?"

"Of course," Florence wrote. "I can't believe she's doing that for you."

"Michelle?"

"Uttamroop."

Santokh didn't text back. And for the first time, Florence thought that, maybe, there was something in Michelle's jealousy of the beautiful student.

$$\overline{\phantom{xxxxxxxxxxxxxxxx}}$$

# Anyone Else Coming?
## TUESDAY, DECEMBER 25

Christmas Day came quickly.

David texted her in the morning, sober, contrite, humble. Asked to see the kids, and Isaac was beside her when the text came and read it, and looked at her with such expectant eyes, Florence couldn't hesitate.

He came at noon, with a Pointsettia and a box of Bernard Callebaut chocolate-covered liquor cherries for Florence and three iTunes gift cards for the boys.

"You can't afford this," Florence wanted to say. But she didn't. Accepted the gifts with gratitude.

Did not open the chocolates. She did not want to share them with him. She hoped he understood why—she didn't say anything about that either.

She watched his tense, exhausted body, and she watched her children's complicated interplay of happiness and pain— even Ethan sat in the living room with the man who had been his father, the only father he had known, for five years.

They loved him.

He stayed an hour. Florence walked him to his car.

"How do you not hate me, Florence?" he asked before he got in. It was, she knew, an apology for October.

"Hate is hard work," she said.

She wanted to know. So she asked.

"On and off," he said. Which meant no. His hands shook. Florence knew he was going to drive to a bar. Or liquor store.

She kissed a shaking hand.

"Your children love you very much," she said. The first year after she left him, she'd tell him she loved him very much too. But then she realized she no longer did, not most of the time, so she stopped saying it.

He kissed her cheek.

Got into the car and drove away.

Florence walked back to the house cold. But... still tranquil. There was nothing she could do about David either. Or rather—she had done what she could do, what she needed to do, ten years ago.

She didn't really think about Will, but was aware that he was at the back of her head... all around her... anyway.

Then, suddenly, roughly, an image of Will and David, side by side, in a pub, on Christmas Day, neither with his kids and family, a row of glasses... the wave of nausea that hit her bent her over and she had to grab onto the porch railing to steady herself.

*Pull yourself together, Florence.*

A stern command.

She walked into the house chasing the tranquility of the last few days. Finally found it when Martha arrived, carting a bag of presents and two pies, sandwiched between Santokh and Michelle, one carrying a slow cooker filled with Tofurkey, the other a casserole dish with Celebration Dhal.

Uttamroop trailed a few steps behind the trio, looking awkward.

"I'm here," she said to Florence. "Are you still sure..."

"Of course, idiot," Florence said, pulling her into the house. She didn't think they were at a hugging and kissing stage, but Uttamroop fell into her arms and gave a sigh. Florence patted her a little awkwardly.

"Are you crying?" she whispered.

"I am an idiot," Uttamroop whispered back. "Bathroom?"

Florence pointed her down the trailer hallway. Turned her attention to her mother.

"They came to pick me up," Martha told Florence. "Do you think they did it because they think I'm old? And should have my driver's license taken away?"

Santokh gurgled.

"We just wanted to," Michelle said. Exasperated already.

"Hard car ride?" Florence asked. Took the Tofurkey from Michelle's hands and kissed her cheek. "Nice sari."

"No good deed goes unpunished," Michelle murmured. "Well, if she's going to appropriate and misrepresent part of my culture with a turban, I'm fucking going to represent it in a sari."

Florence laughed.

"We just wanted to save you the trip, Martha," Santokh was saying, following Martha into the kitchen. "Why drive when you can be chauffeured? Merry Christmas."

"Lesbians are thoughtful like that," Martha said. "So I've heard."

Florence almost died, and Santokh laughed so hard she had to excuse herself and go to the bathroom. "I'm going to pee my pants," she said.

Michelle looked mildly offended but decided to get over it.

The boys had already set the table, but Martha busied herself re-arranging it. Michelle took the bird out of the oven.

"Meat," she said happily. "Oh, meat."

"Bad Hindu," Florence scolded.

Michelle frowned. "It's not me. It's her."

Florence laughed.

"Is she going to let you eat flesh at Christmas?" Florence whispered into her ear. Michelle sighed. Shook her head. Florence ripped off a leg. "Fuck. Overcooked. Here. Go into my bedroom. Eat."

Michelle laughed. Took a bite. Closed her eyes. But put the leg back.

"We all make sacrifices for love, right?" she said. "I wouldn't cook beef for her. And..." She reached for another piece of meat. But didn't pick it up. "But can you, when you eat it, say how it's overcooked and not very good? It will make me feel better."

Florence laughed.

"I'm pretty sure Martha will take care of that, without prompting," she said. "Ok, people! Take your seats!"

The herding, as always, was chaotic, but Florence had everyone, except for Martha who was butchering the roasted turkey and calling it carving, and Santokh and Uttamroop, neither of whom had come back from her trip to the bathroom, sitting down at the table when the doorbell rang.

"I'll get it!" Santokh called from the hallway.

"Fedex? UPS? More presents?" Isaac asked.

"Maybe it's carollers," Martha said. "Although this isn't the kind of neighbourhood that gets carollers, is it, Florence? Too many brown people," she said to Michelle. Who stared at her with such a gorgeous expression of disbelief, Florence kissed her and loved her.

"Florence."

Santokh was standing in the archway that separated the kitchen from the living room, her arm around Uttamroop. Who looked pale, if a woman with skin that dark could look pale. But also... well, not happy. But cultishly tranquil, Florence thought with a wicked grin. She looked at them both with love too. She was so lucky. So fucking lucky.

Her people. Her family.

"Stop mauling my wife, and go to the door," Santokh said.

"Your Christmas present is here," Uttamroop added. Voice a little funny.

"Fedex or UPS?" Isaac repeated.

Santokh smiled. And so, Florence knew.

Will was standing in shadow of the open door. Wearing a ski jacket and big boots, and a goofy little toque.

"Merry Christmas," she said.

"Merry Christmas," he said. "Jesus. I didn't think. You're sitting down to Christmas dinner."

"We are," she said. Reached for his hands, still hidden in giant gloves. "Come join us."

He looked uncertain, then as if he thought it was a bad idea, then as if he had won the lottery.

Uttamroop was still standing in the little archway that separated the kitchen from the mobile home hallway and entryway, waiting for them.

Will paused.

"Um." He looked at her. Then Florence. "We've had our moment at the door already... I guess it's fucking fitting you already know each other. Which one of us should do the introductions?"

Florence stared from one to the other.

"He knows me as Rosie," Uttamroop said. And Florence's jaw dropped. And then she laughed. And laughed and laughed and laughed.

And hugged Will and Rosie. And laughed so hard, she had to excuse herself and run to the bathroom so she wouldn't be sitting down to Christmas dinner with wet pants.

When she came back into the kitchen, everyone was crowded around the table, Will sandwiched between Uttamroop—Rosie—and Michelle, and opposite Martha.

"Nice of you to finally join us, honey," Martha said. "Any more unexpected guests coming?"

"Only if you invited one of your boys, Mom," Florence said, squeezing in between Ethan and Santokh.

"People in glass houses, Florence," Martha said. "I, however, am thrilled. I finally get to meet the man my daughter has been sneaking off to have sex with for the past year. Of course, I don't know for sure if you are the one. Or the only one. Because she never tells me anything." She looked at him critically. "You're decently good looking, I must say. And the size of your hands bodes well for..." she dropped her eyes low... "other things."

Florence's cheeks burned and she was afraid to look at Will, so she looked at Michelle instead, then Uttamroop. Michelle was biting her lips hard, also not looking at Will. But, Florence saw her put a hand on his hand and squeeze it, at the same time as Uttamroop—she'd have to get used to calling her Rosie... or did she prefer Uttamroop? Goddamn cultist people with double names—reached for his other one. Will smiled awkwardly at Martha. Florence saw it and glowed with affection for him. Rosie. Michelle. Santokh. Her sons. For the world.

Even for her obnoxious mother.

"If she asks the boys what they think of him, I might need to divorce her," Florence whispered into Santokh's ear.

"More potatoes, Martha?" Santokh responded.

"Grandma, here, have some dhal. You have to eat it to prove you're not a racist homophobe," Ethan said at the same time.

And, with her friends and children working together to keep her mother chewing and quiet, Florence got through the dinner without much more embarrassment.

And when she managed to look up from her plate, and saw Will looking at her, suppressed laughter in the curve of his lips as Santokh or one of her kids offered Martha more mashed potatoes, it was worth any amount of embarrassment.

That look was love, fuck it was love.

And it was magical.

It was bliss.

And having Uttam-Rosie there was... it felt right. It felt good. Even when Michelle gave her the occasional harsh look when she and Santokh fell into some yoga jargon or shared a private joke.

"I'm going to call you Uttam-Rosie," Florence told her halfway through the meal. "You already have two names. You can have a third one for me."

"You're so weird, Florence," Uttam-Rosie said.

Will, Florence thought, was performing extremely well. He was natural with Uttam-Rosie, and polite with Santokh and Michelle and the boys, and tolerant of her mother. He obeyed meekly as Martha took charge of the post-dinner clean-up. Not trusted to scrape the plates or load the dishwasher, he swept the floor while Florence, Santokh, and Michelle took care of the leftovers and the boys and Uttam-Rosie were put in charge of the dishes.

Florence watched him, out of the corner of her eyes, watching her, watching the scenario.

And she loved.

Oh-god, she loved him. And she had so many things to say to him she didn't know where to start, and she couldn't endure any more silence...

And so, when he sidled up behind her, as she was putting the last margarine container masquerading as Tupperware into the fridge, and whispered, "What's next on the schedule?" she whispered back, "A walk in the snow?"

"With everyone?" he asked. Not with horror, exactly, but with concern.

Florence laughed.

"No, we've all had enough of my mother by now," she said. "Now we usually watch a Christmas movie, with the volume turned up really high."

"That's so sweet," Will said. "What movie? *It's A Wonderful Life?*"

"*Die Hard*," Florence said. "I have three mostly-teenage boys, remember?" And Will moved in towards her, and she braced herself for a kiss to end all kisses—or rather to begin them, to raise the bar on them—when Martha walked back into the kitchen.

"Florence, I think you and your..." she paused, searching for a word... "man..." she said finally... "should go for a walk. I have just been given a lecture by the lesbians about embarrassing you in front of your..." she paused... "lover," she said, and Florence could tell that she really liked saying the word even though it also embarrassed her, "and so I thought I would come and embarrass you one more time. But also, make leaving us to watch that awful movie without you easier."

"Thank you, Mom," Florence said in a strangled voice.

"Thank you, Martha," Will said.

"You're welcome," Martha said. Graciously. And Florence felt so much laughter gag her throat her knees went weak. "I am aware of my role in this play."

And she strode out.

"Oh-my-fucking-god," Will said. "Is she for real? Was she... is she... an actress?"

"At heart," Florence agreed.

They bundled up in their winter things—Will readjusting her toque after she put it on and wrapping her scarf around her throat, touching the bare skin of her neck before covering it, Florence not wanting to let go of his hands before they disappeared into their big gloves—and went out into crisp December night.

---

# Frostbite



---

It was cold and the air bit her cheeks, but Florence felt hot. Things needed to be said, she knew. Questions asked? Explanations offered? But the hundreds of things she needed to say to Will in the kitchen had all disappeared. All that mattered was that he was beside her. Footsteps crunching in the snow. Beside her. Beside her.

Beside her!

Will maybe felt the same way, because he said nothing either. They walked in silence for five minutes. Ten more. Time didn't matter—the gentle pressure of his hand around hers, through the thick winter glove, did.

"I got your Christmas present," he said finally. Stopping and leaning into the space between her toque and scarf and kissing one exposed, tingling cheek then the other. "Thank you. So very much."

"You're very... very welcome," she said, drinking in the kisses through her skin.

"Do you want to know if I disabled mine?" he asked. Still dropping kisses on her cheeks. Then eyes.

"No," she said. She wanted to add—*it wasn't a tit-for-tat*

*gesture, it wasn't a... it was what you wanted, a gift for you, I don't need, want anything back.* But she didn't. And he understood and pushed her scarf further below her mouth and found it.

And the kiss to end all kisses—the kiss to raise the bar on all future kisses—came.

"Oh-my-fucking-god, Florence, it's minus 30 degrees out!" Will groaned when the kiss broke.

She moved back to his lips.

"Why does that matter?" she murmured, chewing them.

"My penis will fall off." Will sighed. Pulled off her scarf and then suddenly, tightened it until she gasped before he released it again. "And you'll get frostbite on your ass. Your nipples."

"We are not," she said, kissing his chin, and then unzipping his ski jacket so that she could kiss his neck, "going to have sex. Here."

"We're not," he agreed. "There's too much light. We need to go into an alley."

"Will!" she exclaimed as he pulled her into the shadows.

"Fuck, Florence, if you don't want to, you have to stop kissing me," he said. She didn't. So he pulled her into the alley, and pressed her against a rickety garage door, and her legs were around his waist, his teeth on her neck—and then, he tightened the scarf again, fuck—and the cold was crazy and insane and it was all very awkward, to be honest, but also hot, and he was so excited, it didn't last very long.

"I've missed you," he said, pulling out, and pulling her pants up and her jacket down.

"I noticed," she smiled. Then laughed as she watched him drop to his knees.

"I'm not hungry," he said as he crawled around and felt up the ground. "I was selfish and I am completely full and sated for the moment. I will have dessert and give you pleasure later. I'm looking for the fucking condom wrapper. And my gloves. So don't get your hopes up."

She laughed. Dropped to the ground to help him, and found his gloves. But not the wrapper.

"We can just leave it," she said.

"You have no manners," he said. "I'd really expect more from a professional janitor."

And it didn't feel like a sting, and Florence didn't feel defensive, and she laughed and felt so light. And loved.

They gave up on finding the wrapper—"Sorry, Florence's neighbours," Will said. "It wasn't the damn kids, by the way. It was their parents!"—and resumed their walk, hand in hand.

But not in silence.

"Things need to be said?" Will said. Asked. Florence nodded. "Who first?"

"Me," Florence said. Swallowed. Decided to start with something easy. "I know you know I didn't take you to that house on purpose—that I didn't know. So I know I don't have to apologize. But I'm sorry I... however inadvertently... created that. That situation, I mean."

He kissed her.

"I'm sorry I didn't tell you as soon as we pulled up in front of the house where we were. And that I shouldn't go in," he said.

Florence kissed him.

"I'm sorry I didn't wait for you outside the house," she said.

"Oh, god," he said. "No, don't fucking apologize for that. We screamed at each other for two hours. Until Ranveer—that's her fiancé—and his parents and the kids came. And then, you should have seen it, Florence—your mother would have been so proud—we were like, 'Game

Face On.' And I was the well-behaved ex-husband who happened to drop in to pick something up, so very nice to meet you, Mr. and Mrs. Singh, have a nice night. I even shook fucking Ranveer's hand."

"Then why didn't you text me? Get back to me?" Florence asked. That, she decided, needed to be asked. If not answered.

And maybe Will agreed because he stayed silent for a long time.

"Because I wasn't finished being angry with Amanda yet," he said finally. "Does that make any sense? We resumed the fight the next day. She..." he paused... "she had a right to be angry that I was in *her* house. Without her permission. And I had... there were so many things that I had a right to be angry about. That we never talked about before."

Florence nodded. None of those things needed to be said. He agreed. And there was more silence.

"Amanda—Saryang," he corrected himself, "do you know, Florence, she never told me she was going back to her birth name? I guess it makes sense. After she dropped my last name... that she might use the opportunity to reclaim her full birth name. Anyway. Saryang would also like to apologize to you." He stopped walking and slipped off his gloves. Patted his jacket pockets, pulled out a thick envelope.

"There's a letter in there," he said. "Acknowledging..."

*"Oh-my-fucking-god, Will are you fucking my cleaning lady? What's wrong with you?"*

...his voice stalled, and Florence kissed him, to show him that he didn't need to say much more...

"...well, I guess everything that she felt she needed to

say. And apologizing. And asking you to continue to work for her. If you feel comfortable doing that."

"Do you feel comfortable with me doing that?" Florence asked.

Will swallowed and she heard the saliva travel down his throat at glacial speed.

"Not one hundred per cent," he admitted. "But... it's nobody's decision but yours, Florence."

And she kissed him so fucking hard, they ended up falling onto the front lawn of the house they were passing, right at the feet of an inflatable reindeer.

"We are not having sex here," Florence whispered to Will as he rolled on top of her.

"We're not," he agreed. Regretful. "But we're going to lie here for a few minutes while I fantasize."

They got up slowly. Resumed the walk. Florence now remembered the hundred things—well, they were only one thing, really, with a hundred parts—she wanted to say. But didn't know how to begin.

Which was ok, because Will wasn't done yet.

"There is also," he said, "an invitation in that envelope. From Aman—Saryang. To her wedding. Her and Ranveer's wedding."

"Oh."

"I had told her—I told her there was no need for that," Will said. "Because I was going to bring you, to the wedding, as my plus one."

"Oh."

"But she said... she said you were more likely to come if she invited you. Than if I did."

Florence laughed. Fucking Mrs. Doctor. She was right.

"Do you really want me to come with you to your ex-wife's second wedding?"

"Florence, there is nothing I want to do less than go to

my ex-wife's second wedding," Will said. "It will be awkward and embarrassing and probably horribly awful. It will make me long to be back in your house at Christmas, having Rosie of all people open the door, and then listening to your mother pontificate about lesbians, brown people, and the size of my penis. Having you there with me will probably make it even more awkward and embarrassing and horribly awful."

He paused.

"But yes. Jesus, Florence, yes. I want you there."

"Why?" She didn't mean to ask. She meant to say yes. She meant to give him an unconditional yes.

Instead: "Why?"

"Because that's the sort of thing that people," he stopped and kissed her, "in committed, loving relationships do with each other. For each other. They endure awkward family events."

And then Florence understood why she asked the "Why."

And kissed him.

And said, "Yes."

No Promises, But Vows,
Of Sorts



"We will practice with other awkward family encounters first," Will promised. "You need to meet my kids. And I'd like you to meet my sponsor. Niko. He's so important to me, I need you to know him. And... like, you and Rosie and I should... get a coffee. Something. I don't want it to be weird. I want the two of you to like each other."

"It will be weird, Will," Florence said. She wondered if she should tell him about the Santokh-Uttamroop-Michelle triangle. Share with him her speculations that Uttam-Rosie was falling in love with Santokh... and Santokh with her. Which would make everything more weird. But that was life. Weird. Awkward.

Magical.

She decided not to mention any of that. Not now. There were more pressing things.

They had to have one more conversation—the hundred things that were one thing that Florence carried inside her— and even though she no longer wanted to do it, because she loved and felt loved and was safe and not just tranquil but blissful, Florence made herself talk.

About all the things she was afraid of and didn't want.

Niko, Rosie—she was happy to meet. Well, in Uttam-Rosie's case, to re-meet on different terms.

His kids? The idea of meeting his kids? It fucking terrified her.

She made herself talk about the spectre of a blended family that haunted her. About how she didn't want to ever —she loved him so much, now, she was sure, she knew, she would love him as much, more in the future, but she did not want to, ever—to live together. Much less marry. Be a stepmother, or even a mother figure to his children. Bring him into her children's life as a father figure.

"They already have one, you know," she said. "However broken he is."

She talked about David. Her responsibility towards him. "I had children with him. They are his... and it is so complicated, Will." He listened.

Her ongoing fear. Jonathan. David. Will. What was wrong with her that all of her life's great loves had this awful demon in common?

"I am one of your life's great loves?" Will whispered. And enveloped her in his arms and covered her face with kisses. Got wool bits from her toque in his mouth and tried to rub them off on her parka.

He told her he wouldn't make promises he couldn't keep, that she wouldn't believe he could keep.

"But I fucking fight so hard, Florence," he said. "Seven years now. Before that night—almost ten. I was lucky, Florence. I caught myself early—Amanda helped me, made me catch myself early. And I work so fucking hard."

That, she believed. She rested her head against his chest and felt his heart beating through the down of the ski jacket.

She was out of words. But not out of feelings.

"I'm scared," she said. "I'm so scared."

He held her tight.

"Me too," he said. "One day at a time. Right?"

She smiled.

"One awkward family encounter at a time," he said.

She laughed.

"One text at a time," she said. Half-joking, half-serious.

"One text at a time," he agreed.

It sounded like a vow.

---



*Will Ornot*: Happy New Year's, Songbird. I love you.

**Florence Gunn:** Happy New Year's, lover. To many, many more.

THE END
THE BEGINNING

---

Thank you for reading *Text Me, Cupid*! If you enjoyed the story, please consider leaving a review for it with your favourite bookseller and on GoodReads.

**MORE! IS THERE MORE?**

Turn the page for bonus content: "25 Years Later" and "Awkward Cupid"—the story of Saryang Park's wedding.

To find out what's coming next from M. Jane Colette and to receive a **FREE** copy of *Taste Me: The Thinking Woman's Erotica*—a gift available exclusively to M. Jane Colette's newsletter subscribers—ask her to send you love letters:

**YES! MY LIFE NEEDS MORE LOVE LETTERS!**
**mjanecolette.com/loveletters**

# BONUS: 25 Years Later
## DECEMBER 2042 OR THEREABOUTS

The story you've just read takes place, in my mind, between Christmas 2017 and Christmas 2018—very much in the "here and now." But the happy ending I envision for Will and Florence—I want it to last for decades.

It's not going to be easy. She's always going to be a little prickly and defensive. He's always going to have his demons. They're both, always, going to be a little bit broken. If you've gone through any trauma yourself, you know this. You do get better. But that broken part of you, and the coping strategies you evolve to protect it—it never goes away.

Still. I want you to know—they're going to make it. Their happily-ever-after isn't conventional. It doesn't include a wedding cake. It's full of awkward family encounters (one of the most awkward of which—Will and Florence at Amanda and Ranveer's wedding—follows). It has tears and misunderstandings and even a few "is this the end?" fights. But it's still pretty amazing. And the sex just keeps on getting better. ("You're welcome, dear. It's in the genes," Martha tells Florence once. Florence shudders. "Another thing to put in the 'Things I didn't want to know about my mother' file," she tells Santokh later.)

Florence and Amanda become almost-friends. Not total friends, because, well, I may write fiction, but I like it to be believable. They are, at the core, very much alike: strong, stubborn, sensual. Florence may not be Amanda's clone physically, but Will definitely has a type—he likes his women just a wee bit pugnacious.

Florence does stop cleaning Amanda's house. First, she passes the job on to Santokh. But even that's too close, so Amanda/Saryang Park has to find another cleaner. She goes through a few of them before Martha finds her someone sufficiently pliable. But Florence steps in every once in a while to rein Saryang in and remind her that clients are just as replaceable—perhaps even more so—as cleaners.

Florence's boys don't mind Will. They don't love him or adopt him as their new father—they have a father of their own, however flawed—but they don't mind him. After his eighteenth birthday, Ethan sits Will down for a talk, and tells him that so long as Will makes Florence happy, her sons are happy. "But if you ever hurt her, we will beat the shit out of you. I don't care how often you box and work out—there's three of us, and we will be angrier."

Will never tells Florence about that talk.

Florence does eventually tell Ethan about Jonathan—his biological father. Ethan googles him and stalks him on Facebook for a while. But he never reaches out and makes himself known to his sperm donor. He does, however, go to Jonathan's funeral.

Florence doesn't.

Will and David do meet, formally. It's as awkward as you might imagine.

And Will does go with Florence, and the boys, to

David's funeral. And that's much less awkward than you might imagine.

Jonathan and David die in the same year, six months apart. Florence turns 50 that year, and the events hit her hard. She pulls away from Will, just as he is planning to put cohabitation on the table. Again.

Florence never changes her mind about having a blended family. She likes Will's kids—she has a particular affinity with Matthew, because she knows how to raise boys. Polly scares the shit out of her—but Amanda knows how to handle her daughter. Matthew—well, he's a challenge for Mrs. Dr. Amanda comes to Florence for advice on what to do with the sullen male teen all the time. Florence helps. But she prefers to keep Will's kids at a distance. She stays aware, always, that she used to be paid to clean their rooms and fought with their mother over the mess they left under their beds. And, she has three children of her own. She doesn't want to be anybody's stepmother.

By the way, much to Martha's relief, none of her grandsons becomes a drug addict, let alone dies from an overdose. Ethan trains as a welder and somewhere along the way discovers that he's a damn shrewd business man. He makes a fortune in something to do with cricket protein. Sammy quits high school and gets a job up north on the oil rigs for a few years. Dances a little with coke, but shakes himself clean with a little help from his older brother—they never tell Florence—and starts working with Ethan in his welding business, where he discovers his inner artist. He starts doing amazing things with metal and fire, gets his high school diploma equivalent and goes on to art college—drops out after a year, because the art college is determined to turn him into an art *professor*—and slowly takes over Karma Klean from Florence and Santokh, while making his art.

He's mostly happy, although he continues to have

terrible taste in men. Martha, by the way, is sure that it was wearing a dress at Santokh's wedding that made him gay, and the family gave up trying to argue her out of that viewpoint years ago.

Isaac turns into a total hippie and moves to the Haida Gwaii islands to hunt, fish, and exploit tourists. He ends up with a coterie of lovers and provides Florence with her only grandchildren. Florence and Will go up to visit him on the Haida Gwaii every year. Will wants to buy a vacation house up there for them—Florence won't let him. As a compromise, he buys a Mercedes Benz camper van and insists on calling it their joint property. She lets him, reluctantly.

Will's son becomes a lawyer and his daughter becomes a dentist. Their grandparents are very happy—until Matthew has a spiritual awakening in Peru, quits his law practice, and reinvents himself as an uncertified psychotherapist, energy healer, and psilocybin advocate.

Will never particularly takes to Ranveer or vice-versa, but after a few years, the family does manage to spend Christmas Day together. It's... awkward.

Rosie/Uttamroop and Florence do become really, really good friends. So good, Will is jealous.

Will finally convinces Florence to live with him as they're both nearing sixty. It's a hard adjustment for her, and he never really understands just how hard.

When Niko, Will's sponsor, dies, Florence does understand how hard it is for Will. And she keeps him sane—with a lot of help from Rosie.

Florence's mother, Martha dies quite peacefully and in decent shape, mind sharp as ever, on her eighty-third birthday. All of Florence's boys come to the funeral. Isaac brings two of his lovers and four of his children. Amanda, Ranveer, and Will's kids and their partners come as well, as do Santokh, Michelle, and Rosie/Uttamroop.

It's not awkward at all, until the reception, when three of the elderly gentlemen mourners identify themselves to Florence as her mother's long-time lovers... and discover that none of them was Martha's only one.

"See? This is where I get it from," Isaac tells his lovers. "Except I'm honest about it."

Florence is flabbergasted. Will is amused. And then, worried. Who else got those genes? There's a big fight—but they recover.

There are more things I could tell you about Florence, Will, Rosie, and Santokh... but I won't, because I think I might want to write about those bits sometime in the future, and I'd like some of it to be a surprise.

I do want to reassure you that, twenty-five years later, Will and Florence are still going strong. On their last trip to the Haida Gwaii, they get pulled over on the highway by a twenty-something RCMP officer who can't help but notice the Grandpa's unbuttoned jeans and the Grandma's smeared lipstick. The good news: he's too embarrassed to give them a ticket.

And now, I'd like to share with you a peek at Amanda—Saryang Park's—and Ranveer's wedding. Ranveer, by the way, is a really nice guy. Boring as all hell on the surface, but an animal in the bedroom—Amanda also has a type. He doesn't appear in this story much, but Amanda wants me to let you know that Will's digs at Ranveer's penis size are all unfounded and probably racist.

We clear on that? All right. Let's go to a wedding.

# BONUS: Awkward Cupid
## SATURDAY, FEBRUARY 2

"Awkward?" Will asked.

Florence tried not to wince. She loved him. She was here for him. It was hard for him and she needed to bear up, have a stiff upper lip, and...

"Awful," she whispered into his shoulder. "But wow, you look *hawt*."

"You have a total suit fetish," Will murmured as she rose up on her toes and nuzzled his neck. "Anyway. Ow, ouch, Florence, what are you doing?"

"Biting relaxes me."

"It does the opposite for me. And..." He pulled her in closer and, simultaneously, off his neck. "Let's not fuck at my ex-wife's wedding, ok?"

"Like you haven't fantasized about it a hundred times in the past two months." Florence extricated herself from his arms. "Ok. Let's do this, Mr. Ornot. Game face on. Let's watch the gorgeous Mrs. Dr. get married."

"It might be easier if you hated her, you know," Will said, taking Florence's hand.

"It might be easier if you didn't," Florence murmured.

"Come on, babe. Let's go. Nothing could possibly be worse than meeting your kids. And thinking of them as those slobby brats who don't make their beds or know how to use a clothes hamper—and having them hate me on first sight. Is that fair? They seem to quite like Ranveer."

"They've had a chance to get used to him," Will said.

"Are we going to go in there? Come on. If we wait much longer, we'll be the last ones in. And it will look conspicuous. And people will think we were late because we fucked in the vestibule." Florence stood on her tip toes again, and flicked her tongue at Will's ear. "Like, that one, right over there. Look, it even has a curtain."

"Silence, temptress," Will said, but he pulled her in even closer. And disappeared into her throat. Florence purred. But did not pull him behind the curtain into the vestibule. Instead, she led him—or let him lead her, it was a little hard to tell which of the two of them had more initiative or less reluctance—into the hotel's wedding chapel.

---

Will didn't know why Amanda—Saryang—chose to get married in the inconvenient, out-of-Calgary Canmore. Well, perhaps he did—the views of the Rocky Mountains, when he glimpsed them from the large hotel windows, were spectacular. But the sixty-minute drive from the city was treacherous in February, and dangerous at night, which meant most of the guests—including Will, his kids, and Florence—planned to stay at the hotel overnight. Which would have been ok if it meant raucous hotel sex with Florence—they hadn't had hotel sex yet—but he'd have the kids, so... Yes, they'd be in the next room, but the adjoining door would need to be open—Polly already asked for that—and so... maybe cuddling? Or soft sex?

Could Florence have sex without screaming like a banshee?

He didn't know.

Maybe he'd find out tonight?

No. *Shut the fuck up, penis.* Amanda's wedding. Ranveer's hairy arms. He probably had a hairy back. *OMFG, stop thinking about Ranveer naked. What the fuck is wrong with you, Will?*

*Your ex-wife is getting married and you're at her wedding. You're allowed to be weird.*

Will sighed. Searched for Florence's hand.

The ceremony was, at this point, delayed by some forty-five minutes, because the person who was supposed to officiate—some mutual friend of Amanda and Ranveer's that Will did not know and already disliked—was delayed. By ice on the highway between Calgary and Canmore. Of course. Will resented her, resented the weather—resented everything.

"On her way, but delayed," the usher—who was also some friend of Amanda and Ranveer's that Will did not know—how did Amanda amass an entire separate, new life in the past year?—announced several times over the past forty-five minutes.

Forty-five minutes. Spent sitting on the uncomfortable folding chairs in the wedding chapel, surrounded by Amanda's extended family and school friends, his ex-neighbours—an army of people who used to be his people and who now weren't.

Polite smiles and nods, and not too much conversation.

Florence next to him.

Think about Florence.

She squeezed his hand.

"We so should have fucked in the vestibule," she whispered. "Do you think there's still time?"

He put a hand on her thigh and rubbed it through the thin green fabric.

"What's this made of?" he asked, rubbing it some more. "Oooh, I like it. Are you wearing stockings and a garter belt? Tell me there are no panties under there. But no, there's no time. I see distinct preparation for the walk down the aisle."

"Genuine fake silk, baby," Florence said and shifted her body a little towards him, so both her parted legs touched, straddled his knee.

"Woman, stop." His hand slid down her thigh and grasped her knee. But he felt... Well. If he had to be here, in this crowd of ex-friends? At least he was here with the hottest woman imaginable. Who would totally have sex with him in the—he cast his gaze around the room—in that alcove. Behind that pillar. Mmm, under that table?

"Down, Will," Florence whispered.

He shifted uncomfortably.

"Did you ever think you'd be watching your ex-wife walk down the aisle, down to her second happily-ever-after, with an erection?" she gurgled into his ear.

He went flaccid.

"Did you do that on purpose?" he whispered back.

"You're welcome," she said. And then the music started, and the breathless Justice of the Peace almost ran down the aisle, followed by Ranveer—in a tux, but also an orange-peach turban—and his best man, nondescript. Will didn't know him —wouldn't know him if he saw him again. And then Amanda's maid of honour, Tammy—Will knew her, but couldn't for the life of him remember how. She wasn't a close friend— certainly not her best friend. An odd choice for a maid of honour, he thought—but maybe they got closer after their mutual divorces. The maid of honour's strapless dress matched Ranveer's turban—and the tie of the best man— which Will found a bit funny. And finally, Polly and Matthew

—Polly glowing with happiness and throwing flower petals on the ground, Matthew a little stiff and awkward, very serious.

They both waved at him as they walked past. And pointedly did not look at Florence.

He felt a pang of pain and fear and worry.

Maybe it was a bad idea to bring Florence to the wedding.

It was definitely a bad idea to have her *not* meet the kids until the morning of... but she so did not want to do it before.

Maybe coming to the wedding period was a bad idea. Who came to their ex-wife's wedding, anyway?

"Here comes the bride," Florence whispered as the music changed from an innocuous and muted classical hum to the unmistakable Wagnerian bridal chorus.

And there she came. Decked out in white... looking a bit like a bridal figurine from atop a wedding cake. Will found himself wondering about the white dress. At *their* wedding, she wore a traditional Korean outfit, colourful but—well, unflattering, he had thought so even then. And thought it was peculiar choice, given her very loose relationship with her parents' home country. She did not speak Korean. Did not, ever, cook Korean food. Seemed a little embarrassed by her parents' Korean friends. Habits.

She started taking Korean lessons two or three years ago. Trying to teach the kids, too. What happened?

Was it Ranveer and his much closer, intimate relationship to his parents'—and his own—culture?

He must have been frowning, because Amanda—Saryang—stopped her walk down the aisle beside him.

"I'm so glad you're here," she said. And hugged him. And then reached for Florence. "Florence. Thank you so much for coming."

As the two women embraced across his body, Will felt... really weird. Like he was living in a *Twilight Zone* episode or a Dan Savage column.

So fucking civilized, twenty-first century marriage and divorce. He wondered if he would have to congratulate Ranveer on marrying his ex-wife. Maybe, while everyone mobbed the wedding party—in this case, very small—after the ceremony to offer their congratulations, he and Florence could find that vestibule. Or a washroom.

Or a kitchen. He'd never had sex in a hotel kitchen. What would that be like?

"Down boy," Florence whispered into his ear as they sat down. He slid a hand down her thigh... then between her legs.

It was awkward, but it could have been worse, and there were plenty of funny moments, and on the whole, Florence didn't regret that she had come until they walked into the banquet hall where dinner would be served, and found out that she and Will were sitting at the same table as the wedding party.

"What the fuck?" she said. Not quietly.

"Jesus," Will groaned. "See, at times like this, a normal person would say, 'I need a drink. Or ten.'"

"Let's go fuck," Florence said. "Seriously. There's no way I'm getting through dinner at a table with your kids without having an orgasm first."

But the usher was leading them to the table, and there they were. Saryang's maid of honour and Ranveer's best man were already sitting down. She introduced herself as Tammy. The name fit. He mumbled his name a few times before Florence realized it was John. For some reason, she found this hilarious.

"Do you know, I don't think I've ever met anyone named John before," she said. "Please tell me your last name is Smith."

He flushed. It was and she loved it and laughed, and he didn't like the joke, which, granted, wasn't very funny. But still. It was conversation. She was trying.

"Daddy!" And Polly was in Will's arms. Matthew beside him. They sat down, beside Will, but too close to Florence. She let them have Will's attention and turned to John, who was on her other side.

"So how do you know Ranveer?" she made herself ask. Listened to a mumbled, barely audible account of graduate school. Which seemed to bore John to tell to her. "And do the two of you know each other?" she asked, looking over at Tammy. "Or was today the first encounter?"

They both mumbled something at the same time that might have been "First time" or "Forever"—they were both completely inaudible. Then they looked at each other and looked away.

Florence wondered how someone as dynamic and driven and—well, loud and alive—as Saryang Park ended up with such a milquetoast friend and maid of honour as Tammy. The woman was probably a dental hygienist, Florence thought. Or a dentist, she corrected her inadvertently sexist thought. Saryang probably did not hang out with dental hygienists. Not her social class.

She was going to ask Tammy what she did for a living, but then she realized she'd have to reciprocate the information, and she wasn't sure how she felt about being the quaint cleaning lady at the table of doctors, professors, bankers, and dentists, so she didn't.

And then Saryang, glowing and beaming, and Ranveer,

flushed and happy, came to join them, and Saryang sat down next to her kids, and Ranveer between his new bride and Tammy, and as dinner was served, the need for conversation flagged temporarily.

Florence uttered a sigh of relief and turned her attention to her salad.

---

Polly was happy, Matthew was excited and tried not to show it, Amanda and Ranveer were fucking oozing with happiness, and Will had no idea how he felt. Florence seemed to be ok, chatting with the bland man on her right.

"His name is John Smith, really," she whispered into his ear at some point. He squeezed her hand, then her thigh.

If his kids hadn't been at the table, he would have slid his hand between her legs and treated her to a... little something. But they were, so he didn't.

Instead, he listened to Polly, and tried not to watch Amanda—Saryang—and Ranveer kiss. And was very grateful that there were no speeches.

Between dinner and dessert, Amanda's parents came over to their table to torment the children. Also to torment Will—by looking at him but not saying anything, and very carefully not looking at Florence—but whispering, very loudly, to Amanda that it really was excessive to have Will bring some stranger to the wedding.

Will's jaw tensed and he crushed Florence's fingers and opened his mouth and was about to...

"For fuck's sake, Mother, what's wrong with you?" Amanda's voice was not a loud whisper—it was just loud. "What sort of fake etiquette is he violating by bringing his new partner to his ex-partner's wedding to her new partner?"

And Will remembered why he had loved Amanda.

"Will?" Florence whispered. "You're breaking my fingers."

"Sorry." He kissed her hand. Caught, out of the corner of his eye, a grimace on Matthew's face. Sighed.

"I'm so sorry," Amanda said to Florence after her parents walked away.

"You're so good at apologizing now, Saryang," Florence said and winked. The two women laughed.

"It's nice that the two of you get along," Tammy, the maid of honour, said. Will smiled. He had always thought she was a rather stupid, boring woman, but in this moment, he liked her.

The moment was very brief.

"Although it is very odd. Isn't it? That Will ended up dating your cleaning lady? I mean, what are the odds?"

Will was afraid to look at Florence. There. It was said. Someone pointed out the elephant in the room. Tammy's voice wasn't malignant or acidic. She didn't speak to hurt—Will accepted that. But... he was sure... Florence... he remembered Valentine's Day, and the scene in Aman—Saryang's—house before Christmas and...

"I know, hey?" Florence said. Laughed. "Did Saryang tell you how it all happened? So my mother's former business partner was her original cleaner. And after Will moved out—not immediately, right? A few months later? Anyway, he asked Karla to clean his apartment."

"And I totally freaked out," Amanda said.

"Well, I don't know anything about that," Florence continued. "But I suppose you did. It would be like you to freak out about that."

"I totally did," Amanda said. "You should have heard me. Or read me. Do you still have those texts, Will?"

Will shook his head. A little dumbfounded. He didn't understand women. At all. He listened as Florence and Aman—fuck, he really had to learn to call her Saryang, although she didn't insist, but still, that was the name she was using now, and maybe it would be easier to think of Amanda as the woman from his past and Saryang as the woman in his present?—he listened as Florence and Saryang recited, in turn, the evolution of their relationship. The hiring, the notes, the firing.

Florence downplaying the messy children's rooms a little—and up-playing the hair in the shower drain and the dirty dishes on the counter. Saryang ruefully confessing she never took her shoes off in the house—"So very un-Korean of me," she laughed—until Florence started riding her about it.

"And then one day Will offered to come help me do my Sunday work so we'd have more time to hang, and guess where I took him? Oh-my-god, Tammy, you should have seen the look on his face when we pulled in front of that house. And I'm so stupid—I thought he was just wussy and tired from the first job we did that day."

"And then I walk into the house as they're making out..."

"We weren't actually making out, I was giving him a hug because I thought he was going to pass out, he looked so sick..."

"And I totally freak out..."

"Yeah, you totally freaked out..."

"Anybody else not enjoying this story?" Will muttered under his breath.

"I think it's funny, Daddy," Polly piped in.

Will did not understand women. At all. He looked across the table at Ranveer. Who looked amused.

Maybe he didn't understand men either.

Suddenly, he felt Florence's hand on his thigh. And then, between his legs.

She, he thought, understood men very well. His cock agreed.

———

Florence decided she was going to play Cupid just before the maid of honour and the best man walked off the dance floor. She had been worried, as Ranveer led Saryang onto the dance floor for the first dance, that Will would be weird and awkward while watching the newlyweds dance, but, after the "Oh-my-god, Will, what are you doing with my cleaning lady?" story—which Florence thought that she and Saryang delivered as well as if they had practiced it as a comic routine for weeks, and which now, Florence could admit, made a great and funny story—and after the naked hostility of Saryang's parents and the dressed up politeness of Ranveer's parents, there wasn't much awkward left.

"She wants everyone at our table to go onto the dance floor for the second dance," Tammy instructed them, without looking at anyone. Florence, however, looked at her carefully, then turned to Polly. "Do you want to dance with your brother or your dad?" she asked. "Matthew, if Polly wants to dance with your dad, will you dance with me? I'm a very good dancer. I won't step on your toes much. Really."

Polly squealed and chose Will. Matthew rolled his eyes, but, when the DJ called on the wedding party to come onto the dance floor, condescended to take her arm. She very solemnly placed her left hand on his right shoulder and her right hand in his left palm. He let his right arm dangle at his side for a while, then put the fingertips on her hip.

"My sons hate to dance with me," she said to him in a confiding tone. "But I tell them it's good practice for later.

When, you know, they want to dance with girls." She paused. "Or boys." Matthew looked up at her.

"Is one of your sons gay?" he asked.

"It's kind of early to tell, right? Human sexuality is complicated. Oh, I'm sorry. I'm embarrassing you. I do that."

"I don't mind," Matthew said, and rested his hand a little more comfortably at her waist. Florence smiled. She knew boys. Matthew wouldn't mind her, so long as she didn't try to mother him.

Polly, she thought, looking at the little girl twirling with Will, would hate her no matter what she did.

And then she found herself looking at Tammy and John. Milquetoast Tammy and non-descript John, neither of whom could dance and neither of whom looked as if they were enjoying themselves—and she saw them come apart as soon as the song ended, and then she saw the flash of disappointment on Tammy's face as John released her hands and walked off the dance floor alone.

Interesting.

Florence thanked Matthew for the dance, and turned to look for John.

Suddenly felt voracious hands around her waist.

"Your fingers feel hungry," she said without turning around.

"They are," Will spoke into her hair. "Dance with me and rub a little against my cock. Very subtly so only my ex-in-laws notice."

"Tell me about Saryang's maid of honour. Tammy," Florence said as Will turned her around and pulled her closer.

"Are you trying to kill my nascent boner?" he muttered. "Killjoy."

"Yes," she said, swaying her hips a little, but not quite

grinding against him. "You missed the window for inappropriate wedding sex. I'm thinking she has a thing for Ranveer's best man. Would Saryang know? Is that why she chose her to be her maid of honour? Because she seems an odd best friend for someone like her. I mean..." Florence paused. Felt judgmental.

"They're old friends, but they're not close friends," Will agreed. "I can't quite remember—we've known her forever. Our kids are close to the same age—maybe Am—Saryang met her at a parenting group or preschool or something. I can't remember. And I don't want to talk about it. I want to talk about the post-wedding sex we're going to have."

"We're not, because you're taking the kids for the night, remember? And then for the following two weeks."

"I am a terrible father and I forgot. Ok, let's go find that vestibule and..."

"Tammy. What can you tell me about her?"

"Nothing. She doesn't interest me. You interest me. Look, no one is paying attention to us right now, and we can slip off and..."

Florence settled into his arms.

"You're all talk."

"Probably," he agreed. "But it's much nicer talk than talking about Am—Saryang's boring friend."

Florence frowned. She searched Tammy out—there she was. At the table, alone. John was a few metres away, talking with Ranveer's parents.

Florence didn't see anything particularly special about him. But Tammy—she saw that Tammy didn't have to be boring, bland or milquetoast. She could be sparkling, vivacious.

Wild.

But she wasn't.

Why?

Florence's obsession with Am—Saryang's—maid of honour annoyed Will. He would have understood resentment and anger—Tammy's "what are the odds" remark was ill-judged, no matter how well Saryang and Florence responded to it. Instead, Florence seemed fascinated. She was sitting beside the woman right now—instead of dancing with him—and talking to her. With animation, excitement.

He frowned.

"Come dance with me, Will."

He turned.

"Amanda," he smiled. "I mean, Saryang."

"I told you, you don't have to keep on correcting yourself." His ex-wife laughed. "But I appreciate you trying. Just as I appreciate you coming."

He didn't say anything, but extended his arms towards her and whirled her into position.

"Is Florence having a good time?" Saryang asked.

"She seems to be," he said. "She... she wanted to know why Tammy was your maid of honour. And if she had a thing for John."

"She's perceptive. Yes, she has a thing for John. She's been mooning after him since she met him two years ago. But she won't make a move. And neither will he. I thought—wedding, romance, spending time together at the table—both single. Maybe horny? You know."

"That really doesn't really seem like you," Will said. Flushed. "I mean..."

"I know. A little out of character," Saryang admitted. "Thinking about other people and what not. What can I say? I'm feeling romantic. Wedding and all."

He moved her with practiced efficiency into a turn and a twirl.

"You are a better dancer than Ranveer," she said. "Will? We're going to be ok, right? You, me, the kids—you and Florence? It's all going to be ok?"

"One day at a time, it will all be ok," he said. Looked across the dance floor at Florence. Who was now taking Tammy by the arm and taking her... where?

"Will?"

"Florence is playing Cupid," he said. "I have a feeling this will turn out badly."

Saryang followed his gaze.

"She's not taking her to John," she said. "Where are they going?"

"I don't know." Will moved Saryang into another turn. Then frowned. Should he help? Stop her? Stay out of it?

Ranveer appeared beside them and tapped Saryang on the shoulder. His uncle something or other, he said, wanted to talk to them for a minute. Would Will excuse them?

Will did. He couldn't see Florence and Tammy anymore.

Saw John over by the bar, alone.

Sighed.

*Fine, redhaired witch. Want to play Cupid? I'll be your assistant.*

<hr>

"We are not going to be able to get these two together," Will pronounced at a quarter to midnight. Florence, barefoot, her strappy stilettos on the floor, sighed. The wedding was still going strong—the dance floor was full of whirling and grooving couples—including Ranveer's parents and his ancient aunts and uncles. Polly and Matthew were also tearing up the dance floor.

Tammy and John were sitting at the head table. Sort of

next to each other, but bodies effectively turned away. In silence.

"Fuck it. We're not," Florence finally agreed. She slipped from her chair into Will's lap. "We've tried everything. I've redone her hair and tried to inject her with sexiness and told her how hot she is and how into her he seems to and done everything short of putting her on his dick. Other than getting them drunk and locking them in a closet, the first of which we cannot do for very important and cogent reasons... yes. We've done everything."

Will squeezed her.

"She wants him," she said. "And he seems receptive enough. Every once in a while, I catch him giving her a look. And she's more attractive than she looks, too, you know what I mean? When she relaxes a bit and doesn't pull into herself and look all timid and mousy? She's got good bones, a great figure. I bet she's a wildcat in bed, with the right motivation. No confidence, though. I diagnose overbearing mother and possibly prettier big sister issues. Him, I don't have a clue about—he won't say boo to me. God... what do you think is wrong with them?"

"Nothing. They're just people. Scared people." But Will thought about it for a bit. "Neither is willing to take a risk," he added. "Neither is willing to make the first move, no matter how innocuous. They are both going to die lonely and alone. Fuck them. We cannot give them a happy ending."

"Wait. Wait." Florence leapt up. She remembered Santokh and Michelle's reconciliation and smiled. "I just had the best idea. Thank me in advance. We can't get them drunk, no. But we can... Ha! I'm about to make everyone very happy." She grabbed a couple of abandoned name cards off the table by which they were sitting, and scanned around for a pen. Turned to Will. "Does Mr. Banker have a promo pen in his suit pocket somewhere? I bet he does. Just in case a client needs to sign something over lunch?"

"Fucking witch," Will muttered. Gave her a pen. Florence thanked him with a kiss. Wrote quickly, "Meet me in the wedding chapel. Now." Then wrote it again on a second place card.

"Your job is to get this into her hands," she told Will. "I will get it into his."

"And then what?" Will said.

"Then… I don't know, Will. Last ditch effort. You get a 'Meet me in the wedding chapel' note. You show up. And there's the person you've been mooning over. Surely, you make a move? Or are open to a move? I mean, you've essentially been told the net is unguarded, to use a sports metaphor I've never quite understood."

"Not those two," Will said. "But. For you. I will try. And after we lock them in…"

"We're locking them in?"

"Yes. We're going to bar the door or something. So they can't leave right away. Create a bit of a crisis, pressure. Anyway, and then—that vestibule. I've got about thirty minutes before I'll have to carry Polly up to the hotel room to bed—she's dancing slower and slower, see? Thirty-minute window, Florence—and then no sex for two weeks. So. Vestibule. Now."

"Vestibule?"

"Wasn't that part of your plan? You said you were going to make everyone happy."

"I love you, you idiot," Florence said. "First, final attempt to play Cupid. Then, vestibule." And, not kissing him, went to deliver her note.

Will followed.

———

It wasn't going to work, except for their vestibule sex afterwards. Which would be a little awkward—Will realized he didn't pack condoms. Would Florence be up for lube-free anal in a public place? Saliva only did so much, and while she was often up for lube-free anal for other reasons...

Oh-god, he was at his ex-wife's wedding, trying to set up her maid of honour with her new husband's best man, and thinking about fucking Florence in the ass in a public place.

Well done, Will. Mature. Very grown up.

*Whatever.*

He and Florence effected the note drop-off fairly smoothly. Swung by the table for some casual and awkward conversation—although Tammy seemed genuinely happy to see Florence. John, Will realized, was so painfully shy he didn't know how to be genuinely happy to see anyone. They created a commotion at the table, then started a hangman game, and in the process, ensured both notes were delivered. Will dropped Tammy's note at her feet—and saw her reaching for it. Florence, Will saw, placed John's note fairly conspicuously among the hangman papers.

They smiled at each other and excused themselves.

"So do we go hang out by the chapel now?" Will asked. Holding Florence around her the waist. And rubbing her ass. "Come on. The clock is ticking."

"Pervert," she said. But she ground back at him and followed him out of the banquet hall into the hallway.

The curtained vestibule was dark. Private.

And full of chairs.

"Fucking hell," Will swore.

"Washroom?" Florence gurgled. "I love washroom sex."

"I know you do, you filthy slut." He bit her neck. "No. There was a recess in the wedding chapel. And a pillar. Plus, the lights will be off. Let's go there."

"But the wedding chapel is where Tammy and John..."

"Florence, it's not going to work. They're not going to show. They lack all initiative. Whereas we do not."

And then they were in the chapel, and, without much preamble, she was on her knees and his cock was in her mouth.

"You're so romantic," she whispered.

"I know," he said. "Just tease me a bit. Don't make me come yet. I have plans." He stayed mostly still as she worked her tongue around his head and up and down his shaft. "Just like that. Mmmm. Tease, tease, tantalize. Don't touch my balls—goddammit, woman, can you not follow dir…"

The chapel door opened. Will froze. Florence stopped working his cock and turned her head. He dropped to the ground beside her.

Tammy walked in. Looked around.

"I'm so stupid," she said, loudly.

The door opened again.

"No, you're not," John said.

---

The maid of honour and the best man did not fuck in the wedding chapel. There was kissing and heavy breathing, and some mumbling, and then a quick agreement to go to his hotel room, followed by more kissing and heavy breathing, and the creak of the opening and closing chapel door. At which point Florence dived quickly for Will's cock, and he plunged his fingers into her pussy, and they both burst out laughing.

"Well done, Cupid," Will said, pulling his cock out of her mouth and swapping his tongue for his fingers. She moaned with delight. "Wait. Reposition. Like this… you know, the problem with 69, really, is that if one of you is doing your work properly, the other should not be capable of doing anything. So what we're going to... ouch, aw... oh... woman, what are you doing?"

"Either proving your point or challenging it, I haven't decided yet," Florence said, slurping.

"Just let me... ah... finish. We're going to take turns. I lick. You come. Then you lick and suck. I come. Then, if your performance meets my expectations, I'll lick and chew and fingerfuck and if you're slick enough, maybe fist you until you explode. And then we go get the children and put them to bed. And sleep chastely and celibately. Deal?"

"I'd answer you but your cock is still in my mouth," she mumbled.

"Right." He pulled out. And set his attention to the task at hand.

His plan worked perfectly, except that after he was done "his work" the second time and she exploded, Florence could barely stand, and he had to half-carry her out of the chapel.

Saryang Park's parents were standing in the hallway outside the chapel when they came out. Gave Will a look of distaste. Did not look at Florence.

Florence, however, looked at them and beamed.

"I'm so very, very happy," she said, "that your daughter left Will. Aren't you?"

She adjusted her dress a little, and nipped at Will's ear.

"Bitch," he whispered.

"And you love it," she whispered back.

"I love it," he agreed. "I love you. Let's go gather up the kids."


*Text Me, Cupid* is also available as an audiobook
*iTunes Audible Amazon Google Play & more*

A few words about a word:

Milquetoast is an insult popularised by H.T. Webster's character, Caspar Milquetoast, in the comic strip/series *The Timid Soul*. Milquetoast is a deliberate misspelling of the dish "milk toast"—toast dipped in milk. Yes, as delicious (not) as it sounds. It refers to a person who has a meek or timid disposition, or a colourless character and dull personality.

## Ok, There's A Little Bit More

Florence, Santokh, Michelle, and Uttamroop also make an appearance in M. Jane Colette's noir erotic romance short story, "Violets," coming soon from Coffin Hop Press in the *Baby, It's Cold Outside* anthology.

And, Santokh and Uttamroop's yoga studio—and complex relationship—is part of the backdrop in M. Jane Colette's new genre-breaking series, *Fat Yoginis In Love*, coming in 2020.

**Find out more:**
*mjanecolette.com/FatYoginis*

# About the Author

**M. JANE COLETTE** writes tragedy for those who like to laugh, comedy for the melancholy, and erotica for people who like their fantasies real. She believes rules and hearts were made to be broken; ditto the constraints of genres.

Find her on Instagram, Twitter, GoodReads and Facebook as *mjanecolette*; better yet, to find out what's coming next from M. Jane Colette and to receive a **FREE** copy of *Taste Me: The Thinking Woman's Erotica*—a gift available exclusively to M. Jane Colette's newsletter subscribers—ask her to send you love letters.

## CLAIM YOUR FREE BOOK
*mjanecolette.com/loveletters*

## Also By M. Jane Colette

Fiction
*Tell Me*—an erotic (filthy) romance for people who like a little bit of angst with their hot sex
*Consequences (of defensive adultery)*—an erotic tragedy (!!) with a happy ending
*Cherry Pie Cure*—a "lol rom-com for the sexting and blogging generation"

Non-Fiction
*Rough Draft Confessions: not a guide to writing and selling erotica and romance but full of inside insight anyway*—a non-fiction collection of essays about writing dirty and fulfilling your creative drive

Anthologies
*Queer Christmas in Cowtown*—featuring "Therapy" by M. Jane Colette
*Screw Chocolate 1*—featuring "The Shy Girl's Guide to Texting" by M. Jane Colette
*Screw Chocolate 2*—featuring "Benign Beginnings" by M. Jane Colette
*Baby, It's Cold Outside* (Coffin Hop Press, in press)—featuring the noir erotic short "Violets" by M. Jane Colette
*Passionate Hearts* (Passionate Ink, in press)—featuring "Accidental Cupid" by M. Jane Colette

**mjanecolette.com/books**

*TellMe@mjanecolette.com*
**GOODREADS.com/mjanecolette**
**mjanecolette.com/LOVE LETTERS**

 facebook.com/mjanecolette2

 twitter.com/@mjanecolette

 instagram.com/mjanecolette

www.ingramcontent.com/pod-product-compliance
Lightning Source LLC
Chambersburg PA
CBHW051158190726
48288CB00006B/1713